Hunter

Legend of the Silver Hunter
Book THREE

Kethric Wilcox

ISBN: 0996526536
ISBN-13: 978-0-9965265-3-1

Publisher's Note

Contents

Acknowledgements

Thank you once again, Tiger, for giving me a chance to express my creativity. Your love and support makes every day brighter.

A big shout out to my Beta Reader Lisa Cullinan and to all the fans of Kieran and Cory, this one is for you.

Beauty's Tale

He was within thirty miles of his own house, thinking on the pleasure he should have in seeing his children again, when going through a large forest he lost himself. It rained and snowed terribly; besides, the wind was so high, that it threw him twice off his horse, and night coming on, he began to apprehend being either starved to death with cold and hunger, or else devoured by the wolves, whom he heard howling all round him, when, on a sudden, looking through a long walk of trees, he saw a light at some distance, and going on a little farther perceived it came from a palace illuminated from top to bottom. The merchant returned God thanks for this happy discovery, and hastened to the place, but was greatly surprised at not meeting with any one in the outer courts. His horse followed him, and seeing a large stable open, went in, and finding both hay and oats, the poor beast, who was almost famished, fell to eating very heartily; the merchant tied him up to the manger, and walking towards the house, where he saw no one, but entering into a large hall, he found a good fire, and a table plentifully set out with but one cover laid. As he was wet quite through with the rain and snow, he drew near the fire to dry himself. "I hope," said he, "the master of the house, or his servants will excuse the liberty I take; I suppose it will not be long before some of them appear."

He waited a considerable time, until it struck eleven, and still nobody came. At last he was so hungry that he could stay no longer, but took a chicken, and ate it in two mouthfuls, trembling all the while. After this he drank a few glasses of wine, and growing more courageous he went out of the hall, and crossed through several grand apartments with magnificent furniture, until he came into a chamber, which had an exceeding good bed in it, and as he was very much fatigued, and it was past midnight, he concluded it was best to shut the door, and go to bed.

It was ten the next morning before the merchant waked, and as he was going to rise he was astonished to see a good suit of clothes in the room of his own, which were quite spoiled; certainly, said he, this palace belongs to some kind fairy, who has seen and pitied my distress. He looked through a window, but instead of snow saw the most delightful arbors, interwoven with the beautifullest flowers that were ever beheld. He then returned to the great hall, where he had supped the night before, and found some chocolate ready made on a little table. "Thank you, good Madam Fairy," said he aloud, "for being so careful, as to provide me a breakfast; I am extremely obliged to you for all your favors."

The good man drank his chocolate, and then went to look for his horse, but passing through an arbor of roses he remembered Beauty's request to him, and gathered a branch on which were several; immediately he heard a great noise, and saw such a frightful Beast coming towards him, that he was ready to faint away.

"You are very ungrateful," said the Beast to him, in a terrible voice; "I have saved your life by receiving you into my castle, and, in return, you steal my roses, which I value beyond any thing in the universe, but you shall die for it; I give you but a quarter of an hour to prepare yourself, and say your prayers."

The merchant fell on his knees, and lifted up both his hands, "My lord," said he, "I beseech you to forgive me, indeed I had no intention to offend in gathering a rose for one of my daughters, who desired me to bring her one."

"My name is not My Lord," replied the monster, "but Beast; I don't love compliments, not I. I like people to speak as they think; and so do not imagine, I am to be moved by any of your flattering speeches. But you say you have got daughters. I will forgive you, on condition that one of them come willingly, and suffer for you. Let me have no words, but go about your business, and swear that if your daughter refuse to die in your stead, you will return within three months."

The merchant had no mind to sacrifice his daughters to the ugly monster, but he thought, in obtaining this respite, he should have the satisfaction of seeing them once more, so he promised, upon oath, he would return, and the Beast told him he might set out when he pleased, "but," added he, "you shall not depart empty handed; go back to the room where you lay, and you will see a great empty chest; fill it with whatever you like best, and I will send it to your home," and at the same time Beast withdrew.

Beauty and the Beast, Jeanne-Marie LePrince de Beaumont, English translation, 1757

Mother never refuted this section of the tale. She loved her father, the last man she ever really loved, and I think she wanted to remember him as someone who loved her after the rest of her family abandoned her to her fate. Family rumors abound. The youngest of my uncles, Johan, supposedly had a destiny he chose not to face or was forbidden to face by Grandfather. Whatever the case may be, Johan gifted Mother with the ability to channel Silver magic once in her lifetime in her greatest hour of need. We all suspect she used her spell during the fight with the Beast, but even on her deathbed, she wouldn't revel what she'd done with the spell. Father past many years after Mother. I believe his fear of her kept him from revealing the truth.

From the First Chronicle of the House of Beauty, translated from the original French, 1998

Prologue: Three Weeks Ago

John Mason was surprisingly excited when he got off the phone with Kieran Belle. The boy's excitement about his upcoming wedding and handfasting was contagious. The photography professor dialed his travel agent to arrange for a trip to Maine. As he gave the travel agent his details, John wandered through the living room and stopped before the photographic portrait of Kieran's fiancé hanging over the fireplace. A shirtless Cory Cooper, leaning on a piece of construction equipment, looked back at the professor with a deeply felt love for the man on the other side of the camera. The boys hadn't even begun to admit their feelings for each other when the picture had been taken, but you didn't have to know them to sense what they felt in that moment in time. John's daydreaming was broken by the voice of the agent.

"Sir, are you still there?"

"Yes, I'm sorry. My mind wandered off. What were those flight times again?"

The agent rattled off the flight information between Little Rock and Maine, along with the cost. John agreed and added in a rental car booking, and then gave the agent his credit card information. The agent let him know his reservations were complete and could download his tickets when he was ready. John thanked the man and hung up. He decided he'd call Kieran back when he had his tickets in hand.

Chapter One: Present Time

The transport spell faded, depositing Grams, Kellen, and an unconscious Kieran in the garage attached to the main house. Kellen and Grams made Kieran as secure and comfortable as possible in the back of the family van. Grams stayed in the back with Kieran using her Sapphire magic to heal what damage she could. She was fighting a desperate battle to save her grandson. Between the damage the falling tree had done and the wounds inflicted by the shifters during his defense of the compound, Kieran was an unrecognizable mess. Ebony magic surged in his system from the numerous bites he'd received fighting off the shifters, and now it was fighting her efforts, keeping Kieran on the edge of death.

She dug in. Recalling how some Sapphire mage had locked away the Ebony magic within Cory's blood, she crafted a binding spell. It began to chase down the Ebony magic and corral it, driving it away from Kieran's vital organs. Kellen drove like a mad man, using the reserves of his own magic to keep the tires attached to the road as he raced to the hospital in Bar Harbor.

Back at the Oisín compound, Cory, Brom, and Billy raced back to the cabin Kieran and Cory had been living in, so Cory could get dressed and pack clothes for Kieran to wear. When Cory burst through the open door just ahead of Brom and Billy, he found a man sitting on the couch in the front room. The stranger, who'd brought the attacking shifters to the compound, bristled with weapons and reeked of Ebony magic. Without thinking, Cory leapt at the man, shifting shape in mid-leap to become a silver wolf. He crashed into the stranger, sending him over the back of the couch. Brom snatched up a fire poker as he raced past the fireplace to pin the man down.

"Who are you?" Brom snarled.

"Alex Kincaid, I've come to collect the Master's prize. Where is young Belle?"

"No place you need to worry about, murdering scum," Brom said as he slammed the poker down on the man's head until he was sure Kincaid was unconscious.

Brom turned to find Cory caught in a midway form, between his wolf shape and his human form. Brom couldn't help himself. A vision of the character from the animated version of Beauty's story superimposed itself over Cory's figure. Hysteria got the better of him, and he started laughing at Cory. From his perspective, Cory couldn't figure out what was so funny about the situation until he turned and caught a glimpse of himself in the mirror over the fireplace. His own laughter burst forth, and his shift completed back to human.

When Brom finally got himself under control, he urged Cory to get dressed. Blushing, Cory dashed upstairs to get dressed and toss some clothes in a bag. As he opened the closet, he was confronted by Kieran's tracker armor. Tears sprang to his eyes as he thought about how Kieran might not be hovering on the edge of death if he'd been wearing those enchanted leathers. He tried to sense Kieran through their bond, but only sensed pain. He poured his love down the bond, hoping it would strengthen Kieran's spirit to fight through the pain. Cory dressed in his own clothes, even though he would have loved to toss on one of Kieran's shirts, but while they were the same height, Kieran was narrower in build than he was. He tossed a couple of changes of their clothes into an overnight bag before heading back downstairs. After setting down the bag, Cory wrapped Uncle Brom in a hug, which caught the older man off guard for a moment.

"Are you okay, Cory? This has been a rough day for all of us, but . . ." Brom didn't finish elaborating. They both knew Cory's husband was fighting for his life; toss in Cory's sudden ability to shape-shift at will, who wouldn't be having a rough day.

"I just needed to hold something of Kieran's for a moment to ground myself again. He mentioned a couple of times how much he liked it when you'd hold him when he was here and sad. I guess I needed to feel what he felt for a moment."

Brom hugged Cory tight as he'd done for Kieran so often as a boy.

"I get it, Cory. Kieran is the son I never had. Now, before we go to him, we need to take care of this piece of trash. The sad part is he's human. I want you to go on ahead to the hospital. I'll catch up after I've taken care of Mr. Kincaid and the coroner has come and collected Dad's remains."

"Do you think Kieran caught up to Marissa?"

"Yes, I'm sure he did. My magic is limited at this distance from my forge or another Silver mage, but I can sense a very ancient and nasty Silver magic spell active in the center of the property. I think he cast a spell, which borders on being forbidden. If he did cast that particular spell, neither you nor I want to see it in action. Pray he doesn't remember what he did when he wakes up."

"Okay, I'm going to go to the hospital now."

"Make sure you take a copy of your marriage license with you. In the rush to get Kieran medical treatment, Kellen and Mom may not remember, but you have as much right to make Kieran's medical decisions for him as they do."

"I packed it, figuring I'd need to prove I'm his husband so I could even visit him. I didn't stop to think about medical decisions."

"Kellen and Mom won't let anything bad happen to him, but they aren't going to be thinking about what might happen to you if Kieran isn't going to recover. In that event, their first priority is going to be to transfer the power of the Silver Witch back to Kellen."

"I won't let them hurt Kieran. He has to recover. I can't live without him, but I won't trap him on life support forever."

"Cory, listen to me. Kieran is very tough; he's a descendant of two of the most powerful families in history. I'm sure no one's ever told you how his mother died."

"No, but I assumed she was killed by a shifter while on a hunt."

"No single shifter was ever a match for my sister-in-law. To bring her down took an entire pack of the darkest shifters anyone had ever encountered. In the end, fifty shifters died to take her out. Kieran's maternal grandmother wanted him to be with his mother on that mission, but his two uncles—Eric and Stephen—said he wasn't old enough or ready to go. They went in his place. While they were skilled trackers and experienced fighters in their own right, neither of them was gifted. Miranda used her one shot of Silver magic trying to save them instead of herself."

"But you think if Kieran had been there she would have survived?"

"No, I honestly think Miranda was destined to die that night," Brom said, opening his mouth to continue, but Kincaid groaned. He hit him with the poker again, and then sighed. "Kellen brought Kieran here to get him away from his grandmother because she blamed him for her daughter's and sons' deaths." He paused as if considering his next words, but never took his eyes off Kincaid. "She blamed a ten-year-old boy—for failing to be old enough or skilled enough to go out and die. I spent months convincing Kieran their deaths weren't his fault. Months." He kicked Kincaid for good measure. "I don't want him falling into that pattern over his grandfather's death. There was no way to know Marissa was going to attack any of us like she did." He looked up from Kincaid to meet Cory's amber eyes. "We have to keep him from blaming himself, or we will lose him."

****

Kellen whipped the family van into the patient drop-off for the Emergency Room at Mount Desert Island Hospital. After he parked, he hopped out of the van and raced inside to get medical personnel. Once the desk nurse heard about Kieran's injuries, she summoned immediate assistance, and a gurney was rolled out to the van. Grams withdrew her magic the moment the doors to the back of the van were pulled open. With her magic gone, Kieran began to seize as the pain came crashing back into his body. The emergency team slid a full body board into the van and got Kieran transferred to the board and then onto the gurney. They rushed him into the hospital and into an exam room. Grams moved as quickly as she could to stay with Kieran while Kellen dealt with paperwork, registering Kieran as Kieran Oisín without even thinking about it. Once the paperwork was filled out, Kellen moved the van to the parking lot before going back to find his mother standing in the hall as a team of doctors worked to stabilize Kieran. Monitors beeped and pinged as doctors called out orders for blood typing, meds, and X-rays. The surgical team and operating room were prepped.

Kellen could tell his mother wanted to use her magic to hold Kieran stable so the doctors didn't have to deal with it while they treated his injuries. One glance at his mother and he could see her exhaustion. She'd already pushed herself beyond her limits.

"Mother, come, let's find a place to sit—out of the way of the trauma team. Brom and Cory should be here soon."

"I could still be keeping him stable, Kellen. I can hold him while they fix all the broken parts."

"You're exhausted, Mother. You won't do Kieran any good if you kill yourself trying to do what the doctors can do. He's going to need us all when he wakes up."

"I can't lose him too, Kellen. Not after loosing Aodhfin like that."

"We're not going to lose Kieran; we can't even think those thoughts. He's well-anchored to this world, Mother, by his bond with Cory." His own words gave him pause. "Oh, hell. I wasn't thinking when I registered Kieran into the hospital. I put his last name down as Oisín."

"We need to go fix that right now, Kellen. Cory will be frantic when he gets here. He won't think to ask under only Oisín, not at first anyway."

They quickly made their way back to the Emergency Room admission desk to correct Kellen's error only to find an agitated Cory. He demanded to know where his husband was. Kellen caught him around the shoulders.

"Cory, calm down. They have him in a trauma unit, trying to stabilize him so they can get X-rays and prep him for surgery. I'm sorry I wasn't thinking when I filled out the paperwork and signed him in under Oisín. Mother and I were just coming to fix that mistake and get him registered under Oisín-Cooper."

"Cory, come with me. We'll get something to drink while we wait for the doctors to let us know when we can be with Kieran," Grams said, taking Cory's arm to lead him away from the desk.

"But I need to talk to registration."

"Kellen is taking care of that."

"I have the right to make Kieran's medical decisions. I'm his husband, and see, here's the paperwork, plus his insurance cards, and a copy of his medical records from Little Rock. Please don't take him away from me."

"We're not trying to take him away from you, *mac tíre óg*. I promise you, we'd never do that to you. Kellen will fix the paperwork and get you put down as the primary contact."

Kellen came over with a clipboard full of paperwork and handed it to Cory.

"As his lawful spouse, you need to fill these out and sign them. I'm sorry, Cory. I was worried about my son, and I didn't stop to think about my son-in-law. Let's get these filled out, and let the nurse make a copy of all your paperwork for their records." His eyes shifted away. "Where's Brom? I thought you two would be together."

Cory filled them in quietly, "We ran into a human hunter waiting in our cabin to collect Kieran for someone called the Master. Brom stayed behind to take care of him and to arrange for the coroner to come and take care of Gramps' body. He sent me on ahead, figuring that something like this would happen," he said. "I'm sorry I'm being rude. I don't mean to be."

"We're all on edge, Cory. Once you finish the paperwork, you have full control over what happens to Kieran. We will support your decisions."

"Even if I decide to let him go without letting you take back the power of the Silver Witch?"

Both Grams and Kellen gasped at the thought; it hadn't even crossed their minds yet. They looked at Cory in horror for a moment before Kellen spoke in hushed tones.

"If that's the price I must pay to keep peace in this family, so mote it be."

****

Cory bent his head to focus on the paperwork and in acknowledgement of Kellen's sacrifice. He wondered if Brom had misjudged his brother or if Kellen had a secret plan to draw the power out of Kieran. No time for such thoughts; he needed to focus on Kieran and his treatment. He finished the paperwork and took it to the front desk along with his marriage certificate, Kieran's insurance cards, and the medical records from Little Rock. He signed a few more papers in front of the desk nurse and then watched as she entered the corrections in the computer to generate proper paperwork for Kieran.

When it was complete, Cory went back to sit with Grams and Kellen to wait for the doctors to tell them something about Kieran. Brom arrived a short while later and joined the family in the waiting room. Control of the situation was out of their hands now.

Three hours later, the lead doctor on the trauma team headed out to the waiting room to find the boy's family. The admitting nurse handed him new information on the young man. He flinched when he read the young man was married to another man.

"I should have known someone that pretty and with that much hair was a faggot," the doctor muttered loud enough the nurse heard him.

The nurse remained silent.

"Go get Dr. Mihaylova, and have her come deal with the family."

"Yes, Dr. Miller," the nurse said before leaving to find the young Russian doctor.

The nurse found her in conversation with Dr. Thomas Waffe, the chief surgeon for their tiny hospital. From what the nurse overheard, the patient's chances did not sound good.

"I'm sorry to interrupt, but Dr. Miller sent me to get Dr. Mihaylova to do the consult with the family and bring them up to speed on the patient's condition."

"What brought this about?" Dr. Waffe asked instead. "Dr. Miller was already on the way to meet with the family and brief them on the boy's condition."

The nurse handed over information to explain. "Here's the updated patient information, Dr. Waffe."

"Oh, this is beyond belief. Miller and his prejudices." Dr. Waffe sighed. "So what if the young man is married to another man? Uphold your damn oath." Dr. Waffe turned to Dr. Mihaylova. "Anna, would you prefer to let me handle the family?"

"We can go meet with the family together, Thomas. I think they will appreciate access to two doctors."

The doctors followed the admissions nurse back to the waiting area for the emergency room. They were met with four faces in various states of worry and concern. Relationships were easy to discern for the doctors, the two dark-haired men and the older woman were blood relatives, which left the handsome young blond man as the husband.

"Mr. Oisín-Cooper, I'm Dr. Anna Mihaylova, and this is Dr. Thomas Waffe, our chief of surgery. Let's sit and talk about your husband's condition and how he got injured so badly."

"We were out hiking in the forest and this huge tree began falling," Cory explained. "Kieran shoved me out of the way, but the tree caught him and pinned him to the ground."

"What actually happened, Mr. Oisín-Cooper?" Dr. Mihaylova was short. "He has what appear to be bite wounds on his arms and legs, and his back is torn up with what appear to be claw marks."

"Dr. Mihaylova," Kellen interjected, "if you don't mind, my son-in-law—like the rest of us—is very worried about Kieran. There will be time later to talk about how he received his injuries. Please, Kieran's condition."

The doctor looked up at the tall man and felt a sudden shock of recognition as her amethyst eyes met Kellen's violet eyes. Where did she know him from, and why was she suddenly drawn to him? She sat in stunned silence for a moment until she realized Dr. Waffe was talking to the family. She ripped her gaze away from Kellen's and refocused on the rest of the family and Dr. Waffe.

"Kieran's condition is critical," Dr. Waffe said. "He's taken a lot of damage. Most of his injuries are internal. We need to get him into surgery as quickly as possible. We're only holding off for his CT scan to come back, so we can know if he's suffering from any intracranial bleeding. Honestly, I think it's possible he may have a subdural hematoma since he hasn't regained even the slightest trace of consciousness while we've been running our tests."

"What do you need from us, Dr. Waffe?" Cory asked.

"You'll need to sign the paperwork to give us permission to operate on your husband."

"Of course, Kieran gets whatever medical treatments he needs." Cory practically shouted from the relief of being able to do something for Kieran.

"Good, I'll have the nurse start prepping his head in case we have to relieve pressure in the skull."

"I take it you mean you're going to shave off his hair."

"Yes, please understand, Mr. Oisín-Cooper, we're hoping we won't have to do anything, but we should be ready in case we have to open his skull to stop any major bleeding."

"I understand. Can you save his hair? He always said if I let him cut it, he wanted to donate the length to one of those charities that make wigs for cancer patients."

"Of course we can. I'll have the nurse bag it for you."

"Dr. Waffe, besides the possible head injury, what other injuries does Kieran have?"

"Well, he has several broken ribs, none of which appear to be endangering his internal organs, but both of his legs have suffered severe fractures, which we'll have to set and very likely hold together with pins and rods until the bones knit. Both wrists are fractured too, plus all the damage done by those possible bite and claw wounds. He has a lot of bruising, and until we can get him on the table, I can't be sure how much damage has been done to him internally."

"Thank you, doctor. Please keep us informed," Cory said. "I'll go sign the required forms."

The doctors left to get Kieran prepped for surgery. Cory sat stunned by the extent of the damage. He tried to hold himself together, but the first tear escaped, and after it fell, he couldn't hold them back any longer. Líadáin was quick to wrap Cory in a hug.

"Why didn't he escape before they cornered him? I would have expected him to summon his armor. Why didn't he use his magic to join us in the cavern? We could have helped him hold them off. I can't live without him. He has to live."

"*Mac tíre óg*, he's strong, and while Silver magic can't heal like Sapphire or Emerald can, his magic will hold things together once the doctors get everything back in place."

"Grams, why couldn't you heal him?"

"My Sapphire magic did what it could, dear one. His injuries are beyond my healing abilities. To heal him magically we'd need a powerful Emerald mage who'd be willing to take the risk of burning out his magic in Kieran's healing."

"We'd better get the paperwork signed, so the doctors can do their work, Cory," Kellen coaxed.

"Of course, do you think they'll let me see him before they shave off his hair?"

"We can only ask, Cory," Kellen said, offering his hand to help Cory stand.

The entire Oisín clan rose and went with Cory to the admissions desk. The nurse looked up at Cory's tear-stained face and the grim looks of the three people with him.

"What can I do for you, sweetheart?" the nurse asked.

"I was hoping we could see my husband before they prep him for surgery."

"Oh, honey, of course. Come with me, and we'll try to see if we can do that right now. Sally, will you cover the desk for me, while I take the family back to see the boy in 501?"

"Sure, no problem, Trudy. You go on back. I'll buzz June and let her know you're bringing them back so they can hold off prep for a few minutes."

Interlude: During the attack

Professor John Mason sat in his living room, staring at the photograph mounted above the fireplace. There was a tension in the air, as if something terrible had happened, and Kieran was involved. The professor had some connection to his student since their magic had touched during the Thanksgiving dinner Kieran had helped him with. Without thinking, John found himself dialing Kieran's number, hoping everything was all right. Kieran's phone rolled directly to voicemail. John's worry only grew. He called his travel agent and set about changing his travel plans. After he had new travel arrangements, John called the dean of his college to change his request from vacation time to a sabbatical for the coming academic year. The dean wasn't happy about the short notice, but John's performance was above all the standards, so he granted the sabbatical.

John began packing the things he felt he would need, including a battered old book he'd been writing in since he was a young boy and learning magic from his grandmother. He also made a phone call to his sister Vivian. Her phone rolled to voicemail too, so he left a message for her to call him. He hoped she'd come meet him in Maine.

Kethric Wilcox

Chapter Two: Hours After the Attack

Cory entered into the patient room where the hospital staff was prepping Kieran for surgery. He stared at his husband's battered and broken body. Bruising covered Kieran's beautiful face like a Halloween mask. Monitors beeped and pinged, tracking his vital signs. Tubes and wires were everywhere, and Cory could hardly hold back tears as he moved closer to his husband's bedside. Gently he stroked a strand of Kieran's hair away from his face. Tears rolled down his face as he softly placed a kiss on Kieran's forehead.

"Please come back to me, babe. I need you," Cory whispered in his husband's ear.

Grams, Kellen, and Brom each took a brief moment with Kieran before they gathered up the shattered Cory and led him back out to the waiting room. Elsewhere in the hospital, Dr. Waffe was prepping for surgery and examining the latest round of X-rays and the CAT scan. He sighed in relief as he noted there was no sign of subdural hematoma in Kieran's skull. He had his surgical nurse call down to the room where they were getting Kieran ready to cancel the head shaving. The nurse who took the call was glad not to have to remove the boy's hair, and she carefully coiled it into an extra large surgical cap to keep it from getting into any incisions the doctor made. She then called out to the front desk to let them know the good news. The surgical team came shortly after that and wheeled Kieran off to the surgical bay.

****

Cory paced the waiting room of the small hospital waiting for news on Kieran's surgery. He'd been relieved when the doctor had cancelled the need to shave Kieran's head. News that there was no apparent injury to his brain had brought the whole family relief. Now Dr. Waffe and Dr. Mihaylova were trying to put all the broken pieces back together and stop the internal bleeding around his kidneys. Their goal was to get Kieran stabilized in order to transport him to Eastern Maine Medical Center in Bangor for better care in a larger facility. Dr. Mihaylova had admitting privileges there, so she would be able to transfer with Kieran to monitor his condition, especially if he grew worse.

Interlude: Kellen Plots to Reclaim the Magic

As the days passed after Kieran's initial rounds of surgery with no signs of him regaining consciousness, Kellen began to worry that the ancient legacy of the Silver Witch would be truly lost. He regretted giving Cory his word that he'd let the magic be lost if Kieran didn't recover. Pacing the hallways of the hospital, Kellen began to plan a way to recover the powers and knowledge locked away inside his own son.

Father used a blood bond ritual to give Kieran access to all of his power in case something happened to him. Maybe I can work a similar ritual to let the power pass back to me should the unthinkable happen and Kieran dies. I have to do something. I can't let the heritage of the Silver Witch die with my son.

After swapping places with his brother Brom at Kieran's bedside for a while, Kellen gladly turned over the sad task of watching over his son to Cory. As he was leaving the hospital, Brom stopped him.

"You have that look you get when you're plotting something you shouldn't be, Brother."

"I'm just going home to collect the Grimoire to see if there's anything in it that might help us fix Kieran."

"Be sure that's all you're planning to do, Brother. Remember, you gave Cory your word you wouldn't attempt to reclaim the power of the Silver Witch from Kieran."

"And I intend to keep that promise, Brom. I want my son alive and well, more than I want the legacy of the powers that left him in this state."

Kellen turned and strode out of the hospital under the watchful eyes of his older brother–an older brother who did not trust him in the least.

Chapter Three

After hours of surgery to repair Kieran's internal injuries and to begin setting his fractures, he was finally wheeled into a private room. Cory made sure that Grams got the one visitor chair in the room so that she could sit and rest while being close to Kieran. He stood on the opposite side of the bed running his hand over his husband's head, stroking his long black hair. Kellen and Brom sat on the couch beneath the window. The floor nurse came in to check on Kieran's vitals and meds, taking notice of the worn-out family scattered around the room.

"It's going to be some time before we see if he comes around after everything wears off. Why don't you go home, grab a shower, eat something, and get some rest? We'll call you if anything about his condition changes."

"I brought clothes, this room has a shower, and I can sleep on the couch," Cory protested. "I'm not leaving my husband's side."

Kellen and Brom rose from the couch and moved to help their mother up.

"I picked up a change of clothes for myself and my mother when I went back to the house," Kellen said. "We'll go get a couple of hotel rooms and be back in the morning so you can rest, Cory."

"I'll go back to the compound and pick up some of my things after we book the hotel," Brom stated as he helped his mother from the room.

Cory moved around the bed to settle into the visitor chair. He pushed it up against the side of Kieran's bed so he could rest his head on the mattress and be close to Kieran. The stress of the day didn't take long to catch up to Cory, and he soon drifted to sleep. The nursing staff came and went as quietly as they could, trying not to wake the sleeping young man.

"They're such an adorable young couple," the day nurse said to the evening nurse. "It's so sad to see the shape the poor boy is in."

"What on earth happened to the poor boy?" the night nurse asked.

"The report says a tree fell on him, but he has other injuries consistent with being attacked by animals. Nobody pushed for more details because the boy was in such bad shape, and neither his husband nor his father would answer any more questions until after the doctors had done their job."

"Well, maybe when the boy wakes up after the anesthesia wears off, we can get the full story. If his injuries are that bad, then a police report should be filed." The night nurse's face grew pale as she began to read the patient's chart her. "Oh, this is horrible. I thought the name on this chart sounded sort of familiar. There was a story on the local news about an attack on the Oisín compound and that Mr. Oisín was killed. The police say the attacker used a pack of dogs to try and hunt down the rest of the family."

"The boy was originally registered under the name Oisín before his husband arrived to correct it to Oisín-Cooper. Do you think that the dogs got to him after the tree fell and pinned him?"

"I don't know. It doesn't explain why he's still alive."

"Shouldn't one of you ladies be on rounds?" Dr. Mihaylova asked as she entered the nursing station.

"Yes, doctor, I was just getting up to speed on the new patients."

"Is that what they're calling it these days in Maine? Where I went to medical school, it was called gossiping. I'll take Mr. Oisín-Cooper's chart; there are some items to update while I check on his recovery status."

Dr. Mihaylova walked out of the nurse's station and into Kieran's room. Both of the occupants were asleep, so she tried to remain quiet as she moved across the room. But it only took one step for all that to change. Cory woke suddenly and snarled at her like a wolf protecting its injured mate. At first, she even thought she saw claws at the end of Cory's fingers before a soft silver light seemed to wash over him, and he sank back in his chair.

"I'm sorry, Dr. Mihaylova." Cory mangled the pronunciation of her name. "You startled me."

"Why don't you call me Dr. Anna? It will be easier to pronounce, Mr. Oisín-Cooper," she replied with a small smile.

"If you will call me Cory and my husband Kieran. We're not used to the new last name yet; it's still only a few weeks old." Cory's smile was weak but stunning.

"Then we have a deal, Cory. I'm going to check Kieran's vital signs and make sure everything is going well after the surgery. Have you noticed any sign of his regaining consciousness?" she asked as she proceeded to check vital signs, bandages, and the latticework of rods and pins holding Kieran's shattered legs together.

"No, if he'd stirred, I would have known and buzzed for a nurse," Cory replied around a yawn.

"I'll have the nurse come and make the couch for you to sleep on, Cory."

"Thank you, Dr. Anna. I'm tired, but I don't want to leave him all alone."

"Nobody's throwing you out, Cory. We just want you to be comfortable, so you can be well rested. If Kieran is still in stable condition by late tomorrow, I'll check and see if there's a room available for him at the hospital in Bangor as we discussed before he went into surgery."

"Thank you, Dr. Anna. Please know that the Oisíns have said that cost is not a concern." Cory's response was hesitant when talking about Kieran's family money.

"Just relax, Cory. We're doing everything we can for Kieran. Get some sleep if you can. His vitals are looking good. I am a little concerned about the fever he's running, but it's likely due to his body trying to fight to heal itself. If it doesn't break in a day or two, I'll put him on additional medications."

Dr. Anna finished checking Kieran over, making notes in his patient chart before she left to finish her rounds. She stopped by the nurses station and directed the duty nurse to get the couch in Kieran's room set up as a bed for Cory. Afterward, she continued her rounds, trying hard not to think about what she might have seen.

****

Later in the evening, after the Oisíns had left Cory sitting beside Kieran's bed, Father Ivory de Beauchamps, the hospital chaplain, was wandering the halls checking on patients and family members. He made his way up to the floor where Kieran's room was located and noticed a different feel to this floor; the peaceful calm was disturbed by the ebb and flow of magic. He followed his senses until he stood outside of Kieran's room where he saw the faint glow of Silver magic wrapped around the joined hands of two young men. One was a patient swathed in casts and bandages, the other an attractive blond with red-rimmed eyes from abundant tears. As if sensing Father Ivory's presence, the blond looked up and focused bleary amber eyes on the young priest.

"I'm sorry to intrude. I'm Father Ivory, the hospital chaplain. Would you like someone to talk with?"

"I wasn't expecting anyone other than the nurses to be wandering around this late at night, Father. Neither of us is Catholic, and I doubt you'd approve of us."

"This young man is obviously important to you, and while my church's doctrine frowns on such things, I can tell you're very much in love with him . . . and I think from the way Silver magic shines around your hands the feelings are returned."

"You can see our bond? Kieran told me that only the two of us could see it," Cory replied. Fear of discovery tinged his voice.

"I have a gift related to magic called second sight. While I can't work magic myself, I can see it in those who have it or when it has been used. I think in your case, your love for Kieran is visible to anyone who looks at the two of you."

"What else does your sight show you about us?" Cory asked.

Father Ivory's face went blank for a moment as he looked at the young man in the hospital bed. A vision washed over his sight, showing a glimpse of a glowing man in medieval hunting attire bending over the young man as if to whisper in his ear. Father Ivory blinked, trying to focus on what appeared to be the patron saint of his order, but as he did, the vision vanished. He came to himself as he felt Cory's hand on his shoulder.

"Are you okay, Father Ivory?" Cory asked. "You seemed to have blanked out for a moment."

"Just a momentary dizzy spell. I've never been near anyone so gifted in magic before. I had a vision of my order's patron saint, Saint Hubert."

"Sorry, not a Catholic, I have know idea who Saint Hubert is or what he's a patron saint of."

"Hubert is the patron saint of hunters and protection from rabies, among other things. Kieran was bitten by something; that's how the darkness got into him."

Cory took Father Ivory by the arm, turned him around, and escorted him from the room. "Thank you for your visit, Father, but I think it's time for you to go check on other patients. It's been a long day, and Kieran is scheduled for more tests in the morning. I'd like to get some rest before they come to take him down."

Before he could speak, Father Ivory found himself staring at the closed door to the hospital room. Something told him he'd be back again. He could still feel the magic inside the room.

Chapter Four

Kellen, Brom, and Grams found Cory curled up on the couch asleep when they returned the next morning. Grams quietly settled into the chair at Kieran's bedside while her sons went to see if they could find some additional chairs. Líadáin stroked her grandson's right hand, trying to work the healing aspect of her Sapphire magic into the shattered wrist, but she found her power blocked by a swirl of Ebony magic. She focused and let her power scan Kieran's body. She shivered as she discovered the pools of Ebony magic near all of Kieran's major injuries, especially one waiting at the base of his skull, blocked by a powerful shield of Silver magic. So deep was she in trance that when Cory's cellphone rang, she nearly screamed.

Cory groped blindly for his phone as he struggled to wake up. He thumbed it into accepting the call and answered. "Cory Cooper, can I help you?"

"What's wrong, baby?" Cory could make out the sudden concern in his mother's voice.

"Kieran's in the hospital, Mom." Cory's voice cracked as tears began to flow. "He's been through a massive round of surgery, and he still hasn't woken up."

"Oh, Corwin, are you all right? What happened?" Tamara asked.

Cory knew his mother would be pacing the kitchen at home, trying to figure out how she could fix things from Arkansas.

"I can't give you all the details over the phone, Mom. We were attacked, and Kieran ended up pinned under a massive tree. The doctor hopes to move him to a larger hospital over in Bangor this afternoon if he's still stable."

"Oh my god, Cory, I'm so sorry. Why didn't you call us sooner? Your father and I will change the flight plans we made to come for your wedding and be there as soon as possible."

"I haven't had time to focus on calling anyone, Mother. I've been busy filling out paperwork and dealing with doctors and trying to understand all the things they've been telling me regarding Kieran's condition, and today will be filled with making the arrangements to move him to a different hospital."

"Corwin, take a deep breath and slowly let it out." His mother soothed him over the phone. "That's better. Now, sweetheart, why don't you let his family do what they need to do—"

"I'm the one who has to make the decisions," Cory exasperated.

"What?" she asked. "You two aren't getting married until the end of the month."

"No, Mom, we're getting handfasted at the end of the month." The reminder shook Cory. "Oh lord, that will have to be postponed and all the guests notified." Cory started pacing the room until Grams stopped him and sat him in the chair by Kieran's bed. She took the phone from him and placed Kieran's battered and broken hand in Cory's hands before speaking into the phone.

"Mrs. Cooper, I'm Líadáin Oisín, Kieran's grandmother."

"Mrs. Oisín, where's Corwin?" Tamara asked.

"Cory is sitting beside Kieran's bed here in the hospital," she said, ready to break the rest of the news. "The boys married three weeks ago in a civil service at the courthouse here in Bar Harbor. As Kieran's husband, Cory has the right to make the medical decisions, and he has us here to support him. I think, however, he could use some support from his own family."

"My husband Jonathan is changing our travel arrangements as we speak, Mrs. Oisín. We'll call Corwin as soon as everything is set. Would you please have him call us with an update when you get Kieran settled into the new hospital?"

"Of course, Mrs. Cooper. Someone will call you as soon as all the arrangements are made. Please let us know what your flights are, and we'll arrange to have someone meet you at the Bangor Airport."

"Thank you for looking out for Corwin. I know you have a lot to worry about while taking care of Kieran."

"Cory is my grandson's husband, and even before they married, I considered him family, so don't worry. He's in good hands," Líadáin said, seeing the nurse entering the room. "I'm sorry though. I need to let you go so I can hear what the nurse has to say about moving Kieran."

As Grams hung up, the nurse handed a clipboard full of documents to Cory. The paperwork needed to be reviewed before Kieran could be transferred. Cory looked overwhelmed by all the forms and records. He looked up from the clipboard as Líadáin reached over to take it from his grasp. She looked at the forms and the invoice for the cost of moving Kieran to Bangor.

"These fees and charges are ridiculous. I know we've said cost wasn't an issue, but we won't be robbed by a bean counter padding the bill," Líadáin said, thrusting the clipboard back into the nurse's hands. "Take these back to your hospital accountant and tell them to try again without all the phony extras."

When the nurse left, Cory leaned forward. "Grams, do you think we really need to move Kieran?" Cory asked. "It seems like Dr. Anna has everything she really needs here."

"I don't know, Cory. We'll discuss it with Kellen and Brom when they get back, and then talk it over as a family with Dr. Mihaylova. Staying here would certainly be easier on us to drive back and forth from the estate and to put up guests there."

And when Kellen and Brom returned, the family did just that.

"What did we miss, Mother?" Kellen asked while setting his chair down next to the one Cory sat in.

"The hospital just brought the paperwork and the invoice to move Kieran to the hospital in Bangor. I sent it back when I saw how many unnecessary items they'd tossed in on just the first page. Cory and I were just discussing the possibility of keeping Kieran here and using the compound to house Cory's family and any other guests."

"Well, the compound isn't in bad shape physically, just the broken window in the dinning room of the main house. The only area to take major damage is where Kieran made his last stand," Kellen replied, quick to lower his voice on the next part. "Our major problem is all the magical defenses are gone, and without Kieran or the power of the Silver Witch, the best I can do is ward each building separately."

"We could ward a bigger area if we work together using my forge as the focus of the spell," Brom said. "I'm nearly at my original power level when I'm working at the forge. We could use Kieran's new warding spell and tie it to the physical structure of the forge; that way it would be harder to destroy."

"I'm not sure we could work Kieran's spell without him," Kellen argued. "It took four of us to cast it the last time, and one of those people was the Silver Witch. Dad's gone and Kieran's powers—along with those of the Silver Witch—are locked in his head. We're safer moving to Bangor and warding hotel rooms."

Brom held back a glare. "I've worked spells Kieran's created before without him being present, Kellen. The warding spell is just a spell. Ours won't be as big and powerful as the one Kieran cast when he had all of us helping him."

"What about the shifter blood?" Kellen asked.

"Cory, would you be willing to come back to the compound with us for a day and give us some of your blood so we can make the place safe again?" Brom asked.

Cory's eyebrows shot up. "Don't you need to ward against dark shifters, Brom? My blood is only laced with Silver magic, and you want to stop shifting based in Ebony magic . . ."

"It has to be fresh blood in order to work." Brom sighed, defeated.

Cory remembered his nephew. "Billy is still at the compound, because I didn't think the hospital would have appreciated a wolf camped out in Kieran's room. He might be locked in wolf form, but if you ask him and tell him it's for Kieran, I'd bet he'd let you draw some of his blood."

"Oh, dear goddess, I forgot all about Billy!" Grams had a sudden look of panic on her face. "The poor dear must be frightened and hungry. Brom, please take me back to the house. I'll ask Billy if he'll help us."

Behind them, a sudden silver glow around Kieran's right hand caught their attention but quickly faded away. Beneath his hand on the bed, a small silver hatpin appeared. Cory turned in his chair and leaned close to Kieran.

"Babe, are you awake? Can you hear me?" Cory pleaded with his husband.

Kieran laid still; the only sign of life was the slow rise and fall of his chest as he drew breath. Cory took up the hatpin and handed it to Kellen. Kieran's father looked at the pin closely, and his face grew blank as he was drawn into a trance. The rest of the family watched as his eyebrows shot up in surprise.

"Somehow, Kieran has channeled the essence of the spell into this hatpin. If Billy will let us draw his blood with this, then Brom and I can cast Kieran's warding spell over Brom's forge and cabin, my cabin, and the main house since they're the closest structures," Kellen said as he came out of the trance.

"How can he do magic but not talk to us?" Cory asked, his voice cracking.

"I don't know, Cory. I'm just worried it might cost him dearly," Líadáin said. "Kellen, I had to push Ebony magic away from all his wounds when we were bringing him here. I thought I'd driven it out of him along with the blood that was pooling. Now, I can sense that there's a pool of it at the base of his skull, as well as around his wounds. Kieran has his brain shielded to keep the Ebony out."

"That may explain why he's still unconscious," Kellen said. "He's holding off the Ebony poisoning his system and trying to keep it from damaging his magic. I'll check the grimoire; perhaps there's a spell for removing it."

Kieran's body suddenly tensed and started to convulse, setting off all the monitors keeping watch on his vitals. Nurses came running, and Dr. Mihaylova wasn't far behind them. The Oisíns drew Cory back out of the way of the hospital staff so that they could help Kieran. Líadáin sent a trace of Sapphire magic into Kieran to try and sense what was happening. Inside her grandson, a battle raged between Silver magic and Ebony magic as Kieran fought to seal the tiny breach created when he'd shaped the magic hatpin. Still in great pain from his injuries and weak from battling the poisonous effects of the Ebony magic in his system, Kieran was having a hard time focusing on closing the breach. Líadáin thrust a block of Sapphire magic into the breach to buy Kieran time, and realized as she did so that the Ebony magic in his system was a dark spell that was learning as it acted. Kieran sealed the breach, but the Ebony magic had learned to block and destroy Líadáin's Sapphire magic. The monitors returned to their normal sounds as Kieran's body settled down and his heart slowed to a normal pace. His temperature was still high, as if his body fought off an infection.

When she was sure Kieran was out of danger from cardiac arrest, Dr. Mihaylova turned to face the family. The expressions of worry and fear on their faces tugged at the doctor's heart. She wanted to promise them that Kieran would be just fine, but she didn't know what was keeping the young man in his catatonic state. By every test she'd run, the young man should've been awake and talking by now. Behind her, the nurses cleaned Kieran up and made him comfortable again before leaving the room.

"Dr. Anna, please," Cory begged. "Tell me what's wrong with Kieran."

Tears were streaming down Cory's face as he looked desperately at the doctor, hoping for some miracle of science to save his husband. Cory could barely sense Kieran's pain through their bond now.

Something deep inside him told him that Kieran must have been shielding the bond to protect Cory from the pain.

"Honestly, Cory, I don't know what just caused that. I'd like to run a new MRI and CAT scan on him. I'm worried we missed some kind of internal trauma."

"Whatever tests you need to run, Dr. Anna, just please save Kieran," Cory said as he collapsed on the couch in tears. "I can't lose him."

"My son-in-law is correct, Dr. Mihaylova. Run whatever tests you need to run." Kellen added.

"I'll go order the tests right now. An orderly should be up to get Kieran in about an hour. Why don't you take Cory and get him something to eat?"

"No!" Cory screamed. "I'm not leaving Kieran."

"Sshh, Cory," Líadáin urged, wrapping Cory in her arms. "You and I will stay right here, *mac tíre óg*, while Kellen and Brom go find us something to eat and drink. I'm sure that Dr. Anna will make sure you can go with Kieran for all his tests."

"Of course, I was only suggesting you keep your strength up, Cory. It won't make Kieran better if you collapse from hunger or dehydration. You have to take care of yourself while I take care of Kieran. Okay?"

Cory sniffed. "I promise I'll eat something."

"That's all I ask. Now, let me go get these tests scheduled."

Dr. Mihaylova left the room, and the members of Kieran's family looked at each other with deep concern, both for Cory and for Kieran.

"I know you scanned Kieran while he was having that attack, Mother. What did you sense?"

"The Ebony magic in his system isn't just residual poison from shifter bites. It's a spell, a powerful one that can learn how to fend off lesser magic. I won't be able to use my magic to help Kieran until the Ebony magic is gone from his body. I had to buy him time to rebuild his defenses, so the spell now knows the feel of my magic."

"We'll need to keep Kieran from using his magic outside of his body until we can break this spell," Cory said.

"Let's hope he doesn't need to do so again, Cory," Kellen said. "I'm going to go down to the cafeteria and bring back food and water for all of us. Brom, I think we're going to have to try Kieran's warding spell. I don't want to risk moving him to Bangor."

"I'll go back to the compound and start making preparations after you get back with the food and we've all eaten," Brom replied.

"I'll go with you and take care of Billy," Grams said. "Cory, is there anything we can bring back for you so that you will be comfortable here with Kieran?"

"Would you bring back his hairbrush and comb? I'd like to keep his hair clean and free of tangles. My brushing his hair always seems to help him relax."

Her face softened. "Of course, dear. I'll make sure to get those for you and maybe a couple of leather strips so you can braid and tie his hair back, so it's out of the way for the nurses."

Cory gave the older woman a big hug. "Thank you, Grams."

****

Deep beneath the drugs coursing through his system to keep the pain dulled and to fight off any infections, Kieran's mind drifted. He was torn between active defense against the Ebony magic pulsing through his system with every beat of his heart and thoughts. Emotions ranging from sadness about his grandfather and his sisters to pleasant ones of being curled up with Cory followed. He needed strength to maintain the shield he'd built up around his mind, so he focused on the pleasant thoughts. His happiest memory was of Cory accepting his marriage proposal. His heart swelled with joy when the love of his life had said yes to becoming his husband. His mind began to flow along the memory path leading to their brief honeymoon in Bar Harbor.

The memory replayed, *Kieran dropped his pack, sank down on one knee, and presented Cory with a small box. Cory glanced at Kieran, stared at the box, and back at Kieran again. His heart fluttered. Was Kieran thinking the same thing he'd been thinking all week? Kieran smiled and opened the box to reveal a gold ring set with a moonstone and a matching set of gold rings etched with the Gaelic phrase, Deo mo chroí, forever my heart.*

"Corwin Samuel Cooper, will you do me the honor of becoming my husband?" Kieran said as he took the moonstone ring from the box and placed the ring at the tip of Cory's left ring finger, since the soul mate band, which had once occupied the finger, was gone.

Cory eyes, actually brimming with tears, gazed down into Kieran's silver eyes. He smiled and answered with one word. "Yes."

With these happy memories playing in his mind, Kieran drifted off to sleep.

Chapter Five

The ride back to the family compound was quiet. Each of the Oisíns was lost in thought. Kellen was focused on trying to figure out a way to convince Cory to let him try to tap the powers of the Silver Witch locked away in Kieran without hurting his son in the process. Brom was trying to figure out if there was a way to extend the area they could cover with Kieran's warding spell using only the personal power of two Silver mages. Líadáin was trying to keep her thoughts focused on getting Billy the wolf's assistance in their plans and reassuring the boy trapped inside the wolf that his Uncle Kieran would be all right. She fought desperately to keep her thoughts away from images of her husband lying dead on the floor of their dining room.

"Brom, what did you do with your father's body?" Líadáin asked her eldest son.

"The county coroner came and collected it, Mother. It wasn't easy, since the coroner notified the sheriff, who sent out a deputy to take a statement. I lucked out that the coroner sent Joey McIntire to collect dad's body and the deputy who came out was Sammy Petersen. Together we came up with the report about wild animals attacking Dad."

"How did you explain away the human hunter's body, Brom?" Kellen asked.

"Joey and Sammy were too busy with taking care of Dad and making sure his remains were given proper respect that they didn't bother to search the rest of the buildings. When we get back home, you'll have to use a transport spell and dump the body someplace out to sea, Kellen."

"We were very lucky that Aodhfin commanded so much respect in the community, otherwise we might be stuck in a very messy investigation," Líadáin said.

"Yes, and with Joey and Sammy having been part of my circle back when I could work magic helped as well. I just needed to remind them that exposure of Dad's magic could expose them as well. No one wants a modern-day witch hunt," Brom said.

"How long is the coroner going to hold Dad's body?"

"Until one of us calls in to claim it. Despite the obvious cause of death, he still has to perform an autopsy. Goddess, I hate the idea of anyone doing anything further to Dad's body."

"It's just an empty shell now," Líadáin replied with a hitch in her breath. "Your father's spirit is with the goddess and the god. We will celebrate his life once Kieran is recovered. I'll call the coroner and have him turn the body over to the Bragdon-Kelly Funeral Home. Your father and I prearranged our basic funeral services with them."

"Okay," Kellen said, voice cracking as tears began to seep from his eyes. "Let's change the subject before I wreck the car. Besides some shifter blood from Billy, what do we need to work Kieran's warding spell?"

Wiping back tears, Brom replied, "From what I recall of the casting, the blood and the focus item were all the material components to the spell. I already have a hiding place in the forge where we can stash the focus and ground the spell the way Kieran did with his saber."

"Do you have whatever you need to bring your magic to full power, Brom?" Kellen asked.

"I already have all the materials to begin working on new sabers for Kieran. If you can help out Mother, I'd like to add Sapphire magic to the blades this time to keep them from being melted."

"You know I'll do whatever is needed. Perhaps, I can get Emma Handler to come out and help you as well. Can you add Ruby magic to your plans for Kieran's blades?"

"Yes, I think I can adapt the enchantment on the blades to add Ruby to the Sapphire and Silver magic mix. I'm not quite as good at adapting magic as Kieran is, but I've picked up a few tricks from my nephew."

"I'll see what I can do to help you adapt the spells, Brom. The grimoire has a few enchantments for binding multiple forms of magic together for stronger results. I don't know if I can work them without being the Silver Witch, because they're very old spells and very powerful."

"Kellen," Líadáin warned, "don't even think about trying to link to Kieran to get the power back. From what I saw while I was helping him after he created the focus, any breach in his defenses puts him in danger of losing to the Ebony magic."

"I have no intention of going back on my word to Cory. I won't put Kieran's life in danger." Kellen choked. "He's all I have left."

"He's going to be fine, Kellen," Brom tried to reassure his brother. "Think about it. Once we get the Ebony magic out of his system, he's going to heal rapidly, in part because of the latent shifter genes in the House of Beauty's bloodline."

"Kieran also invited an Emerald mage for the Handfasting," their mother added. "Perhaps he'll be able to help us heal Kieran."

"That's asking a lot from a stranger, Mother. Let's find out what information is in the grimoire and go from there. Right now, we need to focus on getting some of the defenses back up if we're going to use the compound as a base of operations," Kellen said as he turned the SUV onto the long driveway leading up to the Oisín home.

"It will take me a while to get the furnace in the forge up to a working temperature, Kellen," Brom said. "That should give you and Mother time to find Billy, get his cooperation, and check over the grimoire. When you come to the forge, bring water and food besides whatever supplies you need for working the ritual. I'll set the forge's wards and then leave the doorway open for you."

Once the SUV was parked and they'd gotten out, the members of Kieran's family spread out, each going to their chosen task. Líadáin went to her kitchen without passing through the dining room. Kellen headed for his father's library where he'd put the family grimoire after reclaiming it from Kieran's cabin on an earlier visit. Brom headed for his cabin and the forge nearby to begin lighting and heating the furnace. What time they had to prepare was short

Kethric Wilcox

Interlude: The Master Gets a Report

The Master lounged in his giant four-poster bed. Between his outstretched legs, his current apprentice-slave—blindfolded and bound in tight leather—sucked on his thick, uncut cock. Once known as William Harkrider, the slave had traded away his freedom and his family's greatest treasure to obtain lessons in the dark arts. It had been with great delight that the Master had plundered Harkrider's virginity in all forms. The mewling mass of flesh could barely recall its name these days. While he was being serviced, the Master received a message spell from his primary apprentice, whom he'd sent to watch over the operation to collect the Belle boy from Maine.

Master, it is with great displeasure that I must inform you of the failure of the hunter and the shifters to secure your prize. While the owl-bitch managed to destroy the defenses and kill one of the Silver mages, she paid for it with her life. Kincaid and his shifters tore the place apart looking for the targets, but only found the boy you wanted as a prize. The boy is the most powerful Silver mage I've ever felt. He's also something else besides a mage, because he fought off the majority of the shifters with weapons. The boy cut them down like he'd trained with hunters. In the end, the pack took him down and infected him with Ebony magic from their bites, but he unleashed a spell of destruction that nothing could have survived. His family found Kincaid and dispatched him. I'm sorry, Master, but your prize is dead.

Ebony magic swirled around the Master's hands and hurled the helpless slave across the room, smashing him into a wall. The mage stormed from his bedroom, dark magic swirling around him to cloak his appearance as he moved to his ritual chamber. Slaves and servants alike fled in terror from their dark master. He seethed, and those not fast enough to escape his path died. When he reached his ritual space, he uttered a few syllables of an ancient language, and a pool of Ebony magic glimmered before him like a mockery of a magic mirror.

"Show me where the boy I seek is. My dark magic dwells in his blood now thanks to the bites of those shifters. Show me!"

The magic pool swirled and rippled before parting to show Kieran lying in a hospital bed hooked up to monitors, arms heavily bandaged and legs under the blanket. His beautiful face was a mass of bruises, and his long silky hair was a mess. Beside him, the Master glimpsed a blond youth, but before he could focus on either boy further, his spell shattered. His vision was lost, but not in memory.

Chapter Six

John Mason paced in the terminal of Little Rock's William and Hillary Clinton National Airport, hoping that Kieran would pick up his phone. Professor Mason's nerves were nearly shot when a female voice answered the phone.

"Hello?"

"Hello, I'm trying to reach Kieran Belle." John fought to keep his voice calm. "Do I have the right number?"

"Yes, this is my grandson's phone. How do you know Kieran?" the woman asked.

"I'm his photography professor at the University of Arkansas at Little Rock, and he invited me to participate in his handfasting, Mrs. Belle?" John's voice rose in question, not sure of the woman's identity aside from her mention that Kieran was her grandson.

"Oh heavens no, I'm not his maternal grandmother. I'm sorry, Professor. I'm Líadáin Oisín, Kieran's paternal grandmother. I didn't catch your name."

"It's John Mason. Am I correct in guessing Kieran isn't available to come to the phone?"

"Yes, I—I—I'm going to give the phone over to Cory. He'll explain."

John listened as the phone went static for a moment before a young man's voice came across the line. As the young man started to speak, the airline began to announce the boarding of John's flight.

"Hello, Professor Mason? Are you there? This is Cory Cooper."

"Cory, I'm at the airport in Little Rock, and they've just announced that they're ready to board my flight. What's happened to Kieran?"

"There was an accident, and Kieran was severely injured. The doctors are doing what they can, but there are conditions I can't talk about over the phone. Are you coming here to Maine?"

"Yes, I have to change planes in Charlotte, North Carolina and Washington D.C., but I'm suppose to arrive around five o'clock tonight in Bangor."

"Keep us posted on your progress, Professor, and I'll have Kieran's uncle pick you up at the airport when you arrive in Bangor."

"I'll call again from D.C., Cory." John ended the call and shut off his phone as he moved to get in line to board the flight from Little Rock.

Flying from Little Rock to Charlotte was uneventful, and there was plenty of time for his layover. On the flight to D.C., John fidgeted in his seat, seeking a comfortable position as chills crept up and down his spine. The feeling of Ebony magic made his skin crawl as he tried to locate the source without giving himself away. His nerves had been on edge from before he'd talked to Cory and learned of Kieran's accident. Somehow, he felt it was something more than a simple accident, especially since Cory wouldn't give him details over the phone. The chills grew stronger. *Where the hell was the blasted Ebony mage?* With caution, he let a trickle of Emerald magic loose to seek out the dark magic. *It's in first class, third row, not a mage, but a dark object.* John was thinking he needed to get closer when two men boarded the plane. They wore dark suits, sunglasses, and had an ear bud in their right ears. The lead flight attendant escorted him and his carry-on baggage to the two dark suited men. They escorted him off of the plane. With them went the dark object, and John found he could relax and breathe easy again. The flight departed shortly afterward, and John stretched in his seat as much as possible. He tried to focus on his book, but his mind kept drifting to the question of what had happened to Kieran. *Nothing you can do until you get more information, John. Stop trying to figure it out*, he thought to himself.

When he arrived in D.C. and found his gate, John placed a call to Kieran's phone and waited for Cory to answer. He was surprised when a deeper, older, and seriously sexy voice answered the phone instead.

"Kieran Belle's phone, can I help you?"

"Um, this is Professor John Mason. I was calling for Cory Cooper."

"Cory is finally getting a little rest now that Kieran is back in his room from the latest round of testing. I'm Kieran's uncle, Brom Oisín. Cory said you'd call when you reached D.C."

"Yes, my flight arrived just a few minutes ago. I won't depart for a while if everything stays on schedule. I was hoping to get an update on Kieran's condition and what happened, Mr. Oisín."

"Call me Brom, Professor."

"Only if you'll call me John. Kieran won't call me anything but professor or sir."

"No problem, John. I can't tell you too much over the phone; it just isn't safe right now."

"I get it. Did Kieran tell you why he chose me for his handfasting?"

"Yes, he mentioned your photography uses a *green* process." Brom emphasized the word green.

"That's correct, Brom. He requested my services to capture their ceremony so they would have something to admire on their *silver* anniversary," John replied.

"Well, we're glad you're coming, although it looks as if the ceremony will have to be postponed. Kieran's accident was severe, and unfortunately, my father was killed in the same accident. I will meet you at the airport when you arrive in Bangor. Give me your flight information, and I'll keep an eye on the arrival status so you don't have to hang around the airport long."

"My condolences," John said before giving Brom his flight information. "I appreciate your help."

"I appreciate yours," Brom replied, and the two hung up.

After the conversation, John went to a food court near the gate. He picked up a sandwich and drink to hold him over until the airline announced boarding of the plane for the final leg of his trip to Maine. John was amazed as his last flight arrived in Bangor, Maine on time. He hadn't flown in several years, and it surprised him that—despite all the additional security measures—the airlines could still manage to get a plane where it was supposed to go on time. Once he was off the plane, he made his way down to baggage claim to retrieve his luggage and look for Kieran's uncle. John wondered what he looked like, and he'd been daydreaming up an image since hearing his voice. *Brom Oisín, the man has a voice for audio romance novels. I didn't talk to him long, but that voice could induce orgasm just reading the phonebook,* John thought as he scanned the crowd for someone who might match the voice.

Behind him, the warning buzzer sounded as the carousel began to move. John turned his attention to finding his luggage. His bag came around the carousel, and John snatched it up and then turned to see if he could find Brom. Having seen all the crime shows where the person on the other end of the phone sex line had the voice of an angel and then turned out to be someone's grandmother instead of the hot twenty-something-year-old, John scanned the crowd looking for a short, dumpy guy, who looked like he'd be cast as a homeless guy. He spotted a man fitting that description not too far away and was headed toward him when he stopped short as a man in jeans, a light blue dress shirt, and hiking boots entered the terminal and turned toward baggage claim. He lifted a sign with John's name on it. The man was stunning in his looks. Before John stood Kieran, grown and mature, or at least he was a possible future version. Short dark hair merged into a neat and trimmed beard, framing the face of a model. John drew near enough to see the man's silver eyes as they locked with his own emerald green eyes. The man's eyes lit up as he smiled at John. *Oh bright goddess, he's even more attractive than Kieran,* John thought as he pushed himself forward to meet the man.

"I'm John Mason, you must be Brom."

"I am, a pleasure to meet you in person, John. I'm sorry it couldn't be under the happier circumstances you were expecting," Brom replied while extending his hand to shake.

"It's still nice to meet some of Kieran's family," John replied as he shook Brom's hand and felt a tingle of very faint magic. It left John puzzled, because he figured a relative of Kieran's would be a powerful mage, but it seemed as though Brom had the barest trace of Silver magic.

"What hotel do you have reservations at, John?" Brom asked as he led the professor out of the airport and toward one of the family SUVs.

"Oh my, I didn't think about a hotel. To be honest, Kieran offered me the guest room in his cabin at your family's place, but if that's out of the question, I'll see what's available."

"Sorry, I should have realized Kieran would do something like that. You can take the guest room in my cabin at the compound. Kieran and Cory's cabin is currently beyond the limits of the wards."

"I don't want to impose on you. I'm sure I can find something in town."

"You won't be imposing, John. If the room isn't to your liking, I'm sure Mother can put you up in the main house."

"If you're sure I won't be in the way."

"I'm sure. We've hardly been home the last couple of days. Between the rounds of testing and surgeries Kieran's been through, the whole family has been living at the hospital."

"Well, I'll try to stay out from underfoot," John replied.

They reached Brom's SUV, and he opened it, allowing John to stow his bags in the back of the vehicle. While John was lifting his luggage into the car, Brom was studying the man. He estimated John was about six foot two, maybe two hundred and ten pounds; his emerald green eyes had captivated Brom from the moment they'd met. John looked to be in good physical shape, not a gym rat, but someone who took care of himself. His dark hair was a little messed up from his traveling, but he was a very striking man. Then there was the feel of the man's Emerald magic; he was incredibly powerful. Brom could see why Kieran had been taken with the man. Moreover, there was the man's tenor voice, which glided across Brom's brain like silk. Once John's luggage was stowed, they climbed into the vehicle, and Brom started the engine. They drove out of the parking area and headed for Bar Harbor and the Oisín compound. When they were well on the way, John turned enough to look at Brom as he asked about what had really happened to Kieran.

"If I'm going to be of any help, Brom, I'll need to know what really happened to Kieran."

"First, tell me how much you know about Kieran, John."

"I know he comes from a hunting family, although I don't know which one. Kieran has a very powerful gift for Silver magic. I know this, because his gift has touched my own gift for Emerald magic. He's the most talented student I've ever had the pleasure to teach, and if he wasn't my student and didn't have Cory, I'd very likely have found a way to have him in my bed. Is that what you'd like to know?"

"I appreciate your honesty, John. Kieran is my only nephew, but he's more like a son to me. I want to make sure you're the man he said you were. I think you're everything he said you are and more. Ask your questions, John. I'll do my best to answer you with all the truth."

"What happened to him?" John asked.

"Long story short, we were betrayed by someone Kieran thought he could trust within a few given limits. Do you know Marissa Holden?"

"Yes, she's a ceramics student and teaching assistant. A very talented young woman."

"Did you know she was a shifter?"

"No, I never sensed it in her. What did she do?"

"She murdered my father, destroyed the magic barriers protecting our family home, and let a hoard of shifters attack us."

"By the Creator, that's horrible, and again, I'm sorry to hear about your loss, Brom."

"Thank you, John. Kieran chased her down and killed her with an ancient spell that borders on the forbidden. Then, he whisked all of us off to a hidden sanctuary on our estate before taking on every shifter that came with Marissa and a human hunter by the name of Alex Kincaid. We're not sure, but we think that Kieran wasn't able to properly channel all of the new powers he inherited when Dad died, and eventually, it interfered with his personal powers and abilities as a tracker. The shifters ran him to ground, and in the fight for his life, he was mauled by the pack and lost control of his vast reserves of Silver magic. He devastated a huge swath of forest, killed all the shifters, and then couldn't get out of the way of a very large tree, which landed on him, adding to his already considerable injuries."

"What kind of powers could Kieran have inherited that would cause him such problems?"

"Our side of Kieran's family is the last descendants of the most powerful ancient Silver mages. Father was the Silver Witch, and Kieran had only just become his direct heir about a week before the attack. My father bypassed my younger brother Kellen—Kieran's father—as his heir, because he was afraid something might happen and Kieran would need the full powers of the Silver Witch."

"I've only ever heard vague myths and rumors of such a being. The Silver Witch is a character out of fairy tales."

"You don't know the half of it, John," Brom said with a dry chuckle.

"What do you mean?"

"Originally, the Silver Witch was always a woman until some twenty generations back, when the last woman to hold the title decided the best way to preserve her line was to transfer the gift from females to males. She tied the full potential of her gift to the Y chromosome of her youngest son. All of her children carried the potential for Silver magic, but only that one son would ever wield the power and the ancient lore. Shortly after his birth, she vanished. The tales say she died in childbirth, but those tales have been edited by both our family and Kieran's mother's family over the ages."

"I'm lost, Brom."

"Have you ever read the original version of *Beauty and the Beast*, John?"

"I can't say that I have. Why?"

"The original tale by Madame De Beaumont, begins, 'There was once a very rich merchant who had six children, three sons, and three daughters...His daughters were extremely handsome, especially the youngest. When she was little everybody admired her, and called her The little Beauty; so that, as she grew up, she still went by the name of Beauty, which made her sisters very jealous.'"

"Okay, so what does that have to do with all of this?"

"The youngest of the brothers was the child the Silver Witch gave her powers to. Beauty, the focus of the tale, went on to found a line of women, who hunt shifters known as the House of Beauty, or to use the French, *la Maison de Belle.*"

"Belle, as in Kieran's last name. Are you telling me that Kieran is a descendant of the Beast and Beauty?"

"Of Beauty, yes. She didn't transform the Beast back into a man; she killed him. Don't ask, nobody really knows how she took down such a powerful dark shifter. She found the real prince locked away in the castle dungeon and eventually married him to found her line."

"Wow that's a lot to take in. If this House of Beauty is all female hunters, how does Kieran fit in?"

"That's the tricky part of all of this. Normally, Kieran would have served as a tracker for whichever one of his sisters succeeded his mother as huntress. Unfortunately, all of Kieran's sisters either failed the test and died or were overwhelmed and killed."

"Are all these deaths recent?" John sighed. "I don't see how poor Kieran could stand up under all the grief."

"Yes, all his sisters died within the past year. I don't think Kieran would have been able to withstand the grief if he didn't have Cory by his side. With my father's death added on top of everything, I'm not sure what shape my nephew will be in mentally when he wakes up."

"I'll do whatever I can to help Kieran. I promised him I'd be his ally."

"Thank you, John. Get some rest if you can. It's about an hour and a half drive back to our compound."

Interlude: The Master Begins Weaving a Trap

The Master stood in the center of his workroom gathering his magic around him. A giant sphere of black onyx stood on a pillar before him. With a gesture, Ebony magic wrapped around the sphere and created a link to Elihu Hayes, his chief apprentice in Maine.

"I have a task for you, apprentice."

"I hear and obey, Master."

"You must go to the hospital in town and pose as an orderly. Gain access to the boy's room and work on increasing the Ebony magic in his system. We must overwhelm his defenses, so corruption may take root.

"Yes, Master. I will do as you command."

The Master broke the connection to his apprentice and then recast the spell to connect to the dark shifter.

"Child of the ancient Beast, hear me, I am the Master."

"So the spider comes calling from its web. What would you have of me, mage?"

"The son of the House of Beauty lies defenseless in a hospital in Bar Harbor; you could destroy him there and end your curse."

"Once that would have been true, but a condition here has changed. I no longer have the ability to leave this cursed forest. Some of this pack speak of a magical pact between the shifters of this forest and the House of Beauty."

"You aren't of the bloodline of that pack. How is it that you are bound?"

"I am not of their bloodline, but they are of mine, mage. I am the Beast of legend, sent forward in time twice. First by the whining little bitch Beauty and then by a male hunter of her line who was too much of a coward to face me in battle."

"You've somehow been caught up in the magic woven in your bloodline. Something of each side must be bound to the spell. Most likely, it's blood bound and done so with Silver magic. You will have to find out what the other half is in order to break the spell. Send some of your pack to kill the son of Beauty."

"No, I will have the joy of destroying the last of the bitch's bloodline. Have your minions bring him here to me, or better yet, prove your worth to me and bring him here yourself. Now be gone, mage."

Kethric Wilcox

Chapter Seven

Kellen Oisín stood just outside his son's hospital room, trying to convince his son-in-law Cory to go to the Bangor Airport to pick up his parents. Mr. and Mrs. Cooper were due to arrive in a couple of hours, and driving took an hour and fifteen minutes if traffic wasn't crazy.

"Cory, you're the best person to go and pick up your parents. They won't know who to look for if Brom or I go to pick them up."

"I've been away from Kieran for an entire night, Kellen. I don't want to be away from him any longer."

"You still don't trust that I won't try and take back the powers of the Silver Witch while you're gone. I get that, and both my mother and I have told you it can't be done without killing Kieran. I'm not going to lose my son, Cory."

"You're right that I don't trust you not to make the attempt," he confessed. "If I'm not here, there's nothing to prevent you from trying."

Kellen and Cory paused their conversation as a nurse went by on her rounds. The sounds of monitors both in Kieran's room and from other rooms along the hall filled the silence. Once the nurse was gone, Kellen resumed the conversation.

"Cory, there are several things preventing me from trying, one of which is the fact that both Kieran's and your own life would be lost should I try and fail. There's also the massive amount of Ebony magic in his system, which is actually a spell that won't hesitate to attack both Kieran and myself. If we both die, the only person left holding the ancient spell binding shifters to their one form is Brom."

"You can still go get my parents from the airport. Just do what Brom did when he picked up Professor Mason; use a sign with my parents' names on it."

"They're going to be looking for you, Cory, not someone they don't know with a sign. Besides they'll want to ask all kinds of questions, some of which only you will be able to answer. I give you my word on Kieran's life that I will not attempt to make any kind of magic connection to Kieran while you're away."

"I don't trust you after everything you've conspired to do over the past couple of months, but I'll go. You're right about the questions my parents will ask, and I should be the one to tell them all their

plans to keep me from shifting have gone to hell in a handbasket."
Cory started to turn away but stopped. "If anything happens to him
while I'm away, Kellen, I'll tear you apart with my bare claws."

"I promise you, nothing magical will happen to him on my
watch."

Cory walked off toward the elevators for the trip down to the
parking levels. Kellen went into Kieran's room and sat in the visitor's
chair beside his son's hospital bed. Hospital sounds intruded into his
thoughts as he watched his son battered and broken body fight for
existence. He'd read and re-read everything the family grimoire had
on transferring the power from one Silver Witch to another and had
concluded that it wasn't possible to do it, not with the conditions
that existed. The presence of the Ebony magic in Kieran's system
made it impossible to establish a link between them. He was glad he
was alone with Kieran for the moment so that no one else could see
his frustration over being powerless to help his son. Tears stung his
face as Kellen finally let himself feel the loss of his daughters as he
faced the possible loss of the last of his children.

Kellen leaned forward and took Kieran's right hand between his
own. He brought the heavily bandaged hand to his face and held it
against his cheek. His tears continued to flow. "I'm so sorry that we
forced you down this path, Kieran. I wish I could undo everything
that was done to bring about this outcome. I should have done more
to help your sisters pass the test. I could have—No, I should have
given at least Rosie a protection spell to help her become the
Huntress of the House of Beauty."

Kellen put Kieran's hand back down on the bed before he buried
his face in his own hands. The dam on his emotions finally broken,
Kellen let his tears flow.

****

A few hours earlier, Cory had let Kellen convince him to go and pick
up his parents from the Bangor Airport. Against his better judgment,
Cory had taken the minivan and made the drive to Bangor, relying on
the GPS to get him to the airport. He checked the arrival board and
found he was early; his parents' flight wouldn't arrive for at least
another half hour. He found a coffee stand and ordered a coffee and
a muffin. After his order was ready, he found a bench where he could
keep an eye on the arrival board while he ate. He reached for the
bond between himself and Kieran and poured his love down it.

There was the faintest of responses back down the link. Cory could tell his husband was focused on fending off the Ebony magic in his system, but Cory wished there was something he could do to help Kieran.

Cory tossed his trash and began wandering the airport, trying to kill time and not worry about Kieran under Kellen's watchful eye. If Brom or Grams had said they'd watch over Kieran while he was here waiting for his parents, Cory wouldn't be so worried, but Kellen and Gramps had been plotting events in Kieran's life all summer. Kellen hadn't expected his father to cut him out of the succession for the power of the Silver Witch when he'd made sure Kieran would inherit directly from him. While it was true Kellen was the most likely person to preserve the ancient bloodline by having children, Cory worried he'd sacrifice the last of his previous family in order to make sure any new family he eventually sired wouldn't have any rivals. No matter how many times Kellen swore Kieran's life was more important than the power, Cory didn't believe him; after all, he'd let all five of his daughters die so that Kieran would be forced to take up the mysterious destiny of the Silver Hunter in the prophecy. *No, I'm not going to let him toss Kieran to the wolves just to fulfill some ancient prophecy. Kieran doesn't want that life for himself, and I'm going to see that he gets the normal life he wants.* Cory looked up and found that the board was showing his parents' flight had just arrived and that their baggage was slotted for baggage claim on carousel six. Shaking himself from his gloomy thoughts, he made his way to the baggage claim area to wait for his parents.

Jonathan and Tamara Cooper made their way down the concourse from their plane to baggage claim. Tamara spotted Cory hanging about the baggage carousel watching the bags come down the shoot and onto the conveyer belt. She ushered Jonathan forward to greet their son.

"Corwin, here we are," Tamara called out.

Cory turned at the sound of his full name. *Only mother calls me Corwin*, he thought. He waved to them and then wrapped his mother in a hug when she was close enough. "Mom, Dad, it's good to see you. Was your trip okay?"

"We managed two layovers, but the long layover in Washington D.C. was a bit much. We're here for you now. How are you holding up?"

"Honestly, I'm dead tired, and I'm worried that Kieran isn't going to ever wake up."

"What about his family? Aren't they taking turns watching him so you can get some sleep and eat something?"

"Yes, Mom. Kellen, Kieran's father, is with him right now. Can we please wait until we get to the car? This isn't something we should be discussing in public."

"Of course, Corwin." Tamara then turned to find Jonathan trying to catch their bag. "Go and help your father with the bag, please, Corwin."

Cory moved with a grace his mother had never seen in him, and she watched as he swiped up his parents' suitcase with ease. Jonathan looked as his son with a stunned expression before thanking him for getting the bag. Cory led the way out of the airport and over to where he'd parked the minivan.

"Well, I see you boys made it up here with that thing still in one piece," Jonathan remarked as Cory opened the back hatch to put away his parents' suitcase.

"We had to stop a couple of times to have some repairs made, but Kieran managed to get a tracking job wherever we happened to be," Cory replied as he closed the hatch.

The Coopers got in the van, and Cory started it up and headed back to Bar Harbor.

"So why didn't you call to tell us you and Kieran were getting married in a civil ceremony before the handfasting?" Tamara asked. "You know we would have come up sooner."

"We got married on the spur of the moment. Kieran didn't want to wait until the handfasting to have the civil ceremony, and I agreed with him. We wanted something that was just ours. The handfasting is more for Kieran's family," Cory replied.

"It's okay, Son. Your mother and I understand," Jonathan said. "I'm sure the Belles are happy you're already married."

"I don't know about the Belle family, Dad. We've been staying with Kieran's father's side of the family, the Oisín side. Kieran used his mother's last name to keep his father's family hidden. When we got married, he decided to combine his father's family name with our family name. We're Mr. and Mr. Oisín-Cooper."

"We're both happy for you, Corwin," Tamara said. "We just wish we could have been there when you took your vows."

"Mom, you will be there when we exchange our real vows. What we've already done was mostly legal paperwork. There wasn't any major ceremony. This handfasting is the big deal, so you will be there for the main event in my life."

"I'm thinking we're skipping over the shifter in the car, Son," Jonathan said.

"I wasn't the one the gene for shifting was bred out of, but you knew that already, Dad. Your binding spell on my shifter gene broke."

"I can't sense any Ebony magic in you. You're all Silver magic, but your ability to shift still exists. There's never been a silver shifter before."

"Nope, I'm the first. It seems I'm part of an ancient prophecy that has Kieran trapped in a life he doesn't want. I'm Kieran's soul mate and the silver shifter at his right hand. Billy is the ebony shifter at his left hand."

"The prophecy regarding the end of the binding on shifters . . ." Tamara faded away as she thought for a moment. "None of this should be possible if all the stories about Beauty slaying the Beast are true. The Beast is required for the breaking of that ancient spell."

"Well, the Alpha whose taken over the pack that tests the candidates of the House of Beauty is rumored to be a shifter of the Beast's direct line—"

"Cory, Son, you don't understand," Jonathan interrupted. "The shifter version of the prophecy you just referred to clearly calls for the Beast himself to be present. Not a descendant. Something is off with the histories of our family and those of the House of Beauty."

"Are you trying to say that the Alpha might be the Beast from the story?" Cory asked. "How? He'd be hundreds of years old. No shifter lives that long."

"He'd be over a thousand years old if he arrived here following a normal flow of time. And you're right; he'd have died ages ago of old age. Magic must have been involved," Jonathan said.

"I don't know, Dad. That sounds like it would be a very powerful spell. I don't think even Kieran, with all the powers of the Silver Witch at his command, could cast an immortality spell."

"He couldn't. A spell like that would require a caster who could work all the colors of magic, and no mage can do that anymore."

"So, if no mage currently living couldn't extend the Beast's life, who or what could?"

Interlude: A Touch of Darkness

Elihu Hayes, the dark apprentice, sat on a stool in a bar near the hospital where he'd learned a couple of the orderlies liked to hang out after work. He was in a dark and frisky mood as he sat nursing a long neck beer. The Master had given him an important task to increase the dark magic within the prize. Elihu relished the idea of breaking the young Silver mage into a sex toy for the Master. He spotted the young orderly, who—according to his sources—had just started working on the floor where the target was kept. The boy had prey practically written on his innocent face. The orderly was new enough that the duty nurses on the floor wouldn't be familiar with his face. He gave the young man a while to relax before having the bartender deliver a fresh beer to the young man. When the young man looked over to where Elihu sat at the bar, the apprentice flashed him an inviting smile. Elihu's prey smiled back and waved the man over to his table. Elihu gave the bartender an order for a pitcher of beer. He asked that the beer and two mugs be delivered over to the booth where the orderly was sitting. The dark apprentice rose from his stool and sauntered over to meet his prey.

"Hi, I'm Elihu, and you'll be taking me back to your place tonight, so I can fuck your brains out," Elihu said as he slid in beside the stunned orderly instead of across the table from him.

"Wha-a-at?" The orderly shook his head like he hadn't heard correctly. "I think you got the wrong impression, Elihu. I'm not looking for anything like that."

"Oh, sorry to hear that." Elihu pouted. "But tell me, how often do you have a hot guy not only buy you drinks, but also tell you he plans to fuck you into a coma? If I'm not the first one, then I'll just go back to my place at the bar and the pitcher that's headed this way is all yours."

"No, no, you're the first guy to do that; it's just that I have a blind date coming, and well, I guess when you sent the drink over, I thought you were him."

"But up close I don't match the image of this mystery stud? Am I sexier looking than mystery guy?"

"Oh god, by a huge factor. You have to be the hottest guy I've ever seen."

"Then take me home and let me fuck your brains out. I promise I'll be the best you've ever had."

"Wow, so much confidence. What happens when I say no?"

"Oh, but we both know you're not going to say no to me." Elihu's dark eyes focused on his hapless victim, and the boy sank into the depths of the dark pools. "You're going to tell me you're ready to go home with me."

"Let's go back to my place," the young orderly said.

Elihu slid out of the booth, drawing the entranced young man with him. The waitress was just arriving with the pitcher and two mugs as they got out of the booth. Elihu drew the orderly closer to his body. He reached into the young man's back pocket and found his wallet, which he drew out and opened. He pulled out some cash and handed it to the waitress.

"There should be a guy coming in and looking for his blind date; settle him in here and pick him out a cute boy toy," Elihu whispered into her ear with a trace of Ebony magic.

The waitress looked blank for a moment before grinning at the young couple before her. She nodded and turned back to her work. Elihu lead the entranced young man outside and then whispered the command to lead the way home. The orderly started walking toward his apartment while holding Elihu's hand. The walk was only a few blocks from the bar and close to the hospital. He led the dark mage up the outside stairs to his apartment. Elihu gave the place a sneering once over as he entered behind his little toy. He gave the boy a sharp twist and brought them face to face as he released the enchantment while he locked lips with the startled kid. The boy gasped when Elihu broke the kiss for a moment. The man's hand on the back of his neck squeezed as it drew the poor little toy in for another kiss. Elihu's other hand reached up and grabbed the neckline of the kid's T-shirt, and he pulled down with enough force to rip the shirt open from neck to naval. The boy squirmed in Elihu's grip as he struggled for the air the man was drawing out of his lungs. A fist slammed into his solar plexus, driving the last of his air from his lungs. As the boy struggled to breathe, Elihu dropped him to the floor. He kicked the kid in the ribs a couple of times. When he was sure the boy wasn't getting up in a hurry, he moved on to the kid's bedroom and found a couple of pairs of hospital scrubs and a backpack. He stuffed the scrubs into the backpack before going back out to the living room where his victim was finally starting to draw a deep breath. Fear drove the kid's eyes wide open like a deer in the headlights. He tried to scramble back away from Elihu, but the man made a gesture, and Ebony magic wrapped around the boy's body and pulled him into the bedroom.

Kethric Wilcox

Chapter Eight

Cory had taken his parents by the hospital for a brief introduction to Kellen and so that Tamara and Jonathan could see Kieran for a moment. They'd arrived at the Oisín compound and driven to Cory's cabin, where he'd shown them to their room and given them a brief tour of the cabin. He also showed them the path to the main house and let them know that dinner was served at six o'clock at the main house. Cory then left his parents to settle in while he went to visit with Grams.

Brom stood at his forge pumping the bellows to get the burning charcoal within the desired temperature for forging. He'd gotten up earlier than usual and had waited until he was outside to put on his heavy socks and steel-toed boots. His jeans came down over his boot tops to keep any stray coals or hot metal from dropping directly into his boots. He wore a lightweight cotton T-shirt that stretched tight across his chest and biceps. Over all of this, he wore a heavy leather apron. As the temperature of the forge rose toward the desired levels, Brom felt his magic rising with it. He gathered the materials he needed to continue his work on Kieran's new swords. The blades were already taking shape, and both Líadáin and Emma had added magic to the swords to help protect them from the kinds of damage Kieran often did to swords. With the help of some of Kieran's notes on adapting magic and Kellen's research in the grimoire, Brom had been able to wrap both the Ruby and Sapphire magic into the weave of Silver magic to create a protection spell. It would keep Kieran's blades from being melted once they took on their final form.

Brom checked the heat of the forge and found it where he wanted it. He drew on heavy leather gloves before picking up his tongs and using them to grip the steel of the first blade. He slid the blade into the forge to heat it up so that it could be worked. Brom wanted to be working when Kellen came to cast the barrier spell. They would need their powers at full strength, and only when he was actually working metal did Brom's power come to its full potential. He let his mind begin to drift into the trance state he often entered when working.

****

The ringing of metal on metal woke John Mason from his restless sleep in the spare bedroom of Brom's cabin. It took him a moment to focus on what had awoken him before he recalled that Brom and

Kellen were supposed to be working a new barrier spell over the compound today. He wanted to watch the working, because he'd never seen Silver magic being cast before. John also wanted to watch Brom's muscles flexing as he crafted Kieran's new weapons. The man was haunting his dreams in a way no one had done since before his long-time partner had passed. John dressed in the clothes Brom had suggested he wear if he ever came out to the forge. Jeans, heavy socks, a cotton T-shirt, and leather work boots borrowed from Brom. John grabbed a cup of coffee from the pot in the kitchen on his way outside to the forge. As he neared the forge, the sound of ringing metal grew louder and was mixed with the sound of chanting. Just as he reached for the handle of the door John felt powerful magic wash over him as it rippled outward from the forge. The hammering stopped for a moment, and John overheard Kellen and Brom in conversation.

"I wish we could do something to restore your magic to what it should be, Brom. You so seldom use it, I forget how powerful you are."

"I sacrificed my magic a long time ago to try and keep Kieran from the path destiny and Dad seemed to feel he should walk. I don't regret it. Besides, I'm more focused here doing useful things."

"Well, thank you for helping me cast the new barrier spell again. I didn't sleep well knowing I'd let Cory's parents stay in the boys' cabin when it was outside the barrier. I'm going to walk and see if it extended as far as we thought it would. We need to know how far the perimeter goes past the boys' cabin now."

John knocked as he pulled open the door to the forge. "I'm not interrupting anything, am I?" he asked as he nodded to Kellen and Brom.

"No, Professor Mason, I was just leaving. If you'll excuse me, I have some things to do around the property," Kellen said, heading for the door without waiting to hear a reply.

"You will have to forgive my brother, John. Kellen is trying to keep himself occupied. I think he regrets giving Cory his word that he wouldn't try to regain the powers of the Silver Witch from Kieran. He wants access to the ancient lore that's not in any of the books we have. That way, he can find a way to bring Kieran out of that spell."

"I've been giving it some thought, that spell, and I'd like to carefully scan Kieran with my magic. I think if several of us work together we might be able to pull the Ebony magic out of Kieran and dispose of it."

"Let me get things cooled down enough to leave them unattended and then grab a fast shower. I don't think the hospital staff would be happy if I came in all covered in sweat and soot."

"Well, it's a sexy look, but I don't think they'd let you in the front door of the hospital," John said as a suggestive smile stretched his lips.

"So you find sweaty and dirty guys . . . attractive, Professor?" Brom said with a smirk made brighter by the soot covering his face. "Must be that ivory tower existence you lead."

Brom leaned in close to John and slipped his hand behind the man's neck; drawing him in for the kiss they'd both been shying away from for days. One of John's hands came up and wrapped around Brom's neck, holding them together in their kiss as it deepened into a war of tongues. His other hand slipped down the broad back, tracing the spine until he reached the top of the tight-fitting pants. At the same time, John felt Brom's free hand cupping his ass and felt his body collide with Brom's. It was hard to tell through the thickness of the leather apron and the jeans beneath if Brom was physically as excited as John himself was, but he'd guess from the way the other man was refusing to let go that the attraction was mutual.

Brom finally broke the kiss he'd wanted to steal since he'd picked this gorgeous stud up at the airport. He had to have this man in his bed or at least his shower. John had started to back away to regain his breath and balance when Brom reached out and grabbed him just as he was about to lean against the anvil and the blades resting on it.

"Careful, John, that anvil is hotter than it looks, and so are those blades."

"They aren't glowing like they're hot," John said, stretching his hand toward the anvil and blades.

Brom captured him by wrapping him in a hug from behind, which pinned John's arms to his sides.

"Both the anvil and the blades are still very hot, about 700 degrees or more. They're in a state known as black heat, where they look cool but would leave you with a very nasty burn. Trust me, I've got a couple of scars to prove how stupid it is to assume metal around a blacksmith's forge is cool enough to touch."

"I'll have to trust the master knows his craft and its dangers," John said, leaning back against Brom's chest.

Brom let his hands begin to wander across John's body while his tongue traveled across the man's neck, tracing a trail up to his left earlobe where he gently began to nibble the soft flesh, eliciting a moan. He stroked his left hand up to grip the firm right pectoral while his right hand slid down across firm abs to rest just above the man's belt buckle. John moaned and ground his ass back against Brom's body, only to be frustrated by the leather apron still between them. Brom's fingers tweaked the firm flesh of John's right nipple through his T-shirt while his tongue snaked into John's ear, making the man squirm and bring his crotch right into the grip of Brom's questing fingers.

The deep moan that escaped from John's throat as Brom's fingers gripped his cock through his jeans only served to enflame Brom's lust further. John felt the hand fondling his nipple slide down his body to join its partner at his waistline. He felt himself being pulled tighter against Brom's body as the man wrenched open John's belt and then went to work on the fastener of his pants. Soon, the jeans, a wallet, and a cellphone went sliding down John's legs, and he was moaning even more as he felt Brom's calloused hands grip his raging hard cock through the thin cotton fabric of his boxers. Before he could focus, there was skin on skin contact, and a rough calloused hand was wrapped around his hard cock and stroking, pulling back the already partly withdrawn foreskin. John gave up any hope of taking control of the situation and melted back against the firm body, which was the only thing keeping him upright. The hand stroking him dragged his foreskin back up and over the head of his cock, lubricating it with some of the copious pre-cum that was leaking from his aching shaft. This man knew his way around a cock, and it wasn't long before John found himself panting on the edge of orgasm only to find that the talented hands bringing him there also knew how to stave off that same orgasm and prolong the pleasure. Twice, Brom brought John to the edge of orgasm only to ease him back from the brink before leading him back to the edge. When Brom felt that he'd ramped the sexy professor past the point of all control, he teased the man to the point that even though Brom removed his hand from the man's hefty cock and locked it around his waist, John still blew his pent up load totally hands free. Brom watched the thick heavy load blast from the man's throbbing cock in five jets, reaching to the base of his anvil before subsiding into minor pulses. Those landed in the jeans pooled around the man's ankles. John signed deeply as the last traces of his orgasm finally faded and let his mind return. He turned his head toward Brom and found his mouth captured by a deep kiss.

Brom broke the kiss and whispered into John's ear, "Pull up your pants and follow me to the shower."

It took John a moment longer than he would have liked to focus enough to follow the directions Brom had just given him. He'd never been so out of it during a sex act. This man was addictive and commanding. John had always been the more active partner with his late lover, always the one in control, but Brom had ripped away any thought of control John might have thought he had. He bent down and grabbed his jeans, hiking them back up to his waist before he followed Brom's muscular ass. Thankfully, Brom's cabin wasn't very far from the forge. John wasn't sure he'd survive the embarrassment of being caught like a naughty teenager.

He slipped in the backdoor and made his way to Brom's room where he heard the sound of water running from a shower. As he walked into the bedroom, he found himself wrapped in Brom's strong arms, but at least this time he was facing the man. Silver eyes locked on the beautiful face of the sexy professor. Brom drank in the features of this man who was perfection personified. The slightly curly hair was matted to the man's forehead by sweat generated by both the heat of the forge and the heat generated while getting a load jacked out of his cock. Brom brought their faces closer together, and then teased the already sex-swollen lips with a gentle sweep of his tongue. They parted of their own accord. John lost his grip on his jeans, and they slid back down his legs as he reached around Brom to hang on for dear life. This man was going to be his undoing. At least the heavy apron was gone and he could feel the heat and the thickness of the other man's package. John slid his hands down first to cup the muscular ass and then to move them to where he could fumble with Brom's belt and pants.

Brom let his own hands wander down John's back to slip beneath the man's boxers and let his calloused hands roam over the soft and lightly furred ass. Slowly, he stroked in toward the cleft and gently gripped each cheek, pulling them apart slightly, just as his own pants slipped loose to pool around his ankles. John was moaning into his mouth as their tongues danced. Both men let their hands roam upward, catching the T-shirt the other man wore and working it up until they were both trying to remove the offending garment from the other and getting twisted up in them because they didn't want to break the kiss. Brom used his strength to break the kiss and strip John's shirt away before removing his own. Now both men were naked to the waist and panting with deepening lust.

John let his hands roam over Brom's work-defined chest and through the heavy coating of hair that covered his pectorals before narrowing into a trail over his abs to the waistband of his boxer briefs. The bulge in that underwear promised a cock at least as thick and long as John's own. Brom, for his part, was taking in the lighter covering of hair on John's defined chest. There was just enough hair dusting the upper chest to make him sexy. John's treasure trail began at his naval and vanished into his boxers. Brom used his bigger frame to move John back toward the king-sized bed that dominated his bedroom. John found himself falling backward as his knees connected with the bedframe. He lay sprawled on Brom's bed, reminded that he was wearing heavy boots as his feet dangled off the edge of the bed. Just as he was about to try and sit up to remove them, he watched Brom drop to his knees and begin unlacing them. They were soon undone, and Brom gripped them and John's jeans. He pulled them off, leaving the man in his socks and boxers. Brom then fumbled with the laces on his own boots as he gazed up the long muscular legs of the smoking hot professor sprawled on his bed. Once his laces were loose enough, Brom rose and toed the boots and his jeans off, leaving himself in his socks and boxer briefs. Soot from the furnace left him with a pseudo farmer's tan. He reached his hand out and drew it up the inside of John's left leg until it slipped into the underwear and came to rest cradling John's balls. The professor's thick, heavy cock started to regain its hardness as Brom teased his calloused fingers over the shaft. John tried to reach over to give attention to Brom's cock, but found his hand captured and pinned. Brom leaned down over John and whispered in his ear, "I want to watch you melt in pleasure again, John. I'll let you have a chance to service me later." The bigger man then locked his lips over John's, keeping him from replying as Brom took a firmer grip on the professor's throbbing cock and began to stroke.

John melted under the sensations coming from his cock, as the rough callouses were so different from his own smooth hands. The feel of Brom's bearded face against his own clean-shaven one was very different from the last time he'd kissed anyone. His partner had always kept his face smooth. With all the differences from the last person he'd ever had sex with, John was rapidly on the edge of a second orgasm. This time, Brom didn't tease him by stopping when he sensed the moment was near. Instead, the man increased the friction and brought John over the edge in a smashing orgasm. If Brom hadn't had his lips locked to John's, both men were sure John's scream of pleasure, as his load fired from his cock, would have reached the main house. As Brom slowly released John's now sore cock with a few last strokes to milk out the last bits of his load, John shuddered at how sensitive his cock was. Brom stroked his hand up John's abs to his chest, smearing cum as he did so. John shivered under the touch as Brom kissed him once more before standing up and offering his hand to John.

"Come on, sexy professor, time we hit the shower so we can get to the hospital before Cory thinks we've abandoned him."

"I'm not sure I can stand up after all that. Are you sure you don't want me to return the favor now?"

"We need to talk about a few things before I let you have your way with me, John," he replied, kindly. "Right now isn't the time for that discussion. Let's get cleaned up, go check on Kieran and Cory, and then I'll take you out to dinner and we'll talk about safe sex between mages."

Kethric Wilcox

Interlude: A Touch of Gold?

Elihu Hayes double-checked that the sedative had been added to the food he was bringing to the mongrel shifter that watched over the Master's prize as he pushed the trolley of hospital meals toward Kieran's room. The dark apprentice needed to be sure he could work undisturbed while enhancing the Master's dark spell inside the prize. He'd been quietly studying the routines of the floor staff as well as the prize's family. The one he most needed to watch out for was the prize's so-called husband. The shifter very rarely left the prize's bedside and spent each night sleeping on the couch in the room. The dark apprentice knew he had to strike tonight because the local news had reported the discovery of the orderly's body earlier in the day. It wouldn't be long before the cops started asking questions at the hospital. Elihu arrived at the prize's room and knocked to announce his arrival with the dinner tray.

"Come in," Cory called from his usual spot next to Kieran's bed. "Hello, Joshua." He'd read the man's nametag earlier in the week. "So what are they serving tonight?"

"Hello, sir. Dinner is soup, a roll, pudding, and a coke," Elihu replied.

"Not very filling, but it's nice that Dr. Anna lets me order in."

"Yes, sir. Has there been any change in your husband's condition?"

"No, no change. Thanks for asking. You can leave the tray over there," Cory said, pointing at the moving tray table.

The dark apprentice set down the tampered tray and then left the room to continue his routine.

****

Late that evening, Elihu made his way quietly back to his target's room, where he checked to make sure the shifter was fast asleep from the drugs. Slipping into the room, the dark apprentice made his way to the bedside where he examined the prize. He could sense the stalemate between Silver and Ebony magic inside the young man. The Master's spell was powerful, but the prize seemed to have vast reserves of power to draw on to prevent the spell from taking hold. Elihu pulled back the sheet covering Kieran's waist and then flipped up the hospital gown to reveal Kieran's flaccid cock. The catheter tube running from the end spoiled the view, but it was still an impressive cock.

"I hope you enjoyed your little shifter's ass, because once the Master has you in his possession, that pretty cock is going to vanish into a permanent chastity device. Now let's start breaking down those shields of yours so the Master's spell can do its work."

Elihu began to chant the enhancement spell, and Ebony magic started swirling around his hands. As he reached out to touch Kieran's forehead and groin, he sensed another presence in the room. He looked up to find Father Ivory standing in the doorway.

"What are you doing?" Father Ivory called out as he spotted Elihu hunched over a nearly naked Kieran.

Snarling in frustration, Elihu raised his magic-shrouded left hand, and threw a bolt of Ebony magic at the priest. Father Ivory instinctively raised his hands in a warding gesture as he muttered a prayer to St. Hubert. The room was engulfed in brilliant flash of gold. Elihu screamed as the gold washed over him, snuffing out his Ebony magic. Cory awoke as the light cleansed the drug from his system, and Father Ivory passed out, slumping to the floor. Both Cory's and Elihu's eyes were drawn to Kieran's body as the golden light lifted him from the bed. They watched as the Ebony magic within Kieran was burned away and the broken bones knit together. The light set Kieran down on his feet right in front of Elihu, whose eyes grew large with terror when he realized Kieran was wide awake and his eyes were glowing with Silver magic. Before Elihu could scream, Silver magic wrapped around him and he heard Kieran's voice. They were the last words he ever heard. "Be my message to your master."

****

Over a thousand miles away, Elihu's smoking corpse crashed to the floor at the foot of the Master's throne-like chair where the Ebony mage sat holding court over his minion. They all drew back at the feel of Silver magic wrapped around the body. Before their eyes, a silver shade arose in Elihu's form and faced the Master.

"I bring a message for the mage who calls himself the Master. The Silver Witch is done dealing with your pathetic minions. You have a choice: leave him and his alone, or suffer the fate of your lowly apprentice."

The shade vanished, and the body exploded, spreading gore across the room.

Chapter Nine

Magic raged just outside the barrier he'd created to protect his mind and powers from the poisonous Ebony magic in his system. Kieran felt and heard everything the dark mage was doing to him but couldn't respond. He knew that something must have happened to Cory since this mage didn't seem worried about him. Then had come the shocking surprise in the form of Father Ivory's arrival. The dark mage had tried to attack the priest only to be stopped by a blast of a magic that shouldn't exist anymore. Gold magic had flooded the room, canceling out all the Ebony magic and freeing Kieran from his self-imposed mental prison. It healed his shattered bones and other injuries, including the burned control channels over the powers of the Silver Witch. He found himself standing and facing his would-be assassin. Power blazed through him and fueled an ancient spell that used the enemy as a message. It surged up, giving him just enough time to tell the enemy mage to fuck off before it sent the burning remains back. Not quiet as nasty as the spell he'd used on Marissa but not pleasant either.

Now he stood wobbling on legs weakened from disuse. Kieran tried to turn to face Cory, but that proved too much for him. He started to fall. Cory caught him in a fierce embrace, keeping him from hitting the floor. His husband held him tight, drowning his hospital gown in tears.

"Wolf, can you set me back on the bed?" Kieran's voice sounded drier than he remembered it being. "I'm not really ready for all the standing."

He felt Cory lift him up and gently place him back in the bed. As his head sank into the pillow, the shrieking alarms from his vital sign monitors finally made its presence known. Cory had just settled Kieran when the first responding nurse arrived, nearly tripping over the fallen Father Ivory.

"We need a gurney; something's happened to Father Ivory," the nurse called out as she jumped over the priest to get to Kieran. She was surprised to see the young man staring at her with bright silver eyes.

"I seem to have dislodged a couple of my monitor leads when I came to," Kieran said with a weak version of his normally devastating smile. "Is Father Ivory okay?"

Before the nurse could answer, Dr. Anna arrived along with a trauma team. Part of the team stopped to check on the fallen priest, while Dr. Anna crossed the room to begin examining Kieran. Cory stood out of the way, but Kieran could feel his anxiety through their restored bond. He pulsed his love down the bond and watched Cory relax a little bit.

"So give it to me straight, Dr. Anna, will I be able to dance the Viennese Waltz?"

"That will have to wait until your legs heal, young man."

"Well, I guess I have something to look forward to, since I couldn't do it before my legs were broken." Kieran's grin was a mile wide as he heard Cory groan at his lame attempt at a joke. He focused on the doctor again. "Do you think we can get the casts off and the rods and pins out soon? They itch something fierce."

"It will be weeks before the bones in your legs have healed enough for us to think about removing the pins and rods. Then you'll be doing months of physical therapy to recondition the muscles."

"I think you'll find that my legs and other injuries are healed, Dr. Mihaylova." Kieran's tone was harsh. "Perhaps we can at least schedule some X-rays."

"Which one of us is the doctor and which is the patient?" Dr. Mihaylova snapped back, her Russian accent starting to thicken.

"Better question, doctor, which of us is the mage who knows the condition of his body down to the cellular level?" Kieran said as his eyes began to blaze solid silver and a glow began to form around his right hand.

Dr. Mihaylova drew back as the silver glow dissolved the cast around Kieran's right hand, and it flexed like it had never been broken. The glow spread to his left hand and repeated what had happened with his right hand. Kieran then flexed both hands through the motions of a person used to wielding a bladed weapon. The staff was drawing back in fear. Cory darted forward and took Kieran's left hand in his own so that their wedding rings touched.

"Babe, calm down. You're scaring everyone." He leaned in and whispered, "They don't know what you are." In a louder voice, he continued, "All they know is that you came in here with devastating injuries. They didn't witness the miracle Father Ivory's prayers to St. Hubert brought about."

Kieran blinked at Cory in confusion, which was enough to break his focus on his magic so that it faded away. Suddenly, comprehension dawned on Kieran.

"I'm sorry, Dr. Mihaylova, I'm still in shock over my sudden recovery. I do believe I felt the touch of St. Hubert bringing me a miracle. Please, is Father Ivory all right?" Kieran turned a pitiful look on the doctor.

"He seems to have fainted. I'll check on him in a little bit. I want to check all your vitals personally; then I'll order some tests, including X-rays and a full CAT scan. I don't believe in miracles any more than I do in magic."

Dr. Mihaylova pulled herself up, her logical and scientific mind already erasing the strange events as the shock of finding her unconscious patient fully awake and able to engage in conversation. The realist in her already shoved all thoughts of miracles out of her conscious thought. She walked out of the room and began issuing orders regarding tests for Mr. Oisín-Cooper. Once the duty nurse had finished reattaching all of Kieran's monitor leads and had left, Cory turned to his husband.

"Okay, we both know that you're totally healed, but Kieran, you don't have to go ballistic on these people."

"I'm sorry, Cory. I'm still a bit stressed about coming out of that nasty spell face-to-face with a dark mage out to kill or enslave me. Then, there's the shock of being saved by a priest with Gold magic. Nobody has Gold magic anymore, Cory."

"Well, I guess it really was a miracle then. Maybe that's what the prophecy was referring to when it talked about the rising of the gold revealing your fate?" Cory said.

"I don't even want to think about it. What are the odds of a priest dedicated to the patron saint of hunters being assigned to this hospital just when someone like me is admitted? Especially when said saint's area of miracle working is curing people infected with rabies. Trying to figure out this prophecy gives me a headache."

"Just rest, babe. I'm sure Dr. Anna will be back to start running her battery of tests on you sooner than we'd like."

"One thing before I try and get some real sleep."

"You know all you have to do is ask, Kieran."

"Kiss me, Wolf."

Cory leaned over the bed and bent down to kiss Kieran deeply. When they broke their kiss, Cory scooped Kieran up and shifted him over in the narrow bed. He then slipped in beside him and pulled him tight against him.

"I'm not letting you sleep alone, babe," Cory said as he wrapped Kieran in his arms.

"Thanks, my love. I don't think I could sleep without you by my side."

"Sleep, Kier. I'm here to keep watch."

The lovers managed to get a few hours of sleep before Dr. Mihaylova returned with an orderly to help get Kieran ready for the first few tests. Cory was just stepping out of the restroom when she came in.

"Mr. Oisín-Cooper, we're going to start with X-rays and the CAT scan before we start drawing blood and doing more invasive tests."

Kieran looked up at Dr. Mihaylova with a faint smile. "Mr. Oisín-Cooper is my husband; you can call me Kieran."

"Well, at least your sense of humor seems to have survived the injuries," she replied.

"Can you do something to fix that, Dr. Anna? He tells the worst jokes, and he's not half as funny as he thinks he is," Cory said.

"Maybe you should ask that question to Father Ivory, since you claim he can work miracles."

"How is Father Ivory?" Kieran and Cory asked in unison.

"A little dehydrated and confused. He doesn't remember a thing about last night past visiting with Mrs. Hyde-Green on the third floor."

"That's a shame. He won't be able to report the appearance of St. Hubert to his order."

"Probably for the best. I don't think the administration would be happy about the hospital suddenly becoming a pilgrimage site. Have you called your family to let them know that Kieran's awake, Cory?"

"Oh, no, I'd better do that right now," Cory said, reaching for his phone and punching Kellen's contact line.

While the phone rang, the orderly set about moving Kieran's IV from the stand next to the bed to a pole attached to the bed. The monitor cords were unhooked and laid beside Kieran on the bed. He then unlocked the wheels of the bed and raised the rails on both sides. Kieran just relaxed as he listened to his husband talk to his father on the phone. When Cory hung up, the orderly began pushing the bed out of the room and off to X-ray. Shortly after they departed, the elevator chimed, and a burly sheriff's deputy exited. He made his way over to the nurses station, flashed his badge, and identified himself as Deputy Petersen.

"Have you seen this man?" He showed a picture of the real Joshua. "I'm told he works as an orderly on this floor."

****

Kieran was exhausted when the orderly wheeled his bed back into his room. Dr. Mihaylova was talking with Cory, Kellen, and Líadáin as the orderly got him hooked back into the monitors and moved the IV bag back to its separate stand. Líadáin moved to the bedside and took Kieran's hand.

"We were all so worried about you, *mo stór*. It's good to see you awake again."

"It's nice to be able to interact again, Grams. How are you holding up?"

"Like the trooper your grandmother is," Kellen interjected. "Once we got her to rest and eat, she was back to her usually busy self. She's thrilled to have people to look after and feed. Between Cory's parents and your Professor Mason, she's having a blast entertaining."

"Professor Mason is here?" Kieran asked. "I figured he'd stay in Little Rock when someone told him I was injured and the ceremony would have to be postponed."

"When he heard you'd been hurt, he changed to earlier flights and put in for sabbatical instead of vacation time," Kellen said. "He's staying in the guest room in your uncle Brom's cabin. They seem to enjoy each other's company. Brom says they'll be along later; he was trying to finish up something at the forge when Cory called with the news. The Coopers should be here soon."

"Could you ask them to come back later? I'm worn out from all of Dr. Anna's poking and prodding," Kieran said.

"I'll let Mom know that maybe tomorrow would be better," Cory said.

"Thanks, Cory," Kieran said around a yawn.

"Okay, time to let the patient get some rest. Cory will let you know when Kieran is up to visitors again," Dr. Anna said, ushering Kellen and Líadáin out of the room and closing the door behind them.

Kieran was starting to drift off when he felt a surge of love and worry through the bond as Cory settled down in the chair at his bedside. He forced his eyes open and gave his husband a smile as Cory took his hand. Cory reached out and stroked Kieran's hair. Kieran drifted off to sleep at his lover's touch.

****

Cory bolted upright at Kieran's screams of pain. He groped around and found the call button, pressing it to summon the duty nurse. He gently stroked his husband's hair trying to calm him down enough to learn where the pain was most intense.

"Sshh, love, the nurse will be here in a moment with something for the pain. I'm right here with you; share the pain through our bond if you can."

Kieran whimpered in pain and tried to reach for the bond with his husband. Cory fell back into the chair as pain from the pins and rods in Kieran's legs took his own out from under him. Cory ground his teeth and hung on to his sense of self as the nurse arrived.

"What's the matter?" the nurse asked.

"The pins and rods are causing him a lot of pain. Can you get him something to ease it, please?"

"Let me check his chart. Dr. Mihaylova was supposed to leave instructions. Yes, here they are. Okay, you hold on, dear. I'll be just a moment."

Cory continued to hold Kieran's hand and bear his part of the shared pain as they waited for the nurse to return. It wasn't a long wait, and she added pain medication to the IV drip. After a few minutes, Cory felt the pain fade from his own legs and knew that Kieran was relaxing back toward sleep. The nurse checked Kieran's vitals and made a note on the chart about giving the pain medication.

"He should sleep now. Dr. Mihaylova should be by on her rounds soon."

"Thank you," Cory said as he settled back in the chair still holding Kieran's hand.

Chapter Ten

Dr. Mihaylova waited to check on Kieran as the last patient on her rounds. She still couldn't believe the X-rays and the results of the CAT scan. Kieran was totally healed. She'd have to schedule an operating room to get the pins and rods out of him so that the bones in his legs could finish healing. He'd still need to do physical therapy to restore his muscles. The doctor had figured that by the time she reached Kieran's room his family would be visiting, and she was right. The room was packed with visitors. She entered, and most of the people moved back out her way as she started checking Kieran's vitals. Pleased with what she found, Dr. Mihaylova faced the family.

"I'm not a believer in miracles, but we seem to have experienced one, because Kieran's X-rays and CAT scan came back showing that all of his injuries have been healed. All that remains to do is to remove the rods and pins we put in to hold his legs together when they were shattered."

"How soon can you schedule the surgery, Dr. Anna?" Cory asked.

"We can do it as soon as I can get a surgical team together. I know you must be starving, Kieran, but can you go a while longer without food?"

"I can manage, Dr. Mihaylova. Grams and Mrs. Cooper have promised to stuff me to the gills with food when I get home from here."

"Well, you wont be leaving right away, Kieran. Your leg muscles will need exercise to get strong enough to support you again after being immobilized for the last couple of weeks."

"I promise to do my exercises, Dr. Mihaylova. I have an important event I plan on walking to," Kieran said as he took Cory's hand in his own.

"Okay, I'm going to go secure an operating room and a team. I think your visitors should say their good-byes for now so you can rest before my team comes to prepare you for the surgery."

Dr. Mihaylova left, heading off to schedule the OR for Kieran's surgery. The Coopers, Kellen, and Líadáin followed her out in short order. Brom and Professor Mason stayed just a while longer before heading out for their dinner and discussion. Cory scooted Kieran over in the bed and curled up beside his husband.

"I can't wait to get home to a real bed," Cory said as he laid his head on Kieran's shoulder.

"Yeah, this bed is way too small for both of us. Besides, if we're home, it will mean I don't have all this metal in my legs, and we can make love," Kieran replied.

"I think that Dad, Grams, and Professor Mason will help speed up your healing, Kier."

"You know I like the new pet name you have for me, Wolf," Kieran said, turning his head enough to kiss his husband.

"Good, because I plan to use it a lot," Cory replied when the kiss broke.

"When we get back to the compound, I want to see you as your wolf," Kieran said, taking Cory by surprise.

"How did you know?"

"I can feel him through our bond. He's as curious to meet me as I am to meet him."

"Kier, you realize the wolf is still me and not a separate entity, right?"

"It is and it isn't you, Cory. The ability to shift is still new to you, and you haven't really accepted your wolf as part of who you are. When we get out of here and I'm strong enough, we need to go spend time in the woods. You can let the wolf out and get used to him."

"But we'll have to wait for a full moon to do that."

"I don't think we will, Cory. You're something new, a shifter whose power comes from Silver magic. You aren't bound by the spell my ancestors cast. Focus on your right hand and will the change."

Cory turned his gaze from his husband to his right hand, and he willed it to become a wolf's paw. Pain flowed through his hand as the bones shifted and flesh reshaped itself. In just a few moments, his right hand was a wolf's paw, complete with fearsome claws. He stared in awe at his transformed hand, and then willed it back to human shape.

"That's going to take some getting used to."

"Well, we now know that you're the shifter on my right, which makes Billy the shifter on my left. We're going to have to relocate to the Belle estate once the doctor clears me. I'm going to have to find the hidden archives the family historians have kept. I need to know the secrets they've kept from each huntress."

"We'll do the handfasting, and then send Mom, Dad, and Professor Mason home to Arkansas. Then we can take your dad, grams, and uncle Brom to the Belle estate with us," Cory said.

"Actually, Professor Mason and your dad might be useful, but we can discuss any plans later, Wolf. I need to rest," Kieran said, snuggling into Cory as best as he could.

Some hours later, the surgical prep team knocked on the door before entering. A couple of them grinned at how cute the two young men looked curled up together in the tiny hospital bed. The lead nurse of the team gently woke Cory.

"Mr. Oisín-Cooper, we've come to prep your husband for surgery. I'm afraid you'll have to slip out of bed. Dr. Mihaylova feels the surgery will last about four hours, so if you'd like to go get yourself something to eat . . ."

"Will you be bringing him back here after the surgery?" Cory asked.

"As soon as he comes out of the anesthesia in the recovery room, we'll bring him right back here," the nurse replied.

Cory slipped out of the bed, trying not to wake Kieran, but he found his husband's silver eyes locked on him. He leaned over and kissed Kieran.

"Go get something to eat, grab a shower, and change your clothes, love. I'm in good hands here," Kieran teased Cory.

"Awake only one day and you're already getting bossy," Cory teased back.

"Your stomach is growling, you stink, and you've been wearing those clothes for at least two days. Go home; spend some time with Grams and your parents. Tell Uncle Brom and Professor Mason to come and stand watch. They can wear the pacing path deeper in the tile of the waiting room." Kieran flashed one of his irresistible smiles.

"Okay, but I'll be back before the doctor is done," Cory said as he left the room and called Brom's phone. "Uncle Brom, they're getting him ready for surgery, and he's sending me home. He wants you and Professor Mason to come and pace in the waiting room. Yes, I'm just heading downstairs. Let Grams know I'm headed back. No, he didn't ask for Kellen for some reason. I don't know, I think his mind is on other things. Thanks, Uncle Brom." Cory hung up and stuffed his phone in his pocket as he headed down and out to the minivan.

As Cory crossed the waiting room headed for the exit, he caught a fragment of the local news.

"Police are still looking into the brutal slaying of local hospital orderly, Joshua Prescott, who was found dead in his apartment two days ago by his landlord. If you have any information on Joshua Prescott, please call . . ."

Chapter Eleven

While Elihu Hayes—the dark apprentice—had been attacking Kieran the previous evening, Brom and John had been out to dinner at the Black Friar Inn. Brom treated John to fresh seafood. After dinner, they'd gone for a long walk along the shore so they could have the private talk Brom had promised regarding safe sex between mages. John stopped Brom when they reached the end of one of the piers. Reaching out, he took one of Brom's calloused hands between his own smooth hands.

"So we were going to have a conversation about safe sex between mages," John said, raising one hand to place a finger on Brom's lips to forestall his speaking. "I want you to know that what you did earlier was absolutely amazing. I also want you to know that whatever the reason you're afraid of someone returning the pleasure, you don't have to be afraid I'll walk out. We haven't had a lot of time to get to know each other, and you have things that are more important on your mind than a casual hook-up with a random professor. So just tell me what's on your mind, and we can build something from there."

"You're an amazing man, John Mason," Brom said, looking into John's emerald green eyes. "The last guy I was with got up and walked out before we even really got started when I mentioned safe sex. It seems like nobody practices it anymore. He wasn't much of a mage, more of a hedge witch at best. His talent made what's left of mine look vast, but he seemed to think mages were immune to things being transmitted via sex."

John locked his gaze with Brom's silver eyes. "Go ahead, Brom. I promise to hear everything you have to say, and then I ask that you return the favor."

"I will listen to anything you have to say, John." Brom gave the man a quick kiss before resuming his story. "You know how much I love Kieran; he's the son I never had. When he was born, Kellen was so excited, and it was infectious. In those days, I was father's heir to the powers of the Silver Witch, and my magic ranged free. Father discovered a prophecy in our ancient grimoire that he was afraid referred to Kieran. We investigated, we found that Kieran seemed destined to fulfill this prophecy or at least have to attempt to fulfill it. I was dating a young man at the time that I didn't realize was a dark shifter until I brought him home for dinner to meet the family. He couldn't pass the defense spell that used to cover the grounds. Father met us at the gate when the alarm spell went off. We argued, and I left with my so-called boyfriend and went back to town. We rented a hotel room, and I deluded myself into thinking we were making love—" Brom's choked.

"It's okay, Brom." John ran a hand up his arm to soothe him. "It's in the past. Let it go."

"I thought by taking up with a shifter I could take Kieran's place in the prophecy. I didn't realize that the shifter had known I was a Silver mage and had dark plans for me. We fucked for hours, always with condoms because he insisted on them, afraid of what Silver magic might do to him if it got into his bloodstream. Sometime in the early morning hours, we were going at it one last time before having to split up for some reason. He was fucking me, and I wasn't paying attention. He slipped the condom off and fucked me bare. When I realized what was happening, it was too late; he was blowing his load deep in my ass. The Ebony magic in his blood infected me, battling with my Silver magic, warping and twisting it. I managed to get off one last spell at full power before my magic was crippled forever. I killed him and took most of the hotel with him. I staggered to my car and managed to drive home somehow. Father found me slumped over the steering wheel with a raging fever just inside the gates. He got me back to my cabin and worked some spell that stripped me of my connection to the powers of the Silver Witch. He stopped the spread of the Ebony magic in my system. When we tested my magic after I recovered from my fever, he found that my channels had been ruined. I went out to my forge to console myself by working with hot metal. Something in the process of working metal opened my magic channels, but only while I was working at the forge."

"Brom, I'm so sorry."

"Don't be, I really didn't want to be the Silver Witch, because I wouldn't have been allowed to remain true to myself. I would have been expected to take one for the team and wed a woman to produce a blood heir. Father shifted the heir status to Kellen who already had an heir of the bloodline. I honed my craft, traveling to learn from the best blacksmiths around the world, and fulfilled family tradition by making a fortune in order to inherit my share of the family fortune.

I'd tried to take Kieran's place, but magic prevented me. The problem is that I'm still infected with a taint of Ebony magic, and anyone I have sex with can be infected and lose their powers if we don't use condoms for everything. Over the years, I've learned to enjoy giving my partner pleasure without having them reciprocate."

"I thank you for being honest with me, Brom. I did wonder why you didn't want me to help you get off," John said. "May I ask if you'll let me scan you magically? Silver magic isn't noted for it's healing spells, but Emerald magic is."

"If you wanted to scan me with magic, you could have done so at any time."

"I could have, but my family has always striven to have permission before we do a scan as invasive as this one will be. I think it would be best to go back to your place, as the magic will take a lot of both of us. I want to test out the spell I plan to use tomorrow on Kieran."

"So I get to play guinea pig to your magic?" Brom shrugged at the thought. "Well, for Kieran, I'd do anything, so let's go find the SUV and head home."

John reached out and pulled Brom in for a kiss. When he broke the kiss, he whispered in Brom's ear, "You're the sexiest guinea pig I've ever met."

Chapter Twelve

Kieran was resting peacefully in his hospital bed when Uncle Brom arrived. His uncle slipped into the room as quietly as possible, and he settled into the visitor's chair beside the bed, casually opening a book.

"You seem happier than I've seen you in a long time, Uncle." Kieran's raspy voice startled his uncle.

"I didn't realize you were awake, *mo stór.*"

"You and Cory are a lot louder than you think you are. Even when you don't say anything for fear of waking me."

"I'm sorry for disturbing your rest, Nephew."

"So what—or should I guess whom—has you walking on clouds, Uncle Brom?"

"I'm overjoyed by your miraculous recovery, *mo stór.*"

"Okay, like everyone else in this family, Uncle Brom, you're a terrible liar, even when what you're saying is true but not the real answer. I think you're seeing someone you've met since we've been here at the hospital. Did you find a sexy nurse to ease your pain, or is there a smoking hot doctor giving you a special physical exam?"

"Kieran! It's none of your business."

"Well, that confirms you've found someone who rocks your world. Am I sensing more magic around you?"

Kieran's abrupt change of topic caught Brom off guard. However, before he could respond or Kieran could press further, John Mason knocked on the door to the room before he entered.

"Am I interrupting something important?" John asked.

Kieran caught the gleam of joy in his uncle's silver eyes and turned to find a matching sparkle in the emerald green eyes of his photography professor. His own silver eyes lit up as he started to laugh with happiness. His laughter cut off when a jolt of pain reminded him of his recent surgery. He smiled at both of the older men who were blushing like schoolboys.

"So cute." Kieran chuckled. "You two as a couple is just too much to handle."

"We're not a couple, *mo stór.*"

"What a thing to imply, Mr. Belle." John's voice was in professor mode.

Kieran looked at both men as they tried hard to look sternly back at him. His smile got bigger as their blushing got redder and ruined the effect they were going for.

"Right! So not a couple!" Sarcasm dripped from Kieran's tongue. "But I bet you two have been spending a considerable amount of time together, and Uncle Brom has made you lose your mind at least twice with his reputedly skilled hands. However, I sense the dynamic is changing. You've been working Emerald magic on my uncle, Professor. Uncle Brom has never felt this powerful in all my life. I'd have to get Dad to tell me if you're anywhere near your old potential."

The look that passed between the two men told Kieran he'd hit the nail on the head. Both of them started to say something, but Kieran stopped them both.

"I approve. I think you're exactly what the other needs, even if you're only friends with benefits while Professor Mason visits. I want you both to be happy."

"Well, thank you for your approval, Nephew. Not that we need it since we're both grown men and choose who we see for ourselves."

"You might be my elder, Uncle Brom, but as the Silver Witch, I'm the head of the family." Kieran suddenly choked on a huge lump in his throat as his statement reminded him that he was the Silver Witch because Gramps was dead. Marissa murdering the old man flashed through his thoughts. Tears began to flow. Both Brom and John reached out and gently wrapped him in a hug between them.

"Let it out, *mo stór*. You haven't had time to process your grief. We all miss his strength and presence. He was always so proud of you, Kieran. You were his favorite grandchild."

"I failed him. In the end, I failed him. I brought his killer past the barrier and destroyed him and the only place I've ever felt safe—all at the same time." Kieran sobbed.

"You couldn't know Marissa would turn on you like that. She was your friend, and you gave her the measure of trust you give all your friends. I've watched how you made friends with Mr. Harkrider in class even though you didn't like him taking pictures of you," Professor Mason added in a gentle voice.

"All I've ever wanted to do was create, not destroy, but it seems I leave a trail of destruction in my wake. I should have just stayed home and trained young boys to fight monsters until I died."

Cory's voice cut through the grief and self-loathing. "Kieran Samuel Belle Oisín-Cooper, if you'd done that, then the most beautiful thing in the world would never have been created."

Kieran looked up as the two men holding him let go. His husband was standing at the foot of his bed.

"You created the most beautiful love anyone could have ever known. I'd just be a lonely college student drifting through life if you hadn't come along. Billy would be a tormented kid shifting into a raging monster every full moon if you hadn't met him. Your uncle would not have met the man who's made him not only happy, but also magically whole. Yes, some stuff has gotten broken along the way, but that's life, Kieran. Gramps wouldn't have wanted you to be any different than you are now. He loved you as we all do. So cry for his loss, but do not question your decisions to live the life you chose for yourself."

Tears flowed down Kieran face as he opened his arms for his husband. Cory moved into his embrace and gently hugged his husband, stroking his hair as Kieran cried himself to sleep in his arms. John pulled Brom out of the room so the boys could be alone.

"I was going to speed up the rest of Kieran's healing, but I think he needed this release of his grief even more."

"We can come back later, John. Right now, he needs Cory and rest. I think that since the dam has broken on his emotions, he'll finally mourn his sisters as well as Father."

"What about you, Brom? When will you mourn for your father?"

"It's not time for me to mourn yet, John, but I promise that I'll let you comfort me when the time comes."

Chapter Thirteen

It took another week before Dr. Mihaylova was convinced that Kieran was healed enough to be discharged. He'd been getting antsy once he'd started physical therapy. He'd been upset when his legs wouldn't hold him up on the first day. However, each day he got stronger, and each night Professor Mason, Jonathan Cooper, or Grams worked to speed up his healing. By the end of the week, Kieran was wandering the halls under his own power. Now, he was sitting on his hospital bed, dressed in his own clothes and waiting for the nurse to arrive with his discharge papers. Cory sat watching his husband try not to fidget. A huge grin spread over Cory's face as Kieran gave up trying to sit still and began pacing around the room.

"Grin and laugh if you want. You haven't been trapped motionless in a bed for over a month, Wolf."

"Kier, relax, the nurse will be here any minute, and then you can enjoy the nice wheelchair ride downstairs and out to the car. Then, you can enjoy the ride home to the compound and our cabin." Cory's grin was evil.

"You're being mean, Cory. I've got so much energy pumping through me I need to move. I want to be free in the woods to move and dance with a sword in my hand."

"You're catching some of that from me through our bond, Kier. The full moon is only a few days away, and my wolf is clamoring to get out and run."

"I want to run with your wolf, Cory. I want to know him, learn how he moves."

"Likely I'm going to trip over my own tail and fall on my muzzle. I have no clue how to be a werewolf."

"Billy can come and run with us. He can show you how to be the wolf. We need to learn how to move as a group, how to hunt and fight together."

"Babe, settle down. We aren't going shifter hunting any time soon. You have to build all of your strength back up. We still have to honor Gramps, so that Grams, Kellen, and Brom can all mourn. Then there's our delayed handfasting and the claiming . . ."

When Cory mentioned the claiming, the burst of sexual desire that flowed from him stopped Kieran in his tracks, and a moan of pleasure escaped his throat. He turned to look at Cory, his silver eyes blazing with animalistic lust. Cory felt the lustful sensation rebound on him down the bond, and it was all he could do not to grab Kieran and rip his clothes off right then. Only the fear of being discovered by the nurse kept him from pouncing on Kieran. If he felt this wild a few days before the full moon, what would he be like when the moon was full?

The lovers were saved from being caught in a compromising position by the return of the nurse. She had Kieran's discharge papers, prescriptions, and an orderly with a wheelchair. Kieran groaned at the need for the wheelchair but knew it was hospital policy. He took his seat in the chair and let the orderly set the foot rests. Kieran nearly gagged at the scent of the orderly's cologne. His sense of smell seemed heightened; it must have been part of sharing the bond with Cory and his wolf senses. *I wonder if all that Ebony magic triggered something in my own dormant shifter genes,* Kieran thought as he fought down the urge to vomit at the cloying aroma. Mercifully, the elevator ride was short as was the section of hallway to the exit. Out front in a parking space near the door, the minivan he'd bought with Cory sat waiting for them. Once they were close to the van, Kieran practically launched himself from the wheelchair to escape the overpowering smell. Cory looked amused as he clicked the button to unlock the van so that Kieran could escape. He thanked the orderly for his assistance and then made his way around the van to the driver's side. He opened the door and then slid in behind the steering wheel. He glanced at Kieran and had to bite back a laugh. Kieran was pinching his nose, trying to erase the foul smell from the cologne. Cory reached across the seat and pulled Kieran over and into a kiss, making sure to leave his own scent all over Kieran's face to block out any other smells. When the kiss broke, Kieran visibly relaxed back into his seat. Cory started the van and then backed out of the parking space before putting the van in drive and heading back home.

****

In the kitchen of the main house on the Oisín's compound, Líadáin was hard at work putting the finishing touches on a special welcome home dinner for Kieran. She'd made all of his favorite foods and now was frosting the carrot cake she'd made with cream cheese frosting. Tamara Cooper had been helping earlier with some of the cooking and now was out in the garden setting the large table. The construction crew had done a remarkable job of repairing the window in the dining room, and Brom and John had done a remarkable job of getting the stain of Aodhfin's blood out of the oriental carpet and the floor beneath it. Líadáin just couldn't make herself enter the room yet, but maybe once they'd held his memorial service tonight, she'd feel better about entering the room where he'd died. This place had been her home for over fifty years, but perhaps it was time to move on and settle closer to Kieran and Cory in Arkansas. Tamara had already offered her the use of rooms in the Cooper's home on their farm. The gesture was nice, but she was still a very independent woman, even after sixty years of marriage. She set down the frosting knife and pulled a handkerchief from her pocket to wipe away the tears that threatened to get out of hand. *Tonight, I can let them spill during the ceremony. Aodhfin, my dearest, I miss you, but right now, I have to celebrate the living. Forgive me, my love, but your grandson and heir needs me more than your spirit does.* Líadáin dried her eyes and then picked up the frosting knife and resumed her work on the cake.

****

The crunch of gravel beneath the tires and the smell of clean pine woke Kieran from the nap he'd taken on the way home from the hospital. It was good to breathe in the clean smells of home. He rubbed the sleep from his eyes and watched as the familiar forest engulfed them. It wasn't long before Cory was pulling up in front of the main house and parking. Kellen came down the front steps and opened Kieran's door before he could do it himself. Kieran emerged from the van and into a huge hug from his father. When Kellen let go of his son, Kieran took a small step back and looked at his father from head to toe.

"Okay who are you and what did you do with my real father? You don't get emotional and hug, Dad. What's up?" Kieran said with a puzzled look on his face.

"I'm finding all the emotions I buried along with your mother," Kellen said. "I realized when we almost lost you that I'd repressed the side of me you and your sisters needed most. I buried the caring and loving father along with the loving husband."

"Then I'm glad to have my loving and caring father back," Kieran said as he wrapped his father in a hug. "We need to talk about a few things in the next couple of days."

"I know, Son. Let's honor your grandfather first; then we can deal with the rest of things life has to throw at us. Now come inside before your grams decides to give all the food away to the homeless."

"I think she'd enjoy feeding all of them, Dad. Come on, Wolf, let's go eat. I'm starving," Kieran said, taking his husband's hand and dragging him into the house.

Kellen laughed and followed the boys inside. He caught up to them, and then led them out to the garden where a huge table groaned under the weight of all the food his mother had prepared for her grandson's homecoming. Kellen smiled as their combined family engulfed his son and son-in-law. The entire family laughed when Billy—with all the enthusiasm of a giant puppy—pounced on Kieran, knocking him backward into Cory as he slobbered all over the young man.

"I'm happy to see you too, Puppy. Thank you for leading everyone to me," Kieran said, ruffling the wolf's fur between his ears.

Cory handed Kieran a napkin so he could wipe off some of the wolf drool. Kieran then found himself being hugged by Jonathan and Tamara, before being passed to Uncle Brom and Professor Mason. At last, he stood before his beloved Grams. He swept her up in a hug that lifted her off the ground as they both dissolved in tears of mixed joy and sadness. After a moment of shared emotions, Líadáin thumped Kieran on the shoulders so he would set her down. She then turned to her guests and picked up a glass from the table.

"Today is a day of celebration, both of life and of death. It has always been the tradition of the Oisín clan to mourn a birth and to celebrate a death. We mourn birth, because it separates us from our full participation with the divine, and we celebrate death, for it reunites us with the divine until we are needed again. We also celebrate the living and the miraculous healing given to Kieran. *Mo sheacht mbeannacht ort, mo stór*!"

Kieran, Brom, and Kellen all leaned over and whispered a translation to Cory, John, Tamara, and Jonathan.

"It means, 'My seven blessings on you, my treasure,'" Kieran whispered in Cory's ear before taking up his glass and returning the toast with a blessing in return. "*Go riabh míle maith agat, Maimeó!* May you have a hundred thousand good things, Grandmother."

The combined families settled in to eat dinner and enjoy being together. Kieran made a huge dent in the piles of food before him.

He couldn't believe how hungry he was; he even managed two huge slices of cake. When dinner had been demolished, the gathering broke up as each pairing went to get ready for the ceremony to honor Aodhfin Oisín's life and passing.

Cory drove Kieran and his own parents back to their cabin. When they entered the cabin, Tamara and Jonathan withdrew to the guest room so that Kieran and Cory could have some privacy. Cory led Kieran upstairs to their bedroom, where he slowly undressed his husband and then stripped off his own clothes. Kieran drew Cory into a full body hug, and their hands were soon caressing and exploring each other's body, getting reacquainted with each other. When Cory reached for Kieran's raging hard on, Kieran stopped his hand with one of his own; his other hand touched one finger to Cory's lips to prevent a protest.

"After the ceremony for Gramps, my heart. Then, we can give ourselves over to our passion for each other. Come shower with me, and then we need to get dressed."

"What should I wear, Kier?"

"Wear the nicest clothes you brought with you, Cory."

"What are you going to wear?"

"My tracker armor," Kieran replied as he pulled the heavy leather outfit and boots from the closet.

After they'd laid their clothing out on the bed, they went and showered, each lathering the other and Cory washing Kieran's hair before braiding it as Kieran directed, weaving in the silver chains. They dried off and then dressed in silence before returning downstairs where they met up with Tamara and Jonathan dressed in their nicest clothes. Silence reigned over the group as they returned to the car and drove back to the main house. Kieran led them inside to the library where they were met by Kellen and Líadáin and joined shortly afterward by Brom and John. Kieran picked up the urn containing his grandfather's ashes and handed them to Uncle Brom as the eldest son. To his father, he handed the family grimoire, and to his grandmother, a bell and a candle. He gathered everyone into a tight circle around him and then cast the transport spell, whisking the group to the beach.

Kethric Wilcox

Chapter Fourteen

Kieran stood at the center of the family group on the beach staring out at the sea. Above them in the cliff was the cavern system his grandparents and great aunt and great uncle had created with their magic. *Here is where I will give your ashes to the sea, Gramps,* Kieran thought as the rest of the family withdrew to give him the space he needed. He turned and scanned the faces around him as a large furry body pressed up against his leg. Kieran glanced down to find Billy sitting on the beach leaning against him for support. He reached down and scratched the wolf between the ears for a moment. *Will Cory's fur feel this soft when he's in wolf form?* Kieran wondered. With a sigh, he shrugged back his shoulders, casting his tension to the winds. His eyes fell on Professor Mason, standing very close to Uncle Brom.

"Professor Mason, may I call on your Emerald magic for some assistance in erecting an altar?" Kieran asked.

"Of course, Kieran. Where would you like it and what dimensions?" John asked.

Kieran made a gesture with his hands using Silver magic to sketch the form he wanted John to create. "Just like this if you would, Professor," Kieran said.

Professor Mason took a relaxing breath and focused his magic. Emerald magic swirled the sands of the beach into the shape of the altar defined by Kieran's Silver magic. When he was done, he sagged a bit, but was caught by Brom and led to a log so that he could sit.

Concern made the creases in Brom's forehead deepen. "Are you okay, John?"

"I haven't stretched my powers like this in a long time, Brom," John managed as Brom massaged his shoulders. "The healings I've worked on you have taken a little more out of me than I thought. Shaping earth shouldn't have been so taxing. I just need a little rest and I be fine."

Kieran had turned to Jonathan Cooper and Grams for the next items he wanted. In a few moments, candelabras of ice stood at the four cardinal points of the compass. Kieran then took the grimoire from his father, collected the bell and candle from his grandmother, and lastly claimed the urn containing Gramps' ashes from Uncle Brom. All of these items he set on the altar before making the motion of drawing a sword from a scabbard over his shoulder. As his hand came away from his shoulder, a gleaming blade of Silver magic formed. Kieran then walked to stand just outside the area marked by the four candelabras. Finding east by some internal compass, he began to walk clockwise around them with the point of the sword in the sand scribing a circle. When he arrived back at his starting point, he took a step back to stand before the candelabra. Raising his sword of Silver magic, Kieran saluted the candelabra and spoke.

"All hail the Watchtower of the East. The Element of Air, I do summon and call you forth to guard and protect this Circle." On the top of the candelabra, a small swirling cyclone began to form, and Kieran continued, "Be Here Now." The cyclone became a physical presence, confined to the little platform designed to hold a candle.

Kieran moved to the south and repeated his formula, calling fire. In the west, he called the element of water, and finally, he moved to the north.

"All hail the Watchtower of the North. The Element of Earth, I do summon and call forth to guard and protect this Circle. Be Here Now," Kieran said before returning to the east and completing the circle. He then moved and placed his sword of magic on the altar before taking a pack of matches from his coat pocket. Kieran set the candle upright in the center of the altar and lit it. He took up the bell and rang it three times before setting it back down. Lastly, he placed his hand on the grimoire and chanted a call to the goddess and the god.

"By Bell, Book, and Candle, I call to thee, oh ancient guides of life and death. I call thee to attend this circle and stretch forth thy protection that none save those who serve the light shall enter or leave this sacred space, which stands outside time and space. Into thy care I place this circle and all who enter."

Kieran raised his hand from the grimoire and raised both hands above his head. From his fingertips, Silver magic flared upward until it reached the apex and flared out to form a dome of magic with its edge defined by the circle Kieran had scribed in the sand.

"As defined above, so be it below, by my will, so mote it be."

Everyone present felt the dome of magic become a sphere, and they watched Kieran vanish inside as the dome became opaque. After a few moments, an opening appeared just north of where the eastern marker stood, and Kieran appeared holding his sword.

"Let those who would honor the passing of he who was the Silver Witch come forward and prove their commitment to the light," Kieran said to them.

Kieran's family was approaching the opening when they watched him shudder as if fighting off a possession. When the shuddering stopped, the tip of his blade came up, pointing at Líadáin's throat. They met the fire in his eyes and knew another entity currently held sway. Ancient and powerful, this entity would brook no lies. It spoke now, and the voice was groaned from Kieran, as if air was escaping from a tomb. Cory turned and looked at his mother and Billy, fear in his eyes.

"I am the guardian of the mortal remains of the Witch of Silver. I was called to serve the first Witch, and I will come when the last Witch breathes their last breath. All who would pass must prove their service to the light. The dark may not pass."

"Tamara, I think it would be best if you took Billy and went back to the cabin," Jonathan said.

"We honor the light as much as you do, Jonathan," Tamara replied.

"Honey," Jonathan said, "that being inside Kieran isn't going to understand. It will sense that you're both shifters, and it will kill you."

"Billy and I will just wait here," Tamara replied. "I don't know how to get back to the cabin from this beach."

"Dad, it's okay," Cory said. "Billy will keep an eye on her. This beach is pretty secluded from the rest of the estate."

Jonathan hugged his wife then moved to join the rest of the family before the ancient guardian.

"Speak only the truth of your person and relationship to the Witch of Silver," the guardian rasped.

"I am Líadáin MacGregor Oisín, Sapphire Mage and wife of he who was the Witch of Silver."

"Hail helpmate of Sapphire, enter and be welcomed."

"I am Kellen Kieran Oisín, second son and former heir of he who was the Witch of Silver."

"Hail child of Silver, enter and be welcomed."

Brom hesitated a moment before stepping up to the guardian.

"I am Brom Padraig Oisín, first-born son and former heir of he who was the Witch of Silver."

The guardian's blade flamed bright silver, and it started to draw back to attack Brom; it sensed the Ebony magic within him. Kieran stopped the blade short. His body froze as an internal combat seemed to ensue until Kieran stepped to the side, leaving a ghastly being standing frozen in place.

"Enough, I am the Witch of Silver now," Kieran said. "You will do my bidding and depart from this place. Your service is over. I thank you for it and dismiss you."

"Thank you, master. You are the first to defeat me, as did the first Witch of Silver. You have shown a kindness no witch has ever shown me since she who bound me guard her dead. My name is hidden in your memory. Should you have need of me, you may call on me once without the need to conquer me anew."

"Again," Kieran emphasized, "I thank you for your service, and now I bid you return directly to your realm."

The horror vanished in a swirl of multicolored magic. Kieran looked over everyone still standing outside the barrier. Then he turned to see his father and grandmother standing within. He raised his hand, and with a word of thanks, banished the entire summoning. Everyone looked at him and blinked as all traces of Silver magic vanished from the beach.

"This is what you get when you do things the way Gramps would have wanted it done. Rituals and strange guardian creatures, family and friends in danger when all they want to do is honor a man who has died. Well, screw it, Gramps. I'm done with mumbo jumbo rituals; it's not my way of doing magic." Kieran bent and scooped up the urn holding his grandfather's ashes. "You were Irish to the core, old man. We should be going bar hopping, getting rip-roaring drunk, and telling stupid stories about you, not fighting off demons from the dawn of time."

Kieran bent his arm back, and with a twist of his body, snapped his arm forward, hurling the urn on a burst of Silver magic into the ocean.

"Rest in peace, Gramps." Kieran called after the urn.

Kieran turned to face his stunned family. Grams walked up to him and slapped him across the face. Kieran rocked back in shock; his gentle Grams never hit him. Grams was always his shelter from the vicious world.

"Kieran Samuel Belle Oisín-Cooper, that was the most disrespectful send off I've ever witnessed. Aodhfin loved you more than you will ever realize. You were his pride and joy. Not your father or your uncle. You. I cannot believe you just tossed him away like that." Grams sobbed as she fell into Kieran's open arms.

Kieran wrapped his beloved grams in his arms. All of his love for her and Gramps surrounded her.

"Grams, I'm sorry. The person I disrespected was you. I casually tossed away the love of your life as if he didn't matter to you. I can fetch his remains back for you."

"Don't be daft, boy. Aodhfin's spirit is long gone to the Summerlands. What could I possibly want with his ashes? I have my memories of all our years together and the promise that when it's my turn, he'll be waiting for me in the Summerlands. No, I'm mad at you because you beat me to tossing the old coot into the drink," Grams said with a laugh and a twinkle in her Sapphire eyes.

Everyone around them laughed, breaking the tension as they looked at the stunned expression on Kieran's face. Cory took pity on his husband and moved to stand behind him. He wrapped him in a hug, making sure that his beard rubbed across Kieran's neck in just the spot that sent shivers down his lover's spine. Kieran kissed his grandmother on the cheek and then let her go as he relaxed back into his lover's strong arms. The group gathered around in a circle surrounding the two young men.

"Take us back to main house, *mo stór*," Grams said. "We'll gather in the living room and tell stories about your grandfather."

In a swirl of Silver magic, the group was transported back to the living room of the main house, where they spent the evening swapping stories about Aodhfin Oisín.

Chapter Fifteen

A few days had passed since the memorial service for Brom's father, and John Mason was watching Brom working at his forge through the lens of his camera. There were some small details, which seemed to nag at the back of John's mind. He watched the man who wasn't quite his lover but was more than a friend-with-benefits. It was awkward not knowing what their relationship was. Early on, Brom had opened up to him about why their physical relationship could only be one-sided, Brom giving pleasure with hands or mouth but never full-on intimacy. Ever the healer as his family traditions with Emerald magic required, John had asked Brom for permission to magically scan him to see if his problem could be fixed.

John thought back to that night Brom had brought him home from their dinner date and conversation. He was nervous at the thought of being scanned by another mage. Brom is such a proud man, and it took a lot for him to open up and share his story with me. I had to show him a demonstration of how skilled a healer I am. I remember watching him jump when I slashed that razor-sharp letter opener across my forearm. Who the hell keeps their letter openers razor sharp? The shocked look on his face as the wound glowed green and sealed up before his eyes without leaving a trace was priceless. I melted when he pulled me into that fierce kiss and then held me at arm's length, admonishing me to never do that again. I wonder if that fierce protective streak is a family trait. I think I convinced him I was a healer. He let me do the scan, and he was right about the Ebony magic infection in his blood. I'm not sure how he's lived all these years with the kind of pain it must generate, especially since Ebony magic clashes constantly with his natural Silver magic. Whoever struck that balance between them saved his life, but he became a dull and badly mended blade. He burns so bright when he's working metal, but away from his place of power. He's barely got the power to light a candle. He needs to be melted down and reforged.

They'd spent that night just cuddled up together in Brom's giant bed, eventually falling asleep in each other's arms. In the morning, John had figured out what to do to begin healing Brom properly. He'd dragged the bigger man out to the forge naked, grabbing a small bag from his own room on the way, despite Brom's protests about safety. The furnace hadn't been lit in days, and all the metal in the place was cold. John dragged Brom over to the anvil and looked him straight in the eye.

"Do you trust me to know my craft as well as you know yours?"

"I trust you, but it's not safe to be naked out here, lots of sharp objects."

"Sshh, I trust that you know how to safely secure everything in this place so that no random item can hurt someone, even by accident. For the healing you need, it has to be here in your place of power. Your magic has become tied to this place. I have to melt you down and reforge you, burn away the impurities until your bright shining Silver magic again."

"John, I'm concerned about what that entails."

"It means letting me have control of your pleasure and passion for awhile. It means I'm going to take your body to the heights and depths you've taken others to. Now bend over that anvil."

"John, it's not safe to bring me to orgasm or to fuck me, even with a condom on."

"Did I say I was going to let you orgasm or that I was going to fuck you? No, I said I was going to bring you to the heights and depths of pleasure and passion. Now bend over that anvil."

Brom sighed and bent over the anvil as directed. He felt a whisper of Emerald magic run over his body. It wrapped around his wrists and ankles, binding him to his anvil. Tough vines wrapped themselves around his arms to the elbow and up his legs to the knees before they reached out and twined around each other, holding him firmly in place.

"I never pictured you as the kinky type, John," Brom said.

"Silence, Brom. The only thing I want to hear out of you is moans of pleasure. Your safe word is actually an action. Use your magic and everything ends; the vines will release you the moment they feel Silver magic," John said as he slid his hand between Brom's legs to grab hold of the man's rapidly hardening cock.

John pulled Brom's cock back between his legs, and more vines wrapped around it, holding it in place. A thinner vine wrapped around the man's balls, pulling them away and then wrapping them so that they couldn't draw up and ejaculate. Brom started to speak, but another vine wrapped around his head and forced his jaw apart, thickening into a makeshift ball gag. Brom moaned into the gag as

John stroked his cock from his tied off balls to the tip of the blunt head. John let his hands roam all over Brom's naked and helpless body, drawing moans of lust from the man. He toyed with the idea of letting one of the vines penetrate the man's ass and stroke his prostrate, but felt that would be too much of a violation. He could feel the Ebony magic pulsing along with Brom's heartbeat and Silver magic. He so wanted to run his tongue over many of the places his fingers trailed, tingling pleasure, but knew the danger of contact beyond what he was doing now. It was time to focus on torturing Brom's throbbing cock and overloaded balls until the man exploded. John focused his earth sense and formed a special container that the vines picked up and held just below the tip of Brom's cock. John began to milk the hefty cock. So thick, and those veins will bring so much pleasure rubbing against a prostrate. This beautiful cock will reach so nice and deep. I hope some day I can feel it inside me.

Brom was getting close, and John could feel the fires of passion ramping up to a fevered pitch. Brom was bucking and straining against his bonds, trying to get just the right friction to allow him to fire off his pent-up load. Silver magic was driving Ebony magic before it as it raced to fill the semen churning in Brom's aching balls. This was the moment John had been driving Brom to by bringing him to the edge several times and then denying him release. This treatment would have broken a lesser man, but Brom Oisín was not a lesser man. When he sensed that Brom's churning balls were filled with an Ebony-tainted load, John commanded the vine around Brom's balls to release, and then he made sure all of Brom's tainted cum was captured in the special vessel he'd conjured. Once the vines milked the last of Brom's load from his now-aching nuts, the vessel sealed itself, trapping the Ebony magic within. Brom flexed his hands, and Silver magic flowed effortlessly around him. The vines withdrew as promised. Brom stood and flexed tired muscles before he turned, grabbed John, and drew him into a deep kiss. When the kiss broke, John looked at the silver fire gleaming in Brom's eyes; his magic was free and untainted for the first time in years.

"You, sir, are a knight in shining armor," Brom teased as he sketched a mock bow in John's direction.

"Nay, milord, I am but a humble country healer, peddling the latest in potions and poultices."

The men collapsed against each other laughing. Brom wrapped John in his arms and drew the man close so that they could enjoy the feel of each other's body. Brom nuzzled his bearded chin against John's neck as he caught the healer's ear between his teeth. John's moan of pleasure reminded Brom that this amazing man still hadn't had his own release. He let his left hand stroke down John's body to wrap around the man's throbbing cock and gently drew the foreskin the rest of the way off of the dripping cock head. His right arm wrapped around the man's chest and pulled them tightly together as his fingers found John's stiff left nipple and toyed with it. John was so close that it only took Brom a few firm strokes to bring him over the edge into orgasm. Once his orgasm subsided, John slumped in Brom's arms, lying as if boneless against the other man's strong chest.

"You, my friend, are a menace. When I'm in your grip, I'm of two minds, wanting to never to be free and wishing to escape at the same time," John whispered.

"Well, you will just have to stop being so sexy and easy to capture, mo fíníunacha," Brom whispered into John's ear, making him shudder.

"What does that last bit mean?" John gasped between shudders as Brom's warm breath continued to tease his ear.

"Mo fíníunacha, means my vines, you're a very kinky little witch, John."

"I'm a very kinky mage when I choose to be, Brom. I haven't indulged that side of me in ages. It was the best way to get you to the place you needed to be in order to get the Ebony magic out of your system. Speaking of which, we need to dispose of that quickly," John said, pointing at the sphere held aloft by the last remaining vine in the forge.

Brom glanced at the furnace of his forge, and it came to life under his freed magic. Soon, both men were sweating profusely from the heat of the furnace. When the temperature rose to over 2500 degrees, Brom grabbed his tongs from the rack, grabbed the sphere, and dropped it into the furnace. The sphere melted away in the heat, and the Ebony magic vaporized along with it.

"Now that that's done, let's go inside and get cleaned up before we go soak in my hot tub," Brom said, drawing John out of the forge building.

Chapter Sixteen

The day of Kieran and Cory's handfasting dawned clear and bright. The young men had spent the previous night in separate locations with their families. While it wasn't traditional or even required, they'd agreed to spend one night apart to increase the impact of the ceremony, not just for themselves but for Cory's family who'd missed their actual wedding. Kieran stood in the center of the main house's kitchen as Grams made final adjustments to his wedding outfit.

"Stop fidgeting, Kieran," Líadáin scolded her grandson. "Your hem will be uneven if you don't stand still."

"I'm sorry, Grams. I just never expected to be nervous about going to my handfasting. I guess it's because I figured Gramps would be waiting in the circle to join me with my other half."

"I'm sorry, *mo stór*. You know he's with us in spirit, even if it's a bit soggy," Grams said with a laugh.

Kieran joined her laughter as they both recalled the night of Gramps memorial service when Kieran had flung the urn containing his grandfather's ashes into the depths of the bay.

"I'm sorry, Grams. I really should have let you have the honors of pitching Gramps into the ocean. Have I told you how grateful I am to you for helping speed up my healing so I could get out of that hospital sooner?"

"You have, *mo stór*. Just remember to do the same with Mr. Cooper and Professor Mason. Bringing you back to full health and healing your Uncle Brom took more out of your professor than any of us thought."

"I know, Grams. I'm grateful for what all of you did. I just have to wonder what good it is to have shifter genes if they aren't going to speed up my healing."

"Your father and I think that if Gold magic really did heal you, it pulled all the Ebony magic out of you and turned off your shifter genes."

"I haven't had a chance to question Father Ivory. I only vaguely remember him coming into the room while that dark mage was attempting to pour more Ebony magic into my system and finish the job. Then, there was this sudden flash of golden light, and I was free of the horrible spell and Cory was awake. I'm not sure what the spell

I used to get rid of the dark mage was. It's like I know all this information is up here in my head, but I just can't access it at will."

"Your grandfather mentioned a time or two after he first came into the powers of the Silver Witch that the most ancient of spells only seemed to come to mind when they were needed. He never could access any of the ancient lore he knew was hidden in his mind."

"So all the ancient stuff is locked away like a fire hose in a tall building; you just break the glass in case of emergency." Kieran chuckled as he pictured a giant spell book in a glass case.

"Yes, something like that," Grams said as she smiled at the sound of Kieran's chuckle. "Now let's finish getting you ready. Your Uncle Brom should be along soon to take you to the circle."

Kieran reached out and pulled his grandmother into a tight hug. "I never say this enough, Grams, but I love you."

"And I love you, *mo stór.*"

A knock at the backdoor to the kitchen let Kieran and Líadáin know that Brom had arrived. Brom crossed over to his mother and Kieran taking in the scene.

"So, nephew, are you ready for me to give you away?" Brom asked.

"I guess I'm as ready as I can be since tradition requires a male relative of the Silver Witch or his heir to give him away in marriage," Kieran replied.

"Well, then we should get this show on the road. Mother, the rest of the celebrants are waiting for you out in the garden."

"Thank you, Brom. I will see you in just a little while Kieran," Grams said before making her way out the backdoor to the garden.

"So any last-minute doubts about committing to this handfasting, Kieran?" Brom asked as he moved beside his nephew to escort him out to the clearing they'd chosen for the handfasting ceremony.

"No, Uncle. This handfasting is one of the few things in life I've never doubted. I love Cory with all my being, and I can't picture not getting handfasted to seal that love. I know we're legally married by the state, but being handfasted has that spiritual connection I don't want to miss out on."

"Then let's get you out to the clearing so you can be complete, *mo stór,*" Brom said as he led Kieran out into the garden.

****

"Kieran and Cory, know now before you go further, that since your lives have crossed in this life, you have formed eternal and sacred bonds," Kellen spoke in his role as High Priest. "As you seek to enter this state of matrimony, you should strive to make real the ideals that, to you, give meaning to this ceremony and to the institution of marriage. With full awareness, know that within this circle, you are not only declaring your intent to be handfasted before your friends and family, but you speak that intent also to your creative higher powers. The promises made today and the ties that are bound here greatly strengthen your union and will cross the years and lives of each soul's growth. Do you still seek to enter this ceremony?"

"Yes."

"We invite you all to please stand as we ask for the blessing of the Guardians of the four quarters." Grams voice carried a welcoming lilt.

"Blessed be this union with the gifts of the East and the element of air, for openness and breath, communication of the heart, and purity of the mind and body. From the east, you receive the gift of a new beginning with the rising of each Sun and the understanding that each day is a new opportunity for growth," Uncle Brom voice rang out.

"Blessed be this union with the gifts of the South and the element of fire, for energy, passion, creativity, and the warmth of a loving home. From the fire within you, generate light, which you will share with one another in even the darkest of times," Grams' friend, Gertrude said in a raspy voice.

"Blessed be this union with the gifts of the West, the element of water, for your capacity to feel emotion. In marriage, you offer absolute trust to one another, and vow to keep your hearts open in sorrow as well as joy." Jonathan Cooper's voice almost seemed to sparkle.

"Blessed be this union with the gifts of the North, the element of earth, which provides sustenance, fertility, and security. The earth will feed and enrich you, and it will help you to build a stable home to which you may always return," Professor Mason's deep voice trembled as he spoke.

"We thank the Guardians for their blessings, and now we invite you to sit and witness Kieran and Cory bind themselves in joyous union," Grams spoke with delight. "Kieran and Cory, I bid you look into each other's eyes. Will you honor and respect one another, and seek to never break that honor?"

"We will," the boys said in unison as Kellen draped the silver-colored first cord over the couples' hands.

"And so the first binding is made," Uncle Brom said from the East.

"Will you share each other's pain and seek to ease it?" Kellen asked them.

"We will," came the boys' reply as Grams draped the ruby-colored second cord over their hands.

"And so the binding is made," came the response from the South.

"Will you share the burdens of each so that your spirits may grow in this union?" Grams asked them.

"We will," the boys again responded as Kellen draped the sapphire-colored third cord over the couple's hands.

"And so the binding is made," Jonathan's voice rang from the West.

"Will you share each other's laughter, and look for the brightness in life and the positive in each other?" Kellen asked.

"We will," the boys replied for the final time as Grams draped the emerald-colored forth cord over their hands.

"And so the binding is made," Professor Mason's voice rumbled from the North.

Kieran's grandmother tied the four cords together, binding the boys' hands as they bound their lives together.

"Cory and Kieran, as your hands are bound together now, so are your lives and spirits joined in a union of love and trust. Above you are the stars and below you is the earth. Like the stars, your love should be a constant source of light, and like the earth, a firm foundation from which to grow." Grams and Kellen said in unison as they blessed the couple.

Chapter Seventeen

Following the ceremony, the newly blessed couple led the way back to the main house and celebrated with their family and friends over a lavish dinner created by Líadáin and Tamara. Kieran couldn't resist drawing Cory into a kiss in front of everyone. The level of excitement, joy, and happiness between the young men was at its all-time high. Their families and friends toasted them and wished them luck and blessings. As the evening was winding down, Kellen came forward carrying a tray with two small glasses on it. He stopped before his son and son-in-law and offered the glasses.

"What is this, Dad?" Kieran asked while looking at the glasses.

"You asked me before you got married to cast the spell of the claiming for you and Cory so that you could cement your bond and establish the hierarchy of your relationship. This is how I chose to cast it. Once you drink this potion, you will be transported to the caverns by the sea where you will battle for dominance until one of you claims the other through sexual conquest."

"Kieran, you could easily mop the floor with me with a single spell," Cory said.

"Cory, you could tear me limb from limb if you shifted into a halfway form," Kieran replied.

"This potion will block Kieran's magic and prevent Cory from shifting until the sun rises. You will both be normal humans, filled with all the unbridled lusts and drives man to seek dominance over others," Kellen said.

"We don't need this anymore, Dad. We have everything we ever wanted, and we're happy," Kieran said.

"You don't have a choice, Son." Kellen stiffened. "This potion comes in two parts, and you drank the first part during the first toast. If you don't drink the second part and complete the spell, you'll die."

"Why did you do this, Dad?" Kieran's voice shook. "If I die, the powers of the Silver Witch are gone forever."

"It was never about the powers of the Silver Witch, Kieran. I never wanted them, and I was never meant to wield them. Look at my eyes, both of you. They've always been violet or amethyst as some have called the color. I was meant to fall in love with a witch or a mage of that kind of magic. I did meet her, and my soul knew we were supposed to be together, but I put duty to family first. This is

your test, Kieran. Prove which you love more, Cory or power."
Under the light of the full moon, the gray in Kellen's hair seemed
more pronounced, and his amethyst eyes seemed duller under the
strain as he explained.

Kieran and Cory felt the first twinge of pain from the potion in
their system, and with a look, each grabbed a glass from the tray and
downed the contents. Silver magic swirled around them, and they
were whisked away.

Chapter Eighteen

Cory found himself on the ground deep in the cavern of pools. A rage burned within him that he was yet again the victim of Kieran's crazy family and their magic. He got up and pulled off the robe he'd had to wear for the ceremony, leaving him dressed only in a pair of shorts. The lights in the cavern dimmed and then flared bright as Kieran appeared with a crash in the entrance to the caverns. A barrier sprang up between the two, separating them from each other. His rage grew as he watched Kieran rise, still looking like he could step out of a fashion catalogue. *Perfect as always,* Cory thought. *Why the hell are we here anyways? What do we really have together?*

"What do you really want with me, Kier? Do you really think we have a chance together, shifter and hunter? Are we really trying to make the story of *Beauty and the Beast* over into one that ends happily ever after?" Something felt off to Cory. *Was this part of the effects of Kellen's potion? Did the man add some of his own anger to the potion?* "Do you think you can dominate me, little virgin boy? What are you offering me?"

"I'm offering you a true mating, including the fight for dominance, Wolf. We both have shifter blood in our veins, so a mating either way will bond us both to the other. I'm offering what I've always offered you, Cory. My heart and all the love in my soul."

"Love? No, you're more your father's son than you'd like to believe. This potion was your suggestion, and he tailored it to be a test. He wants to see if you measure up. I don't think either of you have it in you to truly love anything but power, Kieran. So, come fight me if you can do it without your fancy silver weapons or your stinking magic."

I think Cory's partly right, I read over the formula for this spell, and it shouldn't be causing this kind of reaction. Dad did something to twist the intent. I'm going to have to do something to prove to Cory that he's wrong about my loving power, Kieran thought.

During their conversation, Cory had crossed the cavern to stand facing Kieran across the barrier. Kieran stripped to his shorts and lunged through the barrier, wrapping his arms around Cory's waist and dropping them both to the ground. They rolled and split apart, and Kieran bounced to his feet as Cory tried to grapple him. The lovers dodged and swung at each other, getting more and more

worked up. On one lunging pass by Cory, Kieran sidestepped and
sent a sidekick into the back of Cory's legs, sending him sprawling
into the nearest pool. Kieran leapt and landed on Cory's back,
pushing him under. Wrapping one arm around Cory's neck, Kieran
used the other to reach into Cory's shorts and grab a handful of ass
cheek. Cory bucked and rolled, sending Kieran to the bottom of the
pool. Cory's right foot came down on Kieran's chest and pinned him
to the bottom. Kieran struggled to breathe then thrust his right arm
up, grabbing for Cory's cock and balls. Forced to dodge, Cory
jumped back, freeing Kieran to rise to the surface and grab a lung full
of air. Rage and lust burned in Kieran's eyes. His gaze flashed bright
silver as they locked with the equally lust-filled amber-eyed Cory.
Kieran grappled Cory and drew him into a soul-shattering kiss before
biting Cory's lip and drawing blood. They both felt the jolt as the
loose bond between them rose up and fused into a solid chain
anchoring them soul-to-soul, but lust, anger, and frustration still
roiled within them.

Cory reared back, and his fist slammed into Kieran's jaw, driving
him back. Cory then grabbed Kieran's hair and yanked his head back
before slamming his mouth down over Kieran's and returning the
kiss and bite. Kieran jammed his elbow into Cory's solar plexus and
then drove a knee into his groin. The farm boy collapsed to his
knees, trying to get his breath back and cradle his injured manhood at
the same time. Kieran pushed Cory forward and shredded Cory's
shorts, leaving him naked. He dropped his own shorts, and grabbing
Cory's hips, slammed his rigid cock into his lover's ass.

"This was never how I imagined we'd do this, Wolf, but you were
meant to be mine, and so mine is what you will be."

Cory bucked and threw Kieran off. Kieran crashed backward,
striking his head against the edge of the pool. Cory took advantage of
Kieran's dazed state, scooped him up, and dropped him on the edge
of the pool before lifting Kieran's legs up, exposing his hole. Cory
slammed his cock into Kieran's ass and was rewarded with a moan.

"This is the more natural state of things, little hunter. Just lay back
and surrender that sweet ass; it's what you were really born to do."

Recovering, Kieran twisted his legs into a headlock and threw off
the balanced Cory, driving him back into the pool. Kieran followed,
and his fist met Cory's jaw as his lover rose to fight back. Grabbing
the remains of Cory's shorts, Kieran tied Cory's hands behind his

back before bending him over the edge of the pool and slamming his cock back into the blond ass.

"Enough of the foreplay, Wolf. It's time for you to give in and be a good husband. Just relax, and this will be over in an hour or so."

"Like you could last that long, babe."

"So now you're calling me babe again? Well, at least the spell seems to be fading. Now let's finish it off and make it so no one can ever break our bond. Time for you to become my unquestioned mate, Wolf."

Kieran's raging hard cock began sawing in and out of Cory's ass, driving both men into a heated passion they hadn't had since the early days of their relationship. The fight hadn't completely gone out of Cory yet, and he reared backward, slamming the back of his head into Kieran's face and knocking his lover off balance, causing his cock to slip out of Cory's ass. The binding shorts ripped apart, freeing Cory's hands, and he darted forth, lifting Kieran out of the water. He carried him up to the sleeping nook. There he laid Kieran out on his back, straddled his lover's hips, and impaled himself on Kieran's cock. The young lovers both moaned as Cory roughly fucked himself on Kieran's thick prick. Even though he was bottoming, Cory was in complete control of the situation—the Alpha of the relationship, as he'd been from the beginning of their lovemaking.

"Fill me with your seed, babe; bind us together so that we can never be pulled apart again. Please, love me forever and forgive me."

"I claim you as my Alpha lover, Corwin Samuel Cooper. By blood, sweat, and semen, I bind you to me."

"Oh god, yes, Kieran. God you feel so good. Please fill me with your seed, bind us heart, body, and soul. By blood, sweat, and semen, I bind you to me. Transform us."

Kieran finally gave into his pending orgasm and blew his load deep into Cory's ass. He kept his cock buried deep until finally it softened and slid out on its own. He felt the huge pool of cum on his stomach from Cory's still-leaking cock. He grinned and then pulled Cory down and kissed his lover. Cory wrapped his arms around Kieran and held him tight. Kieran drew back and placed his left hand over Cory's heart, and Cory did the same thing. Silver magic streamed out of their chests and formed a sphere between them. They each reached out, and their hands sank into the sphere until they touched inside. They grasped each other's hand, and then the sphere split in half and flowed down to their wrists where the magic transformed itself into bracelets of woven silver with a pair of wolf heads pointing down toward their hands. Kieran and Cory drew each other in for a deep kiss, and the eyes of the wolves opened, reveling that each wolf had one amber and one diamond eye. Cory slid off of Kieran and scooted up the bed to lean his back against the wall. Kieran followed and settled in against his chest as they rested in the sleeping alcove and drew the covers over both of them. Kieran shifted and snuggled his head down on Cory's chest, wrapping his arm over his husband's waist.

"I love you, Kieran. Thank you for fighting for me. I was a jerk."

"I love you too, Wolf. I will always fight for you."

Cory linked the fingers of his left hand with those of Kieran's and stared at the new bracelets on their wrists.

"Are these replacements for the rings we use to have? Is this the same magic that Brom forged into the old rings?"

"That magic broke when we let jealousy destroy our original connection, Wolf. All magic has a condition under which it will fail. The rings only lasted while our hearts were true."

"These feel different somehow," Cory said.

"I think these are a manifestation of our soul bond, Cory. This isn't magic forged by one person looking for his true love; this is magic forged by two souls bound for all time to each other. Nothing save death can break these bracelets. Whatever happens, we're one soul, now and forever."

"I love you, Kieran Oisín-Cooper. I'm honored to be yours."

"I love you, Corwin Oisín-Cooper. Will you make love to me now? I want to be equally yours. We aren't meant to be anything but equals. Claim me as yours as I've claimed you as mine," Kieran said.

"I think we'll do this without all the combat. I want to make sweet love to you as you deserve," Cory said as he bent down and kissed Kieran as a prelude to their lovemaking.

PART TWO
THE HOUSE OF BEAUTY

Kethric Wilcox

Interlude: Secret History

I have discovered a terrible secret regarding Great-Grandmother's pact with the shifters of the forest. She gave her youngest sister to the leader of the pack as a mate. From what I have been able to discover, Great-Great Aunt Ophelia was totally without the gift of Silver magic, a very rare thing only three generations removed from the first of our family. The most terrifying part of this pact is that it must continue each time a new huntress takes over the family. She must give a non-magical sister or cousin of the same generation to the leader of the forest pack as a mate, or the compact between these dark shifters and the House of Beauty will be broken. I am afraid for my twin sister as neither of us were born with the gift of Silver magic. Our eldest sister goes for the test tomorrow night, and if she becomes the huntress, then I fear my sweet sister is doomed to this horrid fate.

From the Second Chronicle of the House of Beauty, translated into English in the 21st century

Fifty Years Ago

Theresa Belle stood with her oldest sister Camille, the new huntress of the House of Beauty, at the edge of a clearing deep in the dark forest on the family estate. In the center of the clearing stood a cottage, which looked like it had been built using plans from a fairy tale. *Why is this here in the forest, and why did Camille bring me here?* Theresa wondered as her sister led her deeper into the clearing. For a brief moment, she thought she felt a tingle on her skin, but it was gone before she could be certain. The door to the cottage opened and a tall, broad-shouldered man stepped out and stood waiting. Theresa felt Camille move to stand behind her and gently urged her forward.

"Camille, what's going on? I don't understand why you brought me out here. Please tell me what's going on. I'm scared."

Camille refused to answer her sister's questions until they were within reach of the strange man.

"Theresa, this is Eugene, leader of the forest shifters. I brought you here today to honor our family's obligation to the compact. You will be Eugene's mate, although you will never bare his children. This arrangement will last so long as I am the huntress or Eugene is leader of this pack."

"What? Why? Camille, I don't understand what you're talking about."

"I'm sorry, Theresa. This is the way it has to be. We must all serve our function to the House of Beauty. You were born without even the potential to pass on our gift of Silver magic. When you were five, your appendix became inflamed and had to be removed, but that wasn't all that was done. Mother ordered your ovaries removed as well. You are barren. She knew you would be the one to take Aunt Mildred's place."

"Why, Camille?" Theresa screamed. Her thin body shook with fear. "Why would you give me to this filthy shifter? Who is Aunt Mildred, and why can't she stay to do whatever it is she's been doing out here?"

"Aunt Mildred was Mother's eldest sister. Like you, she was born without the gift for magic. She can't continue serving, because when mother died and I came to test, Eugene snapped her neck after I killed the previous leader of the pack."

"And this is the fate you condemn me to? So long as you live as huntress, I live as a whore for this abomination?" Theresa's fear was fast becoming anger. "Why don't you kill all the shifters in this forest? Why do they exist at all when our family is dedicated to killing their kind? Why don't you do what you're supposed to do as huntress?"

"Because we must train against their kind if we are to kill them, so that the rest of humanity doesn't have to face their threat. Because you were born useless for any other duty a woman of our house would do. This is your fate, Sister. All your needs will be met, and as long as you live here in this cottage, the Belle side of the compact is honored. The shifters of the forest must honor their side of the bargain and leave the rest of the family in peace."

"I may be a dark shifter, but I still honor my word," Eugene said. "I promise I will never force you, and you may live out your days a virgin."

"What's to keep me from just running away from here?" Theresa asked her sister.

"Magic, for starters. I know you felt it when you crossed the boundary of this clearing. The spell that guards this place prevents all shifters save the pack leader from entering, but in exchange, it prevents those without magic from leaving. Get to know Eugene, Sister; he will be your only contact with the outside world from this day forth."

Camille turned and strode out of the clearing, hardening her heart to the pleas, cries, and screams of her baby sister. She knew the sounds of Theresa's screams and curses would haunt her for the rest of her life.

Kethric Wilcox

Chapter Nineteen

The Oisín family, Professor Mason, and the Coopers arrived at the Belle estate a week after Kieran and Cory returned from finalizing their bond. Kieran strode up the stairs leading to the main doors of the great house that had been his boyhood home. Just behind him, Cory walked at his right shoulder, and Billy the wolf was pressed against his left leg. Behind them, Kieran knew his family and allies watched and followed his lead. He pushed the doors opened with a shove of magic. A mob scene waited for Kieran inside the huge entrance hall. Massive timber support columns reached up to the roof three stories overhead. The Council of the Matriarchs jostled each other, with the exception of Kieran's grandmother and his great-aunt Desdemona, who stood waiting as the forefront of chaos. Around the perimeter of the great hall, Kieran caught sight of his young cousins, both male and female, peeking out around columns for a look at the first male to become a hunter-candidate. Four young boys ranging in age from twelve to fourteen stepped forward from the sidelines and stopped when they were directly in front of Kieran's party. In unison, the boys bowed to Kieran.

"Welcome home, Hunter-candidate Kieran. We await your approval to resume our training so we might aide you as your trackers."

"Greetings, former tracker-candidates. I look forward to continuing the training of those of you who wish to continue when you reach the appropriate age to begin the full training. Until such time, you will resume your regular duties and return to school. When you enter your junior year in high school, I will retest those of you who wish to continue as a potential tracker-candidate. Go and be boys for a while longer."

Beside Kieran, Billy sniffed and whined as the oldest of the candidates approached and knelt at Kieran's feet. The black wolf edged closer to the kneeling boy and sniffed his scent. A huge pink tongue lashed out and licked the boy's face. The boy, taken completely by surprise, fell backward onto his ass and looked up into the glowing amber eyes of the wolf. Billy nudged the young boy, trying to get him to pet him, but the boy cowered in fear until Kieran spoke up.

"It appears that Billy likes you, Cousin. You have nothing to fear from my nephew. Now, if I recall correctly, you are Ian, the boy full of questions. I feel bad for not remembering your full name, Cousin, but you boys have all sprouted in the year I've been gone from this house. I didn't get the time to relearn which branch of the family you come from. Tell me your full name and rank."

"I am probationary tracker-candidate Ian Belle-O'Connell, Hunter-candidate Kieran."

"And how old are you, Cousin Ian?"

"I just turned fourteen last week, sir."

"Well, Ian, you and Billy are close in age. Perhaps you might even convince my nephew to become a boy again instead of remaining a wolf."

"He's a shifter?" came the startled cry from one of the Matriarchs. "You brought a shifter into the House of Beauty?"

"Do not question my actions. I may not look the part right now, but I am the salvation of this house. I don't enjoy it, but I am the Silver Hunter. I have already passed the test of the huntress on my father's family estate and survived. I lead the House of Beauty as Hunter and Belle of Belle, my word is law in this house."

Cory's hand on Kieran's shoulder stopped his tirade at his great-aunts and kept him from crossing the room. His grandmother, still proud in her heritage, came forward from the gaggle of women to meet Kieran.

"Forgive me for not greeting you properly, Huntress-emeritus, but these boys needed attending to first," Kieran said, extending his hand to his grandmother.

The old woman took his hand and stiffened for a moment before bowing as best as she could, given her bad leg. Rising from her bow, she spoke, "Forgive the Matriarchs and I for not giving you the proper courtesy due your rank, Hunter Kieran." There were gasps from the crowd in the hall. "The Matriarchs and I are at your service, my honored grandson."

Kieran was wishing he had been sitting down. Never had he heard such respect in his grandmother's voice. The woman was sincere in her newfound respect. Before he could reply, she turned, stood at his side, and addressed the gathered family.

"Know this, all members of the House of Beauty, this day I acknowledge a new Hunter and leader of the House of Beauty. I present to you my grandson, a hunter who in his test has slain a dozen shifters and retains his magic. Kieran Samuel Belle, I acknowledge you this day as Hunter, Belle of Belle, and head of the House of Beauty. We are yours to command."

"Thank you, Grandmother. The time has come to clean out the forest of the shifter pack and to put an end to the lineage of the Beast. Go about your regular duties and rest tonight. Tomorrow, the House of Beauty prepares for war," Kieran said before turning to face Cory, Billy, and Ian. The young boy had his arms wrapped around the wolf's neck and his face buried in Billy's fur. Cory stood over them looking proudly at Kieran.

Sensing eyes on him, Ian lifted his head from Billy's fur, but kept a tight hold on the wolf, as if he was afraid the wolf would vanish.

"You two seem to have become fast friends, Cousin," Kieran said to the boy.

"We've never had animals in the house before. Is he really a shifter?"

Billy gently pulled loose from the young boy, padded over to Kieran, and rubbed his collar against Kieran's hand. Kieran looked down at the wolf, and silver eyes met amber ones.

"Not here, Billy," Kieran said to the wolf. "I'll consider it once we're settled in." The wolf whined before padding back over to sit pressed against Ian's leg. "Grandmother, will you please have our baggage sent to the hunter's suite. We also need to make arrangements for our guests as well."

"Of course, Desdemona and Fiona will take charge of the arrangements. Where do you want the beast housed?" Grandmother Belle asked.

"If you're referring to Billy, he'll stay with Cory and I in my suite unless we agree to allow him to shift back to human form." Kieran paused to consider his options. "If that is the case, he'll be assigned a bed in the cousins' wing with the other boys his age."

"Very well," Grandmother Belle replied. "Desdemona, see that Hunter Kieran and his husband's things are taken to the huntress' suite, and put Kellen and Líadáin in the blue suite. Fiona, please find suites for the rest of our guests and make sure there is a spare bed in the boys' dorm if it should be needed. Will you take dinner in your suite, Grandson, or would you prefer something more formal?"

"We will all dine in the hall tonight, Grandmother," Kieran said.

"I'll have the cooks prepare for a family gathering then. Will there be anything else?"

"No, Grandmother, that takes care of everything for now," Kieran said as he turned and led Cory, Billy, and Ian off toward the hunter's suite.

Chapter Twenty

Kieran and Cory had taken the suite of rooms reserved for the Huntress of the House of Beauty after their initial meeting with the Matriarchs and the rest of the Belle family. The four boys Kieran had released from their training as tracker-candidates still waited on them as personal servants. It made Cory uncomfortable having servants waiting on him, and he was starting to get surly. On the second full day of their stay, Kieran had finally agreed to remove Billy's collar with Ian as the only outsider present. Kieran knelt and unfastened the clasp on the collar. With a howl, Billy the wolf returned to being Billy the boy. Billy, the naked boy, shivered as the cool air of the house hit his skin. Cory quickly wrapped him in one of his sweatshirts and tousled the boy's hair. Billy rose on shaky legs and walked over to Ian, and then wrapped the startled boy in a hug. Kieran and Cory glanced at each other with huge grins on their faces as the two boys hugged.

"I think you're about the same size as Cousin Henry. Come on, Billy, let's go see if any of his clothes fit you," Ian said to Billy.

Billy glanced over his shoulder at his uncles, who nodded their approval before allowing Ian to drag him off to find clothes. Despite being a year older, Ian was smaller than Billy both in height and body mass.

Ian helped Billy settle into the male cousins' dormitory by rearranging. A couple of the older cousins were reassigned to the servant quarters attached to Kellen's suite, so it was easy. They would see to Kellen's and Líadáin's needs. Once they'd been moved, Billy was moved into the open bunk in Ian's quad. Over the next couple of days, Billy learned the routines and got to know Ian and the other two boys in the quad better. On Billy's third night in the dormitory—around the time dinner for the main family was being called—Cory wandered the halls of the cousins' living quarters looking for Billy so that the boy could eat with them. He found Billy and Ian sitting in the strangest position. Billy was on the floor wedged in the narrow hallway with his bare feet pressed to one wall and his shoulders and upper back pressed against the opposite wall. On his legs, seated in a lotus position, was Ian who was bent over and whispering to Billy. *Wow*, thought Cory, *these two move fast. Wonder if Billy sensed a potential mate. They look so cute like this. I have to get a picture for Kieran to see.* Cory took out his cell phone and snapped a picture of the two boys before he disturbed them.

"It's time for dinner, guys. Kieran wants you both at our table tonight."

Ian looked up with grass green eyes as wide as saucers. Billy merely grinned at his uncle. He'd known Cory was there the entire time and had kept Ian unaware of his approaching uncle. He liked Ian a lot. There was something special between them, and Billy knew that after Uncle Kieran dealt with the evil shifters in the woods, he was going to ask about the possibility of using his collar's magic to lock him in human form instead of wolf form.

After dinner, both boys were invited back to Kieran and Cory's suite, so Kieran could assess how Billy was fitting in. Ian had automatically settled into servant mode when they'd arrived until Kieran had practically ordered his cousin to sit down. There'd been tension in the air, especially around Uncle Cory until that point. Once Kieran was satisfied that Billy was fitting in with the cousins, he'd sent them back to their room. Whenever he was visiting his uncles, Billy paid attention to the mood in the room when Ian or the other trainees were present.

A couple of days later, Billy stopped them just outside their room and checked that no one else was close by. He kicked off his shoes before settling down on the floor with his upper back braced against one wall and his legs braced on the opposite wall. Ian kicked of his shoes and settled himself on top of Billy's powerful legs in the lotus position. He leaned forward to be close to Billy so their conversation wouldn't be overheard, only this time, Billy pulled him even closer until their lips touched and met in a kiss. Ian was startled and almost fell off of his perch. Billy's strong arms caught him and kept him in place.

"Why did you kiss me?" Ian asked, his grass green eyes wide with surprise. "I don't think we're that close."

"I've wanted to kiss you since I switched back to human form," Billy said, locking his deep amber eyes on Ian's. "I really like you, Ian, and I wanted to show you how much I like you. I hope you like me, too."

"Yes, I like you a lot!" Ian gushed.

Billy put a finger to Ian's lips to curb his enthusiasm. "Ssh, we don't want to disturb anyone. We need to have a talk about how you and the rest of your group act around Uncle Kieran and Uncle Cory."

"What? Are we doing something wrong? We've been serving the hunter since we were deemed old enough to begin training to be trackers." Ian was blushing in embarrassment.

"You're so cute when you blush," Billy said as he tapped Ian's nose lightly. "I know this will sound strange to you, but maybe you should let them fend for themselves."

The shocked look on Ian's face at the suggestion stunned Billy who wasn't used to human reactions after several months locked in wolf form. He'd gotten so used to scents telling him what was going on around him that Ian's reactions were confusing.

"I don't understand why you're so shocked at the idea of letting two grown men look after their own needs, especially when your waiting on them hand and foot is driving Uncle Cory nuts," Billy said.

"It's the duty of tracker-candidates to attend to the needs of the Huntress of the House, so she can attend to the larger, more important tasks. Hunter Kieran and his friend are due that same consideration," Ian replied.

"Uncle Cory isn't Uncle Kieran's friend, Ian," Billy growled. "They're married and mated. You aren't a tracker-candidate anymore. Uncle Kieran released all of you from that position. So, it follows that he's not expecting you or the others to wait on him or Uncle Cory. He wanted you to have a childhood, to come hang out with me and play games or read books."

"Billy, I can't ignore what I'm supposed to do just to hang out and do frivolous things. I'm supposed to take care of the hunter, so he can protect the family and the world from shifters." As soon as the last word left Ian's mouth, his hand slammed over it, trying to bite back what he'd just said.

"Right, because we're all evil nasty monsters who are going to attack you and rip your throats out while you're sleeping," Billy snarled. "I thought you'd be different from all the others. My wolf smelled something that drew me to you, but I guess it was wrong. You're as much a bigot as the rest of your family. Only Uncle Kieran seems to be able to get passed his hatred of shifters and see us as people." Billy rose so abruptly Ian was dumped on the floor. Billy stormed down the hallway.

Ian sat horrified that the boy he'd developed a crush on was mad at him. His stomach felt as if he'd taken a punch. He couldn't leave things as they were, so he raced down the hall to follow Billy to try and apologize. The room they shared was at the very end of the hall, so it was easy to follow Billy until he came to the cross hall. *I didn't think he could move so fast. I can't tell which direction he . . . Wait, what's this sensation? It's like I know he went left.* Turning, Ian followed the strange sensation within him right up to the door of the hunter's suite. Loud voices were coming from within. Billy's was one of them, and he thought that Hunter Kieran's voice might be the other voice. He raised his hand to knock on the door to the suite when it was flung open, and he found himself staring at a furious Billy.

"Why are you following me?" Billy snarled. "Come to throw some more insults in my face?"

"How did you know I was out here?" Ian asked.

"I felt your presence. I just . . ." Billy reached out and grabbed Ian, dragging him into the suite as he turned to face his uncles. Ian was swept around in front of him and held protectively tight against Billy's chest. "I don't understand what's going on, Uncle Cory. Part of me wants to beat him to a pulp for thinking shifters are all monsters and part of me wants to protect him from the real monsters."

"I'd say there was a bond forming between you on some level. I also think part of this is an age thing," Cory comforted. "You're still a puppy, and you're seeing Ian as a playmate and rival for attention. We're also in the middle of a strange pack, and we don't know our place in the hierarchy yet."

"It's going to take some time to adjust the thought patterns around here, Billy," Kieran added. "Hatred and fear of shifters has been drummed into the every fiber of poor Ian since he was born. Give him time and patience. He'll come around and be the partner you need in time." Kieran turned to his cousin. "Ian, how did you know where to find Billy? Did you just assume he'd come here, or was there something else?"

"I realized I needed to apologize for my words as soon as I said what I did," Ian replied. "I ran to follow Billy, but didn't know how fast he could move. There was no trace of him in the hallways when

I got to the junction, but then I just felt this pull toward the left hallway, and I followed it here."

A look passed between Kieran and Cory before they looked back at the two boys still in an embrace much like they shared. Kieran gestured for the boys to take a seat on one of the couches in the sitting room of the suite. Cory and he watched in amusement as Billy sat first and then drew Ian into his lap, back against his chest. Cory and Kieran then took the couch across from the boys. They watched as the understanding suddenly dawned on the youths as Kieran sank into the protection offered by Cory's embrace. Kieran couldn't help laughing at the expressions on the boys' faces.

"They're just too cute for words." Kieran laughed as Cory hugged him tight. "Now we know what everyone else sees when they look at us."

"You're right, babe. They are adorable. I think they'll make a wonderful pair," Kieran said before turning his attention back to Billy and Ian. "I have been thinking about your futures. I want you to listen carefully to what I'm proposing. This is a long-term plan, so take a few days to discuss my offers between you. Then, when you've reached an agreement between the two of you, come back to me and tell me which path you wish to pursue."

"You really are kicking me out of the tracker-candidate class, aren't you, Hunter Kieran?" Ian asked.

"Yes, Ian, I am removing you from that path to offer you one I think you're better suited to walk. I am, however, offering you a choice of paths. One leads to lifelong service to the House of Beauty in a very different capacity; the other leads you both away from service to the family and sets you free to make your own way in the world."

"Service or exile is the choice we have to make?" Ian asked.

"No exile, Ian. I have plans to change up how the House of Beauty does business, and some members of the family fit what's coming and others don't. My vision for you and Billy is for you to fill a very important role if you choose to accept it. If you choose to go your own way instead, you will always be family and welcome wherever you come across family. There will always be a set of rooms ready for you both in Cory's and my house."

"Okay, then I think we can listen to your offer, Hunter Kieran," Ian replied.

"When I visited here several weeks ago, you showed an interest in the old chronicles, Ian. Therefore, option one is this: the position of House Archivist is currently vacant and needs to be filled. If you choose this path, the House will pay you to go to school and complete at least your Master's degree in Archival Studies. Once you present your degree to the Council of Matriarchs, you will be confirmed as Archivist." Kieran held up his hand to forestall Ian's question. "The Archivist is very important to this family. Great-Uncle Jonas helped keep me on the path I needed to be on by sharing certain stories with me. If you choose this option, there are traditions that will have to be kept up, but we'll discuss those if you take the job. Now, option two is this: you are free to choose whatever you'd like to be in life, free of any and all obligations to the House of Beauty."

"These both sound like choices for Ian, Uncle Kieran. What are my options?"

"You're both sensing a connection to each other that may well lead to a permanent partnership like I share with Cory. I want to try letting you live your life without the collar. Your ability to shift will be for you to master control of, as part of your schooling."

"You think I can master my wolf?" Billy asked.

"If you apply yourself, we think you can do anything, Billy. If this connection between you develops, I'd like you to study alongside Ian so that you can assist him—if you take option one, that is. If you decide on option two, what you study is totally up to you."

"I don't think you want us both to become professional bookworms, Hunter Kieran," Ian said.

"No, I would like to see you both physically active as well as academically challenged. My recommendation is while you, Ian, get your Masters, Billy goes to the police academy or bodyguard school. That way, he can protect you."

Both boys looked thoughtful for a moment; then, Ian turned to face Billy. He looked up at the dark amber eyes with his own grass green eyes. Kieran and Cory watched as the boys seemed to silently communicate with each other. Ian tilted his head back, and Billy leaned down for a quick kiss before they both focused on the older couple across from them.

"We've decided to take option one. You're right. I'm not cut out to be a tracker, but I do love the archives. I'll need someone to look out for me, but I think we're agreed that whatever self-defense training Billy takes, I'll take it as well. He can't protect me all the time, and if I've had the same training, I'll be able to move as he needs me to move."

"Thank you, Cousin. I do want you both to understand that you can change your minds at any point up to the day you're handed the keys to the archives. Knowing that the archives will be in the hands of someone as interested in them as I am makes me feel a lot better about their future," Kieran said. "Now, both of you run along and be boys; the future will be here before you know it."

Chapter Twenty-One

Every seat around the council table was occupied, except the chair reserved for the Huntress of the House of Beauty. Camille Belle sat one seat down from what had once been her chair, waiting for her grandson Kieran to arrive. There was plenty of murmuring going on, mostly complaints about the presence of the Oisín family at the table. Camille was practically glaring daggers at Líadáin, knowing the other woman had the one thing she'd cheated herself out of years ago: Kieran's loving respect instead of the fear she'd instilled when he was a boy. Now, the women who'd run the House of Beauty for generations sat waiting for the man who would tell them how to they were going to help him save the family.

A small bell, which announced visitors to the chamber, rang, and one of the male cousins opened the great double doors to reveal Kieran with his husband Cory at his side. Kieran was dressed in his impressive set of armored leathers. Cory was wearing heavy denim jeans and a thick denim shirt; sturdy hiking boots completed the outfit. It was hard to decide if the second young man should be considered a threat or a decoration. He was handsome, even next to the beauty that was Kieran. Rugged looks where Kieran was smooth. Then, he moved in Kieran's wake; his stride screamed predator on the hunt. Kieran strode across the room with a glide that reminded Camille of her daughter Miranda and her son-in-law Kellen. Here was a man who could kill you just as easily as let you look at him. The impression of a deadly killer came to an abrupt end when Kieran flung himself into the great chair at the end of the table and sprawled one elegant leg over an arm of the chair. He slouched against the back of the chair. *He's amused that he's annoying me, and those silver eyes of his have always given away his mood,* Camille noted to herself.

"Welcome to the Council of Matriarchs, Hunter Kieran. We are honored to have you grace us with your presence," Camille said, managing not to choke on the words.

Kieran's smile grew larger and his eyes brighter as he watched his grandmother speak the ritual words of welcome. He knew he was already riding her last nerve by his carefree posture and mischievous grin. He caught a small frown of disapproval from Grams and decided he could behave himself. He straightened in the chair before returning his own ritual formula.

"Honored Grandmother, Matriarchs, and guests, I thank you for taking the time out of your busy schedules to attend this meeting. The House of Beauty is in great danger; the pact between our family and the shifters of the dark forest is broken. My sisters have been slaughtered during their attempts to take the test of the huntress. Shifters have ventured to attack me beyond the testing grounds. I have been put to the test of the huntress and come out the other side as the Hunter of the House of Beauty. The time has come to dispose of the shifters who have lived in our woods under our protection in exchange for their taking part in the test. They have broken faith with us and must be put down."

"How do you propose to do that, Hunter Kieran? If you're truly the Hunter of the House of Beauty," one of the Matriarchs said.

"Come and take my hand; you can sense the change in me. I'm more than just the Hunter of the House of Beauty. I'm the Silver Hunter, a child of the line of Belle and of the line of her younger brother, the one who inherited their mother's magic."

"That ancient prophecy called for a three-fold path—tracker, witch, and hunter. Men in our family don't have magic."

Kieran raised his hand, and Silver magic swirled around his hand in sparks like fireflies chasing each other. The magic swirled around him and his chair, and suddenly, he was across the room seated at the other end of the table.

"Does that satisfy you that I have magic? My father, uncle, and other grandmother are here to testify to my having become the Silver Witch. So, shall we get down to business and discuss a plan to clean out our forest?"

There were gasps of surprise from Matriarchs who hadn't been present during Kieran's last visit home. From those Matriarchs who'd been on hand for that last visit, there were both murmurs of approval and disapproval, depending on where they stood in the hierarchy of the council.

"We figured you'd do what huntresses do and just go in and kill them," a Matriarch said.

"Do we have an accurate count of how many shifters live in the woods? From what the magic revealed to me when Rosie went to the test, there were hundreds of them. It took twenty of them to take her down. It took fifty to take down Mother. I don't know if I can take on the entire pack alone, and then there is the mysterious Alpha and the question of a dark mage helping him. I'm going to need backup."

"But if you're entering the forest to face the pack, it will be during the full moon, and they will think you've come to test. You will have to go alone."

"What is with all of you? You let my sisters go into those woods alone to be slaughtered; now you'd send me to the same fate? This is supposed to be a family that hunts shifters. How did it come down to being one person in each generation doing all the fighting while people like you spend your time making the decisions? You old ladies need to go take up knitting or something, save for Grandmother; you aren't worth taking advice from. It's time for a new Council to lead the House of Beauty; this one is dissolved."

The Matriarchs looked at each other and then at Kieran. Voices of protest started to rise against him until Camille slammed her cane down on the table.

"Enough! Kieran is the Hunter; the Council of Matriarchs serves at the will of the Hunter. He has dismissed us from our service. You will accept this and go."

Chairs scraped over the wooden floor as the Matriarchs pushed back from the table and rose. They departed in a parade of long skirts and outraged looks. Kieran only stopped three women from leaving, Grandmother Belle, Great-Aunt Fiona, and Great-Aunt Desdemona. All women who still had their one-shot gift of Silver magic.

"I know you can no longer fight, and I know you don't approve of what I've done, and you certainly won't like my plans for the future, but I need your wisdom, Aunt Fiona, and your knowledge, Aunt Desdemona, and your experience, Grandmother. You three have led this family through some dark times, and we're about to experience something beyond dark. Will you stay and help me?" Kieran asked.

"You ran away a boy, but you have returned a man, Kieran. We were hard on you, because we feared that this is what would come our way. We will do what we can to help you, but we fear that it will come down to you standing alone to face the pack in the end," Great-Aunt Fiona said.

"What do you need from us, Kieran?" Great-Aunt Desdemona asked.

"Of everyone living, Aunt Desdemona, you know the archives the best. I need you to work with Ian and Billy in tracking down everything about Beauty's fight with the Beast and the last hunter's fight with the dark Alpha of his time. I want to know what they did to defeat their opponents. Aunt Fiona, I want you to go play peacemaker with the other Matriarchs and let them know that there are better things ahead for the family. Grandmother, I want you to choose candidates from the younger cousins for a new council. Pick both males and females with a potential to be trackers or hunters. Change is coming to the House of Beauty, and they will help usher it in."

Interlude: The Master comes to Maine

The Master was pissed. The capture or destruction of Kieran Belle could no longer be left in the hands of underlings or beasts. It was time to deal with this personally.

The Master packed a few things he felt he would need before casting a sleep spell over his minions in his lair. Once he was sure none of his servants or slaves would attempt to escape, he cast a transport spell and whisked himself across the miles from Little Rock to Bangor. The spell deposited him in an alley near a major hotel. With a gesture, he altered his appearance from his concealing robes to a finely tailored business suit. His bag became a small suitcase, and he walked around the corner from the alley and made it appear to the valets as if he'd just emerged from one of the cabs. The young valet who was the next on deck took his bag and escorted him inside to the front desk. Here the Ebony mage became the suave businessman he was normally.

"Hello, sir, checking in?" the front desk clerk asked.

"If you have a vacancy, yes. I'm afraid I was called to attend to business at the last moment and didn't have a chance to book in advance."

"We have a couple of suites available, sir. How long will you be staying?"

"That will depend on how long it takes to deal with the business that called me here. At least a week if you have a suite available that long," the mage replied.

"Yes, sir, the Arcadia suite is available for the next two weeks," the clerk replied.

"Then please book me for the two weeks," the Master said, handing over a credit card.

"Yes, sir, if you'll please fill out this registration card please." The clerk handed him a card and a pen, and then waited so that she could enter his information into the computer to book the room.

Behind the mage, the young valet stood holding the man's bag. The mage noted the boy's eagerness and build. He was slender but muscular, somewhere between a gymnast and a swimmer. The tight slacks showed what promised to be a hefty cock and heavy balls. He'd noted the beautiful bubble butt on the way into the lobby. Perhaps he'd indulge himself later. He handed the completed card back to the desk clerk. She smiled at him, hoping maybe she could make an impression. He merely nodded back at her. After a few moments, she ran a pair of blank keycards through the machine and coded them for his suite. She slipped them into an envelope and handed them to the man. She then slid a copy of his receipt to him for his signature.

"Here are the keys for your suite. It's on fifteenth floor. Kevin will show you the way, Mr. Locke," she said. "If you'll sign here, everything will be charged to your card when you check out."

"Thank you, my dear," Mr. Locke, better known as the Master, said as he signed the receipt and slid it back to her.

"Kevin, please show Mr. Locke to the Arcadia suite," the woman said.

"This way please, Mr. Locke." Kevin turned, showing off his tight bubble butt as he headed toward the elevator.

Mr. Locke followed closely behind the young valet. The elevator arrived almost as soon as Kevin pushed the button. Holding the door, he let Mr. Locke enter first and then followed and pressed the button for the fifteenth floor. Once the doors slid closed, Mr. Locke made eye contact with Kevin in the reflection of the highly polished doors. With little effort, he had Kevin turning around to face him directly and locked his gaze on the young man. Kevin was soon in a light hypnotic trance and leaning against the older man. The mage whispered in Kevin's ear, and the boy stood up straight and turned back to face the doors. He remained that way until the elevator chimed to announce their floor, which seemed to break the trance the boy was in. He stepped out and led the way to the Arcadia suite, where he took the key from Mr. Locke and opened the door for the man. He followed the man inside and placed the suitcase on the luggage rack by the door.

"Is there anything else I can do for you, Mr. Locke?" Kevin asked.

"Yes, Kevin, tell me when you get off your shift. I may have some errands for you to run for me."

"I'm off my shift at eight o'clock tonight, Mr. Locke. If you need something before then, I'm happy to be of service," Kevin replied.

"No, that will be fine. Once you're off the clock, come up here and let yourself in," Mr. Locke said, slipping the extra keycard into Kevin's back pants pocket, getting a feel of the tight muscular butt cheek at the same time.

Kevin smiled at the man. "Yes, sir. I'll be here as soon as I've changed and clocked out."

Mr. Locke peeled a twenty-dollar bill out of his money clip and handed it to Kevin for his services so far. Kevin started to thank the man and then froze in place when the man's hand touched his. Mr. Locke maintained his touch on Kevin's hand as he moved around behind the boy and pressed his body up against the frozen youth. He slipped his hand into Kevin's back pocket and pulled out his wallet. Flipping the wallet open, he checked Kevin's age on his driver's license. Finding the boy was actually twenty-one, he put the wallet back and then released the boy. He was the perfect age to meet all of his dark desires. Kevin shook his head when he found Mr. Locke behind him, but he just figured he was tired from working long shifts. "I'll see you tonight as soon as you can get here, Kevin," Mr. Locke said, ushering the boy out of the suite.

Once his reward for the evening was out of the way, Mr. Locke stepped over to his suitcase and then opened it to retrieve his crystal ball and its stand. He set these up on the table in the suite's siting room, loosened his tie, and undid the top couple of buttons on his dress shirt. Ebony magic began to swirl around the crystal ball, and then the connection snapped into place. Staring back at him was one of the most brutish men he'd ever seen. Here was the human form of the legendary Beast.

"So you finally decided to show yourself, mage," the Beast growled, even in human form.

"Yes, I've come to Maine to deal with this in person. I will join you in a few days once I have the lay of the land and an assessment of the defenses around the boy."

"The bitches don't have defenses, mage. The pact between them and this pathetic group of mongrels keeps these sheep bound to the forest. They don't need defenses against shifters."

"As I recall, you're just as trapped by this magical binding as the mangy cur you're trapped with. I want to know what protections the boy has put in place to deal with outside magical threats. He will expect at least my agents to make another attempt. Actually, I'm sure he's expecting me to take a direct hand after his little message drop."

"So do something about him. Once he's gone, the binding spell will begin to unravel, and my kind will be free to shift at will to any shape. I will have my revenge on the bitch's family at long last."

"Soon, one of us will have what we want," the mage said as he broke the spell.

Chapter Twenty-Two

After many days of being cooped up in the Belle mansion, Kieran had finally had enough of meetings with various members of the extended Belle family. Kieran was tired from more than fruitless meetings; he hadn't been sleeping well the last few nights. Dreams and nightmares were plaguing his sleep. The nightmares of a dark-furred monster—half-man, half-beast—were ones he hadn't dreamed since he was ten. To escape the mad house, he grabbed Cory out of their suite, scooped up the new swords Uncle Brom had forged for him, and led Cory outside. He took Cory into a set of woods near the house that wasn't part of the greater forest around them. When they reached the clearing in the center of the grove, Kieran stopped and raised a barrier of Silver magic around the clearing.

"I don't want us to be disturbed. Only you and I can cross that barrier," Kieran said.

"We need one of those on our suite, or at least the bed room," Cory joked.

"Cory, I need to watch you shift. I need to get used to you doing that, so I don't reflexively strike out at you."

"It's not the full moon, Kieran. I can't shift during the day."

"You're different from every other shifter in existence, and I think that if you put your mind to it, you'll find that you can shift at will."

"Is this really necessary, Kieran? You know I'm not much of a fighter," Cory said.

"You're going to have to become something of a fighter or at least learn to let your wolf-instincts take over for you before we go to face the dark pack. You have to be at my side when I face down the Alpha," Kieran replied.

"I'll give it a try, babe," Cory said.

Cory closed his eyes and tried to still his mind to find his wolf within, as his mother had taught him just in case he ever felt the urge to shift. It started as a tingle in his fingers and toes, and it became an itch he couldn't scratch, and then it was a burning pain. His body rearranged itself. He twisted and howled until a beautiful silver wolf stood before Kieran. Until the pain of a cramp in his hands hit his brain, Kieran didn't realize he'd drawn both swords and gripped them so tight his knuckles were white. Slowly, he forced himself to relax his stance and his grip. At the moment, Kieran sheathed his swords, and Cory leapt. His huge front paws crashed into Kieran's shoulders, knocking him backward. Cory's wolf body pinned him to the ground. Silver magic swirled and struck at Cory the wolf, but the power just flowed back into Kieran through their bond. Amber wolf eyes locked on silver mage eyes, and Kieran realized that his magic couldn't hurt Cory in anyway when he was in this shape. Wolf jaws opened, revealing sharp canine teeth before a long wet tongue lashed out and licked Kieran's face. Cory bounded away from Kieran with a wolfish grin on his muzzle as his husband wiped his face on his sleeve.

"I'm going to die by drowning in wolf slobber," Kieran said, rising to his knees. He held out his arms to Cory. "Come here, Wolf."

Cory trotted over and then sat facing Kieran, who moved closer and wrapped his arms around Cory's neck as he buried his face in the thick, soft silver fur. After a few moments, Cory lightly nipped Kieran's shoulder, and Kieran released his hold. He sat back staring at Cory in his wolf form; then, he rose and drew his swords.

"I know this is alien to you, Cory, but we need to learn to move together and to fight side by side. I need to adjust to having a shifter fighting at my side. Will you work with me before we bring Billy out here to work with both of us?"

Cory looked at his lover for a moment before standing and shaking himself before yipping in the affirmative. He padded over to Kieran's right side and waited for Kieran to begin. Kieran began with warming up through several sword katas, partly for himself since he hadn't worked out heavily since his accident and extended hospital stay, and partly so Cory could get a feel for how he moved. Several times, they collided and crashed to the ground before they started to rely more on their bond to sense how the other was going to move. Eventually, they were moving in sync and at greater speeds until Kieran finally reached his full attack speed. They became a whirling blur of swords, boots, claws, and teeth as they lashed out at invisible enemies. Cory urged them to a greater speed as he shifted shape into the halfway form and became a beautiful beast. Cory's movements changed as he became Kieran's opponent in their dance of death.

Claws slashed past soft targets, never striking but showing openings an enemy wouldn't hesitate to rip open. For his part, Kieran's swords blurred past Cory, turning so that the flat of a blade would strike an open target in warning that a shifter could be vulnerable as well. Their sparing went on and on with Kieran moving faster than he'd ever moved before by drawing on his bond with Cory. The bond worked both ways, and Cory seemed to have figured out a way to use it to flow with Kieran's grace and to predict Kieran's moves. Cory noticed that Kieran was tiring, and the scent of a possible victory was driving Cory's hormones into over drive. He wanted to defeat his mate and claim him.

Kieran took a couple of steps back trying to gain some space to reset to go on the offensive, but he stepped into a hole and fell, twisting his ankle in the process. Before he could raise any kind of defense, Cory was on him and not only had him pinned but was actively shredding his clothes. Kieran could feel Cory's intense desires, but his lover was still in partial beast form, and Kieran didn't want to admit it, but this form frightened him.

Silver magic flashed between the two lovers and shoved Cory away from his mate. He landed and then pounced toward his mate again. He crashed into a barrier of Silver magic, but it only slowed him down a little bit. Cory saw Kieran rising to his feet, clothing hanging in rags from his beautiful body, and it inflamed him even more. *Naked, his mate should always be naked,* he thought.

Cory crashed into Kieran, knocking him face first into the ground, and then Cory finished ripping away his mate's clothes. He heard sobbing beneath him as his cock slid along the crease of his mate's ass. He rose up enough to flip Kieran face up. Then, he looked at his mate's eyes and saw fear, not a matching desire. *My mate is afraid of me. Why is my mate afraid of me?* Confused, Cory stopped trying to enter Kieran and forced himself back to fully human. He wrapped Kieran in his arms and felt his husband's body tremble with the fear of his half-beast form; that's when he began to make out the words Kieran kept repeating.

"Please not in this form. Please not in this form," Kieran whispered between sobs.

"Sshh, babe, it's safe. You know I would never hurt you. Please don't be afraid of me."

Kieran wrapped his arms around the human form of his husband and buried his face against the hairy chest. Cory rolled to his back, bringing Kieran to rest on top of him, and caressed his husband until the sobbing and trembling passed.

"Talk to me, Kier. Why are you so scared of me making love to you in my midway form?"

"The nightmares. Always in my childhood nightmares, I saw that form come out of the darkness to rape and abuse me. It was so real that I'd wake up covered in sweat and cowering in a corner."

"Oh, Kier, I'm sorry. The wolf in me saw a victory over my mate and wanted to claim his prize. I didn't know that my midway form was a thing of terror for you. I promise I'll never use that shape when we make love." Cory lifted Kieran's face so that his husband could see the sincerity in his eyes.

Kieran shifted slightly so that he could kiss his husband before snuggling back against him. They stayed like that for a few moments before Kieran looked up at Cory again.

"I didn't know the shift was painful. I felt your pain during the shift from human to wolf form. Once you were moving, the pain was gone when you shifted to your halfway form or when you shifted back to human. Is it because you had to force the change to wolf form?" Kieran asked.

"I think the pain was because I went directly from human to wolf instead of using the midway form first. There are so many anatomical differences between wolves and humans that it's painful when you're consciously making the shift. On the night of full moon, it may not be so bad. The last time I did it, the change happened so fast. I didn't even know I'd changed until Grams talked me down enough to change back."

"You changed the night Gramps died?" Kieran asked.

"Yes, I think it must have happened at the moment you cut loose with all of your power to kill those attacking shifters, or it may have been when the tree fell on you. All I know is that you were in great pain when it happened, and all I could think about was getting to you," Cory replied.

"I love you, Cory."

"I love you too, Kieran."

"Will you do something for me?" Kieran asked.

"You know I'd do anything for you, Kier."

"Shift back to your midway form and just hold me."

"Is that a good idea, Kieran? I've never seen you so afraid before."

"I need to face my fears, to grow stronger. It helps that your fur is bright, not dark like the fur in my nightmares. Please help me to grow stronger, Cory."

Cory gave off a sexy growl; he loved it when Kieran needed him. In a moment, he began the shift toward his midway form. He let his hair thicken into fur, and slowly, he let his muscles and body shift afterward. Kieran snuggled in tighter as Cory's fur thickened, and tried to will himself to remain calm as Cory's body shifted beneath him into the monstrous midway form. Fingernails shifted and became claws, tracing careful lines against his skin as Cory stroked him, trying to help keep him calm. It seemed as if everything was going along fine until Kieran looked up at Cory's face to find the face so like the monster in his childhood dreams. He recoiled in horror. Cory stopped the shift and returned to his human form. He tried to reach for Kieran, but his husband wouldn't let him touch him. Kieran rose unsteadily to his feet and wrapped himself in Silver magic. The magic shifted and molded to Kieran's body starting at his feet. It began hardening, forming boots, and then as it moved up his body. It formed itself into form-fitting armor. As the magic flowed down his arms, part of the magic separated and formed wicked scythe blades starting at Kieran's elbows and extending beyond his hands a matching distance. Cory watched as the magic slowly swallowed Kieran's beautiful face, leaving a mirrored mask facing him. From the shoulder guards, the magic took the form of a cloak and flowed outward to billow in the breeze. Cory had seen Kieran in armor like this before, but there was something different about it this time. As much as he wanted to approach Kieran, Cory knew that any move in Kieran's direction would likely prove fatal.

"Kieran, we can face your fears together. The face scares you the most. You see the monster of your nightmares. Even though you know that the person behind the face you're seeing here is your loving husband, who will never hurt you, that face has promised to do horrible things to you in your dreams for years. Don't hide in that shell of magic. Come share my strength and love. I'll never let the monster get you."

"You can't stop it. The monster comes and he's so strong. I have to be stronger. So many people want me to be so much stronger than any one person can possibly be. This monster is powerful; everyone who was supposed to fight him has run or passed the problem on to someone else. I don't get that choice, Cory. Everything has conspired to leave with only two options: fight and win, or fight and die." Kieran's voice was muffled by the magical armor, but the sob that wracked him was loud, and he crashed to the ground, armor fading away. "I don't want to die, but I can't face that monster."

"We're in this together, Kieran," Cory said as he wrapped himself around his love. "I'm not going to let you face the monster alone. Besides you have an advantage your sisters didn't have when they went to take this test."

"What advantage do I have besides nearly unlimited Silver magic?"

"You're forgetting you've already passed the test. The shifters in the forest are going to be expecting a moment of weakness or something when you've cut down the magical fifth shifter."

"They may expect me to stop fighting since the pact calls for the test to end after five shifters have died. Since we already know they aren't going to stop, we're ahead of the game. You know you're very smart for a big scary monster," Kieran teased, bringing a big smile to Cory's face.

"Well, you're not too bad for a tasty monster snack," Cory teased back before running his tongue across Kieran's neck.

"Oh my, are you going to eat me, Mr. Monster?" Kieran squirmed in such a way that his ass rubbed against Cory's cock.

"Mmm, yes, I'm going to gobble you up, little boy," Cory said as his grip tightened with one hand while the other glided down to stroke Kieran's own rampantly hard cock. "Can you take us back to the cavern at Gram's place?"

Kieran twisted in Cory's grip so that they were face-to-face. He could see the lust and love in his husband's eyes. He nodded and then kissed Cory deeply as Silver magic wrapped around them and whisked them away to the cavern where they'd claimed each other. Kieran even managed to land them gently on the sleeping shelf in the bedchamber. With a groping hand, Cory found the bottle of lube they kept on the little side shelf and flipped the top open. He kept the kiss going as he squeezed lube out to slick up his lover's hole and his own cock. Slowly, he settled so that his cock slipped into Kieran's welcoming ass. Moans of passion began to echo in the chamber as Kieran broke the kiss and let his head roll back against the bedding. Being held in Cory's strong arms or being pinned beneath the strong body always made him feel safe and loved in ways he didn't understand and didn't care to explore further. He just let himself go and let Cory have control of their lovemaking. His skin began to tingle as Cory leaned over him and let his chest hairs brush over his smooth skin. The sensation was different this time, softer somehow. Kieran reached up and ran his hand across Cory's chest and through much thicker hair, the feeling of a dense but soft fur pelt. Kieran opened his eyes and found that Cory had shifted at least part way toward his midway form. The face that looked down at him was still that of his human form, beautiful as always in Kieran's eyes. He watched as Cory slowly let his shift take him from human to half-wolf. The blond hair shifted color to bright silver and spread down his throat and back beneath Kieran's clutching fingers as his lover increased the pace of his thrusts. Soon, Kieran was staring into the face of the monster from his childhood nightmares, but this wasn't the face that caused blind panic; this was his husband who'd never let anything happen to him. He pulled down the face above him, awkwardly kissing the strange mouth that was more wolf than human. When he felt Kieran relax in the arms of his midway form, Cory let the shift fade back to full human, and then set to bringing both of them to the edge of climax several times before finally taking them over the edge. When they came down from their mutual orgasm and had control of their legs again, they made their way down to the pools in the main cavern and set about getting clean. Once they were clean, they rummaged to find something to wear, coming up with a couple of pairs of shorts.

"These are enough to not be embarrassed if there's someone in our suite when we arrive back there," Kieran said.

"That's good. I don't want to scare off the kids. I'm not used to them waiting on us hand and foot, but I do like that they feel so free to come and ask us things. I don't know . . ." Cory paused. "Maybe we should look at having kids of our own someday."

"If it's something you want, Wolf, I'll certainly think about it. I'm not sure I want to inflict my bloodline on an innocent child though."

"We can discuss it another time. We should get back before someone starts sending out search parties, babe."

"Thank you, Cory."

"You're welcome, Kieran."

Kieran stepped into Cory's embrace, and Silver magic swirled around them, whisking them back to their suite in the Belle mansion.

They stepped apart at the sound of a throat being cleared to find Kellen and Grams sitting in a couple of chairs in the main sitting room. Both young men blushed at being caught.

"You're both adorable when you blush like that. Now, go put some real clothes on. We have some important things to talk about," Grams said, while Kellen tried not to laugh aloud at his son and son-in-law.

"Be right back," Kieran said as he turned and fled to the safety of their bedroom, Cory right on his heels.

The lovers found clothes and dressed quickly before returning to the sitting room of the suite. They took their customary place on one of the sofas and waited for either Grams or Kellen to begin the conversation. Silence stretched, making Kieran uncomfortable, but he held back from breaking it, practicing the skills he needed for facing down the Council of Matriarchs. Finally, Kellen cleared his throat.

"Mother and I are worried about the whispers we're hearing from some of the staff about opposition to you from the Council."

"What have you heard, Dad?" Kieran asked.

"Several of the Matriarchs are conspiring to put Camille back in charge of the family, because they don't believe that you've passed the test of the huntress," Grams said. "They refuse to believe that any man could pass the test."

"They're willing to challenge Grandmother's own acknowledgement of my status?" Kieran leaned back. "Wow, I knew they were stubborn old women, but I never thought they'd challenge Grandmother in order to keep things the same."

"Fear of change, *mo stór*," Grams said. "They'd challenge Camille for her seat if any of them had passed the test themselves. You didn't go into their sacred woods and pass the test there, so they don't believe you've faced down a hoard of shifters and emerged the victor."

Kellen settled against the back of the sofa he sat on and crossed one long elegant leg over the other. "You're going to need to convince them that you're in charge and beyond their challenges."

Kieran snorted. "Short of going into the dark forest tomorrow and returning with five shifter heads, I don't think I can convince them I've passed the test. Actually, I'm not even sure they'd believe that evidence, Dad. They'll think I used magic, because only a woman is strong enough to take on five shifters without using magic. Especially since they know I can use magic at will. I don't have to hoard my magic for a really big need."

"You need to do something before you have a challenge on your hands," Kellen said.

"The Council's days are numbered already, Dad. I have a plan to protect and spread the House of Beauty. Like the Oisíns, the Belles have become dangerously concentrated in one place. I'm going to set up each of the cadet branches in their own regions, with training for both men and women as hunters. There will be a new Council made up of the chief regional hunters. This will give us better coverage. I'd like to set up a training school for hunters and huntresses, that will even train non-family members," Kieran said.

"That's a marvelous idea, *mo stór*. Now, all you have to do is convince your current Council to step down and let you get on with the job of transforming everything they've ever known," Grams said.

"I've already started a redesign of the Council. Everyone save Grandmother and Great-Aunts Desdemona and Fiona has been removed. I've asked Grandmother to replace them with younger women and men."

"Well, that will keep Camille busy for a while," Kellen said. "Now we need to find out how to defeat this dark Alpha and the entire pack."

"Plus there's still the Ebony mage out there to be dealt with," Grams added.

Kieran looked around the room, realizing that one of his normal voices of advice was missing. "Has anyone seen either Uncle Brom or Professor Mason since we got here? I'm not even sure what suite Great-Aunt Fiona put them in."

Chapter Twenty-Three

John Mason stood in the sitting room of the suite he was sharing with Brom at the Belle estate. The huge house made him feel uncomfortable. The place was cold, emotionally. Then, there was Brom. The man was just about everything John wanted in a partner, but Brom was beginning to become the one thing John didn't want above all things, possessive and controlling.

The last few times they'd had sex, it had become a battle for dominance, and if John didn't submit, Brom suddenly wasn't in the mood. Just last night John decided enough was enough, and he moved his things into the second bedroom of the suite and slammed the door in Brom's face. It couldn't go on, but John didn't want to desert Kieran when his student might need him most. With one last glare at the door to Brom's bedroom, John stormed toward the door leading to the hallway only to smack straight into Brom as he entered the suite. Angry emerald eyes meet storm-gray silver eyes, and both men's tempers flared.

"Get out of my way, Brom," John growled.

"Where do you think you're going, John?" Brom snarled back.

"To talk with Kieran. I think it's time I went back to Little Rock."

"So after all your talk about being his ally, you're going to cut and run when he's going to need all the help he can get to face an entire pack of shifters that want to rip him to pieces?" Brom pressed up against John with every word.

John shoved Brom away and moved toward the door. Brom grabbed him by the elbow and slammed him into a wall. Emerald eyes flashing with intense anger locked on Brom as every plant in the room tripled in size. Several vines lashed out and wrapped themselves around the man. Silver magic slammed John against the wall and held him there as the vines were slashed. Brom closed in on John and attempted to kiss the man, but John slammed his head into Brom's nose, breaking the man's concentration along with several blood vessels in his nose. When he came free of the wall, John followed up his head butt with a right hook to Brom's jaw.

"Stay away from me, Brom. I won't be manhandled, and I'm not your personal property. I decide when and if I will be the submissive during sex. I am not and will never be a slave or a plaything. If you want to be more than friends with benefits, you will respect my position and limits on the matter."

"Go back to your darkroom then. Kieran needs fighters at his side, not whining little boys." Brom turned his back on John and stormed into his bedroom. He slammed the door behind him.

John looked at the mess he'd made and sighed, sorry for the extra work the maid who took care of the suite would have to do. Turning, he left the suite and went in search of Kieran.

****

Kieran was sitting in the library, reviewing several of the most ancient of chronicles in his search for information on how Beauty defeated the Beast. He even looked for how the last male hunter had defeated the powerful dark shifter of his time. But he wasn't having much luck with the task. When Professor Mason found him, Kieran gave a huge sigh of relief.

"Kieran, I'm sorry to interrupt your research, but we need to talk," John said.

"I always have time for you, Professor. What did you need to see me about?" Kieran asked as he gestured to the empty chair beside him.

John sat down and then looked at his favorite student, trying not to see a younger version of Brom. It was actually easier to focus on Kieran's appearance and block out Brom's, because he'd known Kieran longer.

"I think it's time for me to go back to Little Rock, Kieran."

"I'm going to guess that Uncle Brom is part of the reason," Kieran said bluntly. "I heard part of the argument you had with him last night when I was on my way back to my suite. If you need me to knock some sense into him, I will, Professor."

"That's kind of you, Kieran, but I can fight my own battles on the relationship front, and I think your uncle will realize he's messed up a good thing eventually. However, that's only part of why I think it's time for me to leave. Something about this house doesn't sit right with me. The place is emotionally empty, and for an Emerald mage, it's uncomfortable."

"Let me guess, it feels like all the joy and happiness has been sucked out of the place?"

"Yes, at least in the majority of the house. Around your suite and here in the library, I get a sense of your happiness at least. In here, you were very happy listening to stories told by a very kind old man."

"Yes, Great-Uncle Jonas, the family archivist, whom I deeply miss. Ian kind of reminds me of him. Jonas was the last of his branch of the family, and I think he wanted me to inherit his position. I used to hide in here for hours when I wanted to escape my training to be a tracker," Kieran said, a sad note ringing in his voice despite the smile on his face.

"I don't really want to abandon you when I know you're about to face a great darkness, but I'm not sure how much help I can still offer," John said.

"I think you've done more than enough, Professor. You helped speed up my recovery, and you've given me back the uncle I lost even before I was born. He'll wise up eventually, because I think you two were meant to be together. If he doesn't do it soon, I'll kick his ass until he does."

"Thank you, Kieran. Do you think you'll be back in time for the fall semester?"

"If I survive what I have to do here, Professor, I'll be back for fall semester, so save me a spot in class." Kieran smiled at his professor with one of his dazzling smiles.

"There's always a spot in my class for you, Kieran, just as there will always be a place at my table for you and Cory during the holidays."

"When you get back to Little Rock, Professor, will you do something for me?" Kieran asked.

"I'd be happy to do just about anything for you, Kieran," John replied.

"Find Mrs. Jones for me and ask her how much she wants for the house where Cory and I have been renting," Kieran said.

"I'll see what I can do, Kieran. Do you really think that she'll sell you the place?"

"I'm hoping that she will. It has a good set up for the few members of the family I want living near Cory and I."

"Then I'll see you at the beginning of the semester, Kieran," John said.

"I'll see you in class, Professor Mason," Kieran said.

They both stood up, and Professor Mason grabbed Kieran into a hug before letting him go and escaping the library. Kieran stood there stunned for a moment before returning to his research.

Interlude: The Master meets the Beast

The Master was irritated Kevin the valet hadn't returned to visit his suite last night as promised. He'd wanted that ripe body to work out his tension on; now he must go and meet with the shifter claiming to be the legendary Beast. He rented a car through the front desk of the hotel, and after getting directions to Belle Lumber, he made his way toward the vast Belle estate. When he felt he was close enough, he pulled the car off the road and into the woods. Stepping out of the car, he shifted his clothes from his business suit back to his all encompassing robes. Ebony magic swirled around him, and he vanished and reappeared in the clearing at the center of the dark woods. Before him stood the throne of bones. His apprentice had created it months ago when he'd come here to meet with this shifter, and it still stood. He gathered his robes about him, seated himself in the throne, and waited for the Beast to arrive.

"So the Master mage finally comes to get his hands dirty," a voice rumbled from the edge of the clearing.

"Don't act all high and mighty with me, mongrel. You and your pack of puppies had ample opportunities to kill the entire family and didn't act," the Master replied. "For what you want, you need me, and for what I want, I do not need you."

A huge and brutish man stepped in front of the seated mage and looked down at the smaller man. He reached to grab the front of the mage's robes and haul him out of the throne, but his hand collided with a barrier. He pulled it back as a burning sensation spread from his fingers up his arm. Several lesser shifters, all in human form, moved to attack the mage, but a mere flick of his fingers froze them all in place.

"You cannot hurt me, Beast, but I can kill you and all of these pathetic strays."

"You can't kill me, mage. Hurt me, I will acknowledge, but your Ebony magic can't kill me. I don't even think Silver magic can do the job. So far, all it's ever done is fling me across time from the bitch to her coward of a descendant and now to a mere boy. I'm not afraid of the House of Beauty."

"This boy is more than just a mere hunter. I've been in contact with his magic, and it is old and powerful. He isn't limited to one spell like those you've faced up until now. I've never sensed a mage like him before."

"I do not fear him. He doesn't fulfill either prophecy. No child of the House of Beauty will ever take a shifter for a mate nor are they going to knowingly associate with a shifter."

"You need a better spy network, dog. This boy is very different. He has a shifter for a guard dog, and his husband comes from the same shifter family as his pet."

"It won't matter in the end. He must fight his way through this pack to face me before sunrise on the day he comes to the test. He'll become more of a challenge if he kills five of them before they take him down. Something in the bitch's lineage seems to unlock when they've killed five shifters."

"I gather from all the bones here that this is the place where the test takes place. I shall weave trap spells here; that will slow or stop the boy's progress. I shall also weave a general protection spell from Silver magic over all those who will fight this hunter. On the night of this test, I will also offer the boy a challenge, and he may choose which of our challenges he wishes to accept."

"Do not fail in your tasks, mage, because if he doesn't kill you, I will."

"That's a threat that goes both ways, dog. I bet in your beast shape you'd make an excellent throw rug. In this form, you might make a passible slave once you were properly broken in. I'll be back in two days to begin casting my spells," the Master said as Ebony magic swirled around him, and he vanished. The bargain was struck.

Chapter Twenty-Four

The stack of ancient manuscripts teetered on the table in front of Kieran. The pile had grown over the last few days. He'd read them all and still hadn't found the information he was looking for. The equally high pile of translations and historical notes didn't make any more sense than the dusty old tomes. The tension in the library grew. Kieran's sigh was louder than ever before.

"Does everything have to be couched in riddles and metaphors? Why couldn't the family historians just admit they didn't know what the hell happened?"

"You're only looking at what is available to the whole family, Cousin Kieran." Ian's reply was muffled because he was buried deep in the stacks.

"I don't have much choice in the matter, Ian, unless you or Billy have discovered where Great-Uncle hid the second set of books," Kieran shouted back.

"Where did you get that one on the first male hunter? The one that talked about his choices of armor and why he wouldn't marry the woman his aunts picked for him?" Ian called back.

"Fourth floor, fifth set of shelves, third shelf up from the bottom of the case," Kieran's answered in a mechanical tone. "Why?"

Ian came out of the stacks, dragging Billy with him, which made Kieran laugh considering the size and weight difference between the boys. Billy just grinned at his uncle over the top of Ian's head. The smaller boy was bursting with questions, and both Kieran and Billy knew they wouldn't stop until he had satisfactory answers. When Ian was practically in Kieran's face, Billy drew him back a couple of steps and wrapped his arms around him.

"Easy does it, bookworm. Uncle Kieran will answer your questions. No need to get in his face. I thought your family taught you respect for the hunter," Billy said into Ian's ear.

"Listen, fleabag," Ian hissed back. "This is important, and it must have escaped your notice, so look up and count how many floors there are to this library."

"Boys, no need to fight about this." Kieran pointed up. "Just look. You can see the three floors above this one."

Billy glanced up toward the ceiling and then looked at his uncle before looking up once again. Ian followed Billy's line of sight and then fixed his gaze on Kieran.

"Uncle Kieran, I only see two floors above this one," Billy said, looking back at his uncle.

"I can only see two additional floors as well, Hunter Kieran," Ian said.

Kieran looked at the two boys as if they were playing a joke on him. He turned and whistled toward the stacks on the far side of the room. A moment later Cory, followed by Kellen and Líadáin, emerged from the stacks.

"What's up, babe?" Cory asked as he approached his husband.

"Would you all look up and tell me how many floors you see above this one?" Kieran said to his family.

Cory, Kellen, and Líadáin all looked up toward the ceiling, not really understanding what Kieran was getting on about the number of floors in the library. It wasn't until they looked back down and gave their answers that the confusion began. Cory reported only seeing two floors while both Kellen and Líadáin said they saw three floors above them. Everyone in the group looked at Kieran in confusion.

"All right, Son, what's going on here?" Kellen asked.

"Active magic, or to be correct, the sight of those who have actively used magic. Neither Cory nor Billy have magic, Ian's magic is dormant, and for his and Billy's future, it's better that it stay that way. The rest of us are all active mages in a house where the use of active magic is discouraged save in an emergency," Kieran replied.

"Okay, so if there really is a fourth floor to this library, and you got a book from it that isn't normally available to the rest of the family, why aren't you looking for more such books up there instead of down here?" Ian asked, exasperated with his older cousin.

"Because, until you asked me where I got the book from, I'd forgotten that's where it came from. Great-Uncle always made sure I passed by a particular spot in the library any time he let me borrow a book like the one on the last male hunter. Oh bright mother, I bet that spot has a spell of forgetting on it," Kellen answered.

Kieran paced around the reading area of the library for a moment as if searching for something before he stopped in front of a statue of Beauty. He blinked a couple of times as if something was trying to make him look someplace else. He stepped back a few steps before stepping forward again. When he felt satisfied that he had the right place, he turned and faced his family.

"I take it you found the hidden entrance to the fourth floor, Kier," Cory said.

"Yes, and there is definitely a spell of forgetting on it. The spell isn't very powerful, but it's subtle, and it's Amethyst magic. I'm not going to break it, but I can give Ian and Billy the key to bypassing it. They can keep their memories of the entrance and the fourth floor," Kieran said.

"What about the rest of us?" Kellen asked.

"Neither you or Grams need to remember the place exists once we're done here, Dad. Besides, once Ian and Billy are old enough, I imagine that the library will move to wherever I establish the hunter school," Kieran replied.

"If you'll key us into the spell, then Billy and I can go up and explore the fourth floor and see what we can find," Ian said.

"Come here and I'll give you the key," Kieran said.

The boys crossed the room toward Kieran, and each took a hand he extended when they started to stop and turn away from the statue. Kieran drew them in close and then whispered a phrase to them. They suddenly straightened up and looked at the statue for a moment before moving forward and through the statue. Behind the illusion of a statue, they found an old elevator cage. They got in and started the elevator on its journey toward the fourth floor. The rest of Kieran's family looked at where the boys had vanished and then crossed the room to where Kieran stood. A sharp indrawn breath from both Kellen and Líadáin let Kieran know that the magic had whispered across their minds and coaxed them into forgetting what they'd seen. It raised an illusion of a lower ceiling in the room to hide the fourth floor from their sight. Cory just took Kieran in his arms and nuzzled his beard into Kieran's neck, making his husband giggle with the knowledge that the magic hadn't worked on Cory as well as from the tickle of the beard.

Kieran led his family back over to the reading table he had buried under books and got them to sit. Cory was the first to come around.

"Where did Billy and Ian get off to?" Cory asked as he snuggled Kieran into his lap.

"You don't have to pretend with me, Wolf. I know because of our bond that the spell of forgetting didn't work on you." Kieran grinned as he leaned in and stole a kiss from his husband while waiting for his father and grandmother to come out of the minor trance they were in due to the spell.

"You're being sneaky and giving the boys someplace nobody will disturb them when they want to sneak away," Cory said after their kiss broke.

"Well, they do have to share their room with a couple of other boys, and the whole hall is packed with boys in groups of four. There's no privacy for the occasional kiss or hug. As I recall, there's a private room up there that Great-Uncle used when he wanted to hide out from the rest of the family."

"You really think that they're like us, a bonded pair."

"Yes, they clicked that day we arrived. Just watch them closely the next time they come to our rooms. It's almost like looking into a mirror of us together," Kieran said.

Kellen and Líadáin came out of their trances about that time, and after remembering where they were, they looked around for the two boys.

"Where did Ian and Billy go?" they asked together.

"I sent them off to go be boys for awhile. Plenty of time for them to be locked in dusty old libraries when they're older. For now, they need to have some fun away from the grown ups. I think it's time we all packed it in for the day. What we're looking for is carefully hidden, and my eyes are tired from all the horrible penmanship I've had to read," Kieran said, stretching and grinding into Cory.

****

While the older folk were gathering up their notes and leaving the library's ground floor, high overhead on the mysterious fourth floor, Ian and Billy were just emerging from the elevator. They exited onto a balcony overlooking the rest of the library.

"Okay, so where do we start looking, bookworm?" Billy asked.

"Hunter Kieran said he got the book on the last male hunter from the fifth set of shelves, so I guess we should start there, fleabag," Ian replied with a grin.

The boys made their way to the entrance to the fourth floor's stacks and counted in five sets of shelves. The books here seemed to match the one Kieran had in his suite so they began checking entries in books. The first books they checked were all written in foreign languages they didn't have a clue about, so they kept looking.

"Do you think there's an index or card catalogue around here someplace, bookworm?" Billy asked after a half an hour of looking for books in English.

Ian stood up and brushed dust off his pant legs. "Let's see if there's an office or something up here. I imagine the Archivist must have spent lots of time up here to escape the family squabbles."

The boys started walking up and down the rows of books until they came into an area with several tables and chairs scattered around like some ancient gentleman's sports club. Off to one side was what looked like an office door. Together they made their way toward the door, which they carefully opened. The door opened into a suite of rooms, the first of which was set up as an office of sorts. With a quiet reverence, they entered the room and shut the door behind them. One side of the room was dominated by a huge fireplace of beautiful marble, above which hung a painting of a beautiful woman with hair as dark as midnight and skin as pale as moonlight. Along the entrance's wall stood a heavy bookcase filled with books and scrolls. The far wall had a door leading into the rest of the suite, and the final wall was made of glass and looked out over the library.

"Maybe what we're looking for is here on these shelves, Ian," Billy said.

"Let's be careful. We don't know what other kinds of magic the last Archivist might have used to protect this place," Ian replied.

Together the boys started to carefully check the books on the shelves. The first shelf of books proved to be diaries of the last three Archivists. They found notes in the last diary about Kieran and his sister Rosie.

I have had the joy of finding two potential Archivists in the family of the late Huntress—her son, Kieran, and her middle daughter, Rosalind. They both have a love of history and family lore. The only drawback to either of them is that they have active magic, being of the main line of descent. Young Kieran would be my primary choice, but he's already been in training several years to become a tracker. Only rarely does this post go to a daughter, but if Rosalind could be persuaded to use her magic and then be free of it, she would be a perfect candidate.

Kieran came to me battered and bloody after his test to earn his tracker certification. He told me that the pack had broken the rules of the test and sent two shifters. I worry, the last time a pack broke the rules was during the time of the male hunter. There is an air of destiny about young Kieran. While I don't have magic, I am sensitive to it, and the boy is bursting at the seams with Silver magic. I don't know where it comes from. It can't be the boy's father, not with those amethyst eyes of his, but Kellen MacDonnell has never let me get to close to him. Kieran is a mystery for the next Archivist, since I do not believe that I will live to see the New Year.

Ian noticed that the last entry was in a very different hand.

I came up to say good-bye to Great-Uncle Jonas to discover he's gone quietly in his sleep. I know that he wanted me to take up his position as Archivist, and I would have enjoyed hiding here among all these marvelous books, but my magic calls me to other things. I have a destiny I do not want calling me out into the world. Someplace out there is the other half of my soul. To whoever takes Jonas' place as Archivist, I wish you much joy, but I hope you're not as alone as Jonas was. This will be the only entry I ever write in these journals. I hope they will remember me fondly if I'm ever written about in them.

Kieran Belle, son of Huntress Miranda Belle and a full Tracker of the House of Beauty

"Oh wow, Uncle Kieran was the last person to write in these diaries. He sounded sad that he wasn't going to get to do it full time," Billy said.

"That's because the Archivist is one of the few men in the family that gets to leave to go further their education beyond high school. They have to learn a lot of languages and how to maintain the archives and stuff like that," Ian replied.

"He's offering you his dream job, bookworm. I think you have some big shoes to fill," Billy said as he hugged Ian.

"Well, he's actually offered it to both of us. He didn't want me to be lonely like the last office holder. So we both have a lot to live up to, fleabag." Ian chuckled as he hugged back. "Let's see what's in these other books."

The boys dug into the books on the next shelf and hit a jackpot in the fifth book. Before them, was the story of *Beauty and the Beast* as recorded by the first known author of the tale, broken into sections and interwoven with notes from various chronicles of the family history. Many of the entries were translations from the very first Archivist's chronicles. As they flipped through the book, they found the ending of the tale and the notes from the chronicles, and they were stunned by what they read.

Beauty's Tale

She put on one of her richest suits to please him, and waited for evening with the utmost impatience, at last the wished-for hour came, the clock struck nine, yet no Beast appeared. Beauty then feared she had been the cause of his death; she ran crying and wringing her hands all about the palace, like one in despair; after having sought for him everywhere, she recollected her dream, and flew to the canal in the garden, where she dreamed she saw him. There she found poor Beast stretched out, quite senseless, and, as she imagined, dead. She threw herself upon him without any dread, and finding his heart beat still, she fetched some water from the canal, and poured it on his head. Beast opened his eyes, and said to Beauty, "You forgot your promise, and I was so afflicted for having lost you, that I resolved to starve myself, but since I have the happiness of seeing you once more, I die satisfied."

"No, dear Beast," said Beauty, "you must not die. Live to be my husband; from this moment I give you my hand, and swear to be none but yours. Alas! I thought I had only a friendship for you, but the grief I now feel convinces me, that I cannot live without you." Beauty scarce had pronounced these words, when she saw the palace sparkle with light; and fireworks, instruments of music, everything seemed to give notice of some great event. But nothing could fix her attention; she turned to her dear Beast, for whom she trembled with fear; but how great was her surprise! Beast was disappeared, and she saw, at her feet, one of the loveliest princes that eye ever beheld; who returned her thanks for having put an end to the charm, under which he had so long resembled a Beast. Though this prince was worthy of all her attention, she could not forbear asking where Beast was.

"You see him at your feet, said the prince. A wicked fairy had condemned me to remain under that shape until a beautiful virgin should consent to marry me. The fairy likewise enjoined me to conceal my understanding. There was only you in the world generous enough to be won by the goodness of my temper, and in offering you my crown I can't discharge the obligations I have to you."

Beauty, agreeably surprised, gave the charming prince her hand to rise; they went together into the castle, and Beauty was overjoyed to find, in the great hall, her father and his whole family, whom the beautiful lady, that appeared to her in her dream, had conveyed thither.

"Beauty," said this lady, "come and receive the reward of your judicious choice; you have preferred virtue before either wit or beauty, and deserve to find a person in whom all these qualifications are united. You are going to be a great queen. I hope the throne will not lessen your virtue, or make you forget yourself. As to you, ladies," said the fairy to Beauty's two sisters, "I know your hearts, and all the

malice they contain. Become two statues, but, under this transformation, still retain your reason. You shall stand before your sister's palace gate, and be it your punishment to behold her happiness; and it will not be in your power to return to your former state, until you own your faults, but I am very much afraid that you will always remain statues. Pride, anger, gluttony, and idleness are sometimes conquered, but the conversion of a malicious and envious mind is a kind of miracle."

Immediately the fairy gave a stroke with her wand, and in a moment all that were in the hall were transported into the prince's dominions. His subjects received him with joy. He married Beauty, and lived with her many years, and their happiness -- as it was founded on virtue -- was complete.

Beauty and the Beast, Jeanne-Marie LePrince de Beaumont, English translation, 1757

****

Dear Lord, the fabrications that went into crafting the happily ever after of Mother and her beastly prince. All of it was created out of whole cloth. The entire time Mother spent in that palace was spent trying to hide from the monster that impersonated the prince under a spell. Even in his human form, he was the Beast. Brutish, crude, and violent, nothing could redeem this monster of a shifter. One night, Mother stumbled into the dungeons searching for a hiding place for the night, seeking to escape his attempts to capture and rape her. In a cell far to the back of the dungeon, she found the real prince chained to the wall. She searched the dungeon until she found the keys to his chains, and then she returned and freed him from his bondage. She tended to him until he was strong enough to move on his own. Together they found a way to ambush and destroy the monster. To her dying day, Mother never spoke of how they managed to kill an Alpha shifter of such power. Father never spoke of that day either. I've gone back to the abandoned castle of the Beast, searching the ruins for some evidence of how they freed us from the terror of the Beast. I've concluded that they didn't actually kill the Beast. I'm no mage, I'm not even a hedge witch, but there are traces of a magic so powerful even someone ungifted like me could sense it. I touched the spot where the magic was still strong and saw a vision of a place and time I didn't know or understand. I saw people bowing to a man in strange metal clothes who had the look of my mother in his facial structure. If I had to guess, Mother used her spell to hurl the monster forward to another time where someone stronger could face the creature.

Entry from the first chronicles of the House of Beauty, translated from the original German in the 21st century.

****

The creature came out of nowhere and tore into my trackers as if they'd never fought a shifter before. I've never seen a shifter so dark in color before. This beast was huge and black, as the night itself. I closed with it as quickly as I could, swinging my great sword for its head. The creature swatted my blade aside as if it were a child's toy. It flung me through the air and came at me looking to tear me apart. I reached deep inside and drew on the magic my family is said to posses. Silver swirled from my hand and surrounded the creature. With a twist, the magic ripped the creature away as if he'd never been there to start with. I touched the spot where it had been and where magic still swirled. A vision filled my sight of the beast in a clearing facing off against a young man in silver armor, flanked by wolves, one the brightest silver and the other darkest black. I think this is what I was supposed to have done as the Hunter of the House of Beauty. I'm sorry some future descendant must undertake the task.

A first person account from the hidden chronicles of the first male Hunter of the House of Beauty, translated from the original Spanish in the 21st century.

****

"We need to get this book to Uncle Kieran." Billy found the words. "He needs to know that he's not facing some random dark Alpha shifter; he's facing the legendary Beast himself."

"I don't know how we get the book out of here. I can feel magic on them. It's like they aren't supposed to leave this room, never mind this floor. It might be better to bring Hunter Kieran up here instead," Ian said.

"We're—or at least you—are the new Archivist, so I bet you can take things out of this room if you want to, Ian."

Ian picked up the book and walked toward the door. He reached out to turn the knob, but it began to glow bright red and put off intense heat. He quickly retreated.

"There must be something I haven't done to prove to the spells that I'm the new guy on the job," Ian said.

"Hey, there's blank pages in the last diary after Kieran's entry. Maybe if you write something in the book the magic here will know you've got the job," Billy said.

They looked back to the beginning of one of the earlier diaries and found an entry much like what they'd been thinking about doing. They realized that Kieran's entry had sort of been an introduction to the book as the next writer.

Billy found a pen and a bottle of ink on the desk. He scooped up the last diary and brought it over. He set it on the desk, open to the page with Kieran's entry.

"Time to decide for real, bookworm. Do we want the job and the future Kieran sees for us like we told him we do, or do we want to forget all about it and be on our own with no magic and no shifting?" Billy said as he pulled the desk chair back to let Ian sit.

Ian sat in the chair and stared at the book, pen, and ink for a moment before glancing up at the boy he knew would eventually be his lover when they were older. His decision would affect both of their lives for the long run.

"If we do this, Billy, it's you and me together forever. There's no turning back, no splitting up, and no regretting we committed to this path," Ian said.

"In case you haven't already noticed, bookworm, it's already you and me forever. There's a mate bond like Uncle Kieran and Uncle Cory have growing between us. We're too young for the full effects of it, but in time, the only place I'm going to be found is at your side. The choice is dusty library or the open road, Ian. What do you want?"

"I want this, Billy. I want this dusty library and all the wonders it contains."

"Then make our entry in the book, Ian Belle-Cooper," Billy said.

"That isn't my name," Ian replied.

"It is now. We're not old enough for me to claim you as my bonded mate, Ian, but I'm staking my claim to you, and I hope you'll stake your claim to me and let me be William Cooper-Belle in these journals and eventually out in the real world as well."

Ian swallowed hard to keep back the tears of joy he felt. He grabbed the pen, dipped it into the ink, and began to write.

August 15, 2015

On this day, William Cooper-Belle, my life partner, and I, Ian Belle-Cooper, take up the duties of the Archivist of the House of Beauty. We have been asked to take up this task by Kieran Samuel Belle Oisín-Cooper, Hunter of the House of Beauty, and we hereby accept. We release all other candidates from this role to pursue their own dreams as we now pursue ours.

Both boys felt a tingle of magic as Ian made the last period in his entry and knew the library had accepted them as its new custodians. They left the journal open on the desk so that the ink could dry. Ian picked up the journal they needed to show Kieran and once more headed for the door. This time the door swung open before he'd even reached for the handle. When they were both back out in the reading area, the door swung shut behind them. Billy drew Ian in and gave him a quick kiss on the cheek.

"What was that for?" Ian asked. "Not that I mind you kissing me."

"A promise for our future together," Billy said with a smile. "Now let's go show Uncle Kieran what we've found."

Kethric Wilcox

Chapter Twenty-Five

While Ian and Billy were exploring the fourth floor, Kieran and Cory had returned to their suite of rooms. As Kieran crossed the sitting room to the table and chairs set up out on the balcony, Cory flipped the lock to the outer doors so that no one would disturb them. He had plans for Kieran and would tolerate no interruptions. He toed off his sneakers and then padded silently across the room to come up behind Kieran and wrap him in a tight hug. Kieran sighed and relaxed into Cory's embrace with a giggle.

"What's so funny, babe?" Cory asked.

"You trying to be all sneaky and silent. Even in socks, you walk like an elephant, and all your emotions flow down our bond like water down a drain," Kieran replied.

"Ah well, as long as you always know how much I love you, I'm happy to be a leaky sink."

"You have mischief in mind, Wolf. I can tell."

"Mmm, I might have a little bit of fun in mind," Cory whispered in Kieran's ear as he leaned in to run his tongue around the shell of that pretty ear.

Kieran shivered as first Cory's breath and then his tongue caressed his ear. He couldn't hold back the moan when Cory caught the lobe of his ear between his teeth and lightly tugged. Cory released the tender flesh for a moment and blew warm breath over the damp skin, making his lover tremble. Slowly, he nuzzled along Kieran's neck, eliciting shivers, sighs, and moans from his lover as he undid the buttons of the shirt the man was wearing, exposing the scarred but beautiful flesh beneath. He slipped the shirt down Kieran's arms, kissing and licking along the exposed flesh of the left shoulder before retracing his path, lifting the long ponytail out of the way so that he could trace across the exposed nape to repeat his treatment on the right shoulder. Cory slipped the mass of Kieran's ponytail over his shoulder, leaving his beautiful back bare. Slowly, he licked his way down Kieran's spine, taking occasional side trips to follow one of the many faint scars the crossed his lover's back. In order to continue his journey down Kieran's back, Cory had to kneel behind his lover. He slowly reached around, finished pulling the shirt from the waist of his lover's pants, and then unbuttoned the cuffs to pull the shirt free of the wrists. He teased his way down to the top of Kieran's jeans and then slowly turned his lover around while keeping his tongue pressed to the exposed flesh. Kieran shivered and moaned as Cory turned him around so that they were facing each other, but Cory didn't stop until Kieran was once again facing away from him. The next thing he felt was Cory undoing his belt and the fastenings to his jeans before they were eased down his body to pool at his ankles to reveal that he was wearing a jockstrap. Cory growled in appreciation of his lover's tight ass framed in the straps of the jock. The beautiful curves of Kieran's ass called out to be licked, and Cory began running his tongue over them from where they met the top of Kieran's muscular legs up to his waist. He closed in on the crease between the firm cheeks from the right-hand side before switching and starting over on the left side. Once he'd paid attention to both sides equally, Cory began to tease the crease of his lover's ass with tongue and beard. Kieran was whimpering with pleasure and beyond words as Cory began to spread his ass cheeks apart so that his tongue could have access to the hidden treasure in the center. If there was a coherent thought left in Kieran's head, it shorted out when Cory's tongue laved over his hole. He was holding onto the table for dear life as his husband ravished him with his tongue. His cock was rock hard, and his balls were drawing up as the need to release his load flooded his body without Cory ever coming near to touching his cock. Cory teased the muscles of Kieran's hole until they fluttered open, and let his tongue slide in to tease the inside of his lover. It was more than Kieran could take, and his body arched and tightened in orgasm. Cory caught Kieran as his lover went boneless with his orgasm. While Kieran recovered, Cory finished stripping his clothes off and carried him to the bedroom. He gently laid Kieran on the bed before beginning the tongue bath over again, starting at Kieran's feet and working his way upward until he'd brought his husband to a second hands-free orgasm.

Cory was just starting to remove his own shirt when a frantic pounding on the outer door interrupted. *Oh well, at least I gave Kieran plenty of pleasure before the hoards descended again,* Cory thought as he pulled his shirt back down and headed for the door to the suite. He glanced back, taking in the beauty of his sated husband lying naked on the bed. With a sigh, he went to open the door to the hallway and tell whoever was out there to go away. It seemed like a nice plan, which failed to take into account the two excited young boys on the other side of the door. They blew past him into the sitting room. Billy caught the look of annoyance on his uncle's face and then spotted the pile of clothes on the balcony. Ian was clueless and beginning to babble when a barely coherent Kieran wandered into the sitting room totally naked. Ian stopped in mid-word, blushed, and turned to face in the opposite direction. Billy turned his attention to Ian, while Cory swiftly crossed the room and ushered Kieran back into the bedroom. The two younger boys heard Cory admonish Kieran, "Clothes, babe, we have underage company." Ian looked at Billy with eyes as big as saucers. Billy was as amazed by Kieran's naked beauty, but tried to play it off to help Ian calm down.

"He was naked. I've seen the hunter naked," Ian was muttering.

"Hey, bookworm, it's not like you've never seen a guy naked before considering the showers in our wing are communal. Okay, so Uncle Kieran is a lot hotter than any of the boys in our wing, but he's just another guy," Billy said.

"But he's the hunter," Ian moaned. "It just seems so wrong to see him naked."

"He's human, Ian. He puts his pants on one leg at a time just like you do. I bet he's just as embarrassed at being caught naked as you are at seeing him naked."

"Actually, I'd be surprised if Kieran is embarrassed at all. He has a beautiful body that he likes to show off," Cory teased from the doorway to the bedroom.

"Shut up, Wolf. The boy doesn't need to be teased," Kieran said as he pushed Cory out of the way so that he could reenter the room properly dressed. "Sorry about that Ian, Billy. Cory left me a little out of my senses. I just hope that whatever brought you down here in such a state is worth all the fuss."

Ian gathered himself and picked up the book he'd dropped. "We found a really old record in a one of the journals that shares how the story of *Beauty and the Beast* was created, and it talks about what the first Archivist pieced together about Beauty's battle with the Beast." Ian spit out in one breath.

"Okay, that's important enough to forgive the interruption," Kieran said. "Sit down and show me what you've found, Archivist Ian Belle-Cooper."

"How did you know how I signed my entry?" Ian said, stunned by Kieran's knowledge.

"Because I was the last person to make an entry in those books, and your entry freed me from the obligation to have to go back and fill in all the details of my own life as hunter. Your magic is dormant and buried deep, Ian, but it leaves you with a sensitivity to magic being used around you and to ancient spells that have been laid over items to protect them. All of the spells in that library are delicate; active magic would destroy them all and the library along with them," Kieran said.

"That's why Great-Uncle Jonas wanted Rosalind to use up her magic and why—as much as he wanted you to be his heir—it wasn't possible. Your magic is different from the rest of the House," Ian said.

"Yes, Ian that's correct. Now tell me what you and Billy found."

"Beauty didn't kill the Beast," the boys said in unison.

"What?" Kieran asked, sinking onto the couch in shock. "That can't be right. Everything I've read says that she killed the Beast but would never talk about how she managed to do it. What did she do if she didn't use her magic to kill the Beast?"

"She used her magic to hurl the Beast forward in time," Ian said.

"How far forward did she hurl him?" Cory asked as he sat down on the couch and drew a stunned Kieran up against his body.

"To the age of the first male hunter. Didn't anyone record the man's name? You'd think someone would have written down his name. After all, he was the first guy on the job," Billy huffed.

"The Archivist to his successor did record his name. I found it in later book. He was called Simeon. Why do I have a feeling that history repeated itself and that Simeon did the same thing Beauty did?" Kieran asked.

"Because that's what happened. Simeon fought the Beast, but couldn't defeat him. He panicked and used the same spell Beauty had used," Ian said.

"So the dark Alpha out there in the forest isn't just some powerful shifter that wandered in and took over. The creature out there is the most powerful shifter in recorded history," Kieran said. "No wonder I've had nightmares about facing him since I was a kid."

"You're not facing him alone, babe," Cory said as he hugged Kieran tighter to him. "Billy and I will both be there at your side, just like prophecy says."

"I don't understand why he's out there lurking in the woods then. Why not come and attack us here at the house directly? I'm missing something. I've never understood why this house isn't warded to the max, yet the pack never emerges from the woods," Kieran said.

"They can't leave the woods; it's a part of the pact between the huntress and the Alpha. See, right here in the chronicles," Ian said as he flipped to a page he'd marked in the book.

I have discovered a terrible secret regarding Great-Grandmother's pact with the shifters of the forest. She gave her youngest sister to the leader of the pack as mate. From what I have been able to discover, Great-Great-Aunt Ophelia was totally without the gift of Silver magic, a very rare thing only three generations removed from the first of our family. The most terrifying part of this pact is that it must continue each time a new huntress takes over the family. She must give a non-magical sister or cousin of the same generation to the leader of the forest pack as mate, or the compact between these dark shifters and the House of Beauty will be broken. I am afraid for my twin sister; neither of us was born with the gift of Silver magic. Our eldest sister goes for the test tomorrow night, and if she becomes the huntress, then I fear my sweet sister is doomed to this horrid fate.

From the Second Chronicle of the House of Beauty, translated into English from the original French in the 21st century

"If this is how the pact is maintained, how is it holding right now? Mother didn't have any sisters, and all of her children had magic. Could Grandmother have made the pact with one of her siblings?" Kieran wondered out loud.

"It doesn't sound like it should have held up when your mother replaced your grandmother as huntress," Cory said.

"Ian, has there ever been a case like Mother's and Grandmother's where a huntress was injured and unable to continue in the field?" Kieran asked.

"How would I know? I haven't . . ." Ian's voice trailed off for a moment, and he got a far away look in his eyes, as did Billy. "No, Hunter Kieran, your mother and grandmother are unique in the annals of the House of Beauty," Ian and Billy said in eerie unison.

"How did they do that?" Cory asked.

"We are the Archivist, and we are connected to the knowledge of the library. Ask your questions, Hunter Kieran," the boys spoke together.

"Who did Huntress Camille take to bind the pact?"

"Her youngest sister, Theresa, was offered as the House of Beauty's side of the bargain," the boys answered.

"That would have been over fifty years ago. If the Alpha is killed and replaced by another Alpha, does the pact remain intact, or must the House of Beauty send a new person?" Kieran asked.

"Only if the Alpha is of a bloodline not bound to the pact. Only the death of the huntress or of the sacrifice can free the Alpha from the pact."

"Well, then if Great-Aunt Theresa is still alive, the pact would hold. Grandmother is still living, so her sacrifice would still be valid; the spell that created the pact still views her as the huntress. It doesn't explain how the Beast is bound in those woods though. He can't be of the bloodline of that pack."

"Is the pack of the bloodline of the Beast?" Cory asked.

Ian and Billy hesitated for a moment as if consulting some internal rulebook before answering. "Because you are the mate of the hunter, we shall answer. Yes, this pack like all the packs before them is of the bloodline of the Beast."

"That's how he's bound to the woods. The spell was worked on his bloodline," Cory said.

"That's not a good thing, Cory. Because either he was once able to move in and out of the woods, or he traveled here within the last couple of years," Kieran said.

"What make you say that, Kieran?" Cory asked.

"Billy. Think about how dark his wolf form is. A shifter strong enough to have and hold a midway form raped your sister. My mother died at the hands of a huge pack led by a very dark shifter. I think the Beast was loose and then made his way here. When he took over the pack in the woods, he became trapped by the spell of the pact. Even if Great-Aunt Theresa died, the pact wouldn't be broken, because Grandmother lives and still has her magic," Kieran said before he asked, "Would the pact spell still recognize Camille Belle as the huntress if she uses her one shot of Silver magic?"

"If Camille Belle uses her Silver magic, the pact will be broken until Kieran Belle brings a suitable sacrifice to the Grove of the Secret," came the eerie unison reply.

"I thank you for your advice, Archivist. I have no further need of your counsel at this time," Kieran said.

The distant look in Ian's and Billy's eyes faded, and the boys returned to the present. They looked confused for a few moments as they sat there staring at Kieran and Cory.

"It will take some getting used to, guys. I'm actually surprised that I could trigger the effect. Since Grandmother still has her magic, she's still the huntress. The enchantments around here shouldn't respond to me while she has magic. I'm not fully the Hunter of the House of Beauty. I'm going to have to put an end to that before I go into the forest," Kieran said.

"What do you want us to do, Uncle Kieran?" Billy asked for both boys.

"Stay here with Cory for now. I'm going to go goad Grandmother into using up her one shot of Silver magic, or actually, I'm going to go ask Grams to do it," Kieran said.

"Is that a wise thing to do, Kieran? Grams could get hurt," Cory asked.

"Silver magic isn't going to hurt Grams; she's the widow of the Silver Witch and the mother of his children. There's some Silver magic still in her bloodstream. Should be enough to protect her from Grandmother's one-shot spell. No, if anyone needs protecting from magic, it will be Grandmother," Kieran said with a malicious grin on his face.

Kieran went to search out Grams, Kellen, and Uncle Brom. It was time for the Oisín clan to have a little council.

Kethric Wilcox

Chapter Twenty-Six

Líadáin Oisín made her way across the expansive dinning hall the Belle family used for dinner. She went toward where Camille Belle held her minor court with several of the Matriarchs. Kieran had explained the secrets the boys had uncovered last night over a small family dinner in her suite. He was concerned that Camille knew that all the enchantments around the estate still only acknowledged her as head of the family and was using that knowledge to plot against her grandson. Líadáin was boiling with anger by the time Kieran had laid out all the evidence supporting his theory, including summoning Cory, Billy, and Ian to join them. He'd even put the two younger boys into Archivist mode to convince his father and uncle. By the time they'd finished their dessert, the younger boys were curled up together asleep on one of the couches, and even Kieran was beginning to fade. Wrapped up in Cory's arms, the couple was an older copy of the younger boys. Líadáin smiled at the memory before her frown returned as she thought of all the people, including her late husband and her youngest son, who'd plotted against Kieran all his life. Líadáin was tired of people plotting against her favorite grandchild; it was time some justice was delivered. She paused just outside of the group around Camille and drew herself up to her full height.

"Camille, it's time you and I had a conversation, grandmother to grandmother, about Kieran," Líadáin said.

"Líadáin, of course, please have a seat." Camille waited while Líadáin settled into a chair. "What did you want to discuss about Hunter Kieran?"

"Give some actual respect when you talk about him in that role, Camille. You're holding out on the young man you've proclaimed is the head of your family, and he knows it."

"I have know idea what you're talking about, Líadáin. I've given Kieran all of my support."

"But you haven't truly given him control of the House of Beauty; all the big family enchantments still only acknowledge you as the huntress. I wonder if that little fact is what got your daughter killed, never mind the slaughter of our granddaughters. Why didn't you use your Silver magic to prevent the accident that put you out of commission as an active hunter, Camille?" Líadáin asked.

"Because there was no one else to be offered in place of my sister Theresa to maintain the pact. Miranda was my only child, and she had the gift of magic. All the girls of her generation were gifted. Then, she married your son, and every one of her children came up gifted. I'd hoped that Kieran could be goaded into using up his magic so that he could be sent to take Theresa's place, but his magic proved different, and I figured one of the girls would have to sacrifice her magic and take Theresa's place."

"Then, Miranda died and the girls became more important as potential huntresses, but you still had the question of what to do with Kieran, because you knew he was more than just a gifted tracker-candidate."

"The boy was too talented for his own good, and then he came back from his tracker test with the first real proof that something was wrong with the pact. Two shifters attacked him that night, but the pact of the test allows for only one," Camille said.

"So you started sending the girls in to become the next huntress, knowing something was wrong. Why didn't you go yourself?" Líadáin asked.

Camille gestured for her hangers-on to leave them before she continued. "Because I was afraid that Theresa might be dead, and if I used up my magic, the pact would be broken until a new huntress made the sacrifice. I didn't think about the fact that the test of the huntress doesn't usually take place while the previous one is still living and still has her magic. If I give up my magic, the test must take place immediately; the full moon is only days away. If Kieran doesn't complete the test and make the sacrifice, the pact will be shattered forever."

"Camille, you need to let go of the magic and let Kieran take his rightful place as head of this family. His magic can't be exhausted, and if need be, there are cousins of his generation who can be sacrificed to the pact. I don't think he'll allow it to happen; his plan is to wipe out the entire pack, down to the last pup."

"Líadáin, that's been done before, but the next huntress must be tested, and the use of a pack of shifters makes the magic of the pact necessary."

"Camille, Kieran is the child of two very powerful magical families, and he's very gifted at adapting magic to suit his needs. He's fooled you all for years with the various ways he's used magic to enhance his skills. Now, he has all the power my husband once wielded; give him the last piece he needs to save the House of Beauty from itself."

"I can't take the risk of what happens if he fails," Camille said.

"Then, you leave me no choice, Camille. Your magic has to go so that Kieran can come into his full inheritance as the Hunter of the House of Beauty," Líadáin said.

"You'll have to kill me, Líadáin. I'm not going to waste my magic fighting you. I know your magic isn't over in one spell like mine is," Camille replied.

"Actually, Grandmother, Grams doesn't have to do anything," Kieran said from behind Líadáin. "The brother of Beauty gave your line the gift of one active Silver magic spell, and his line has always held the power to take it back. Give me your hand, and I'll make this as painless as possible."

"Your kindness will get you or those around you killed someday, boy," Camille said.

"It already has, Grandmother, but I choose to remain kind to honor those that have fallen. Now it's time for you to lay down your burdens and let younger shoulders carry the load," Kieran said as he took his grandmother's hand and withdrew her Silver magic.

With the removal of Camille's magic, Kieran found himself overflowing with a new power and perspective on the House of Beauty. The household enchantments locked on to him, and he could sense the bond of the pact. At the moment, he sensed it, the old bond attached to his grandmother shattered, but a new bond attached to him. It somehow took its place, as if the perfect sacrifice had already been on hand in the Grove of the Secret. It was a mystery for another time.

Interlude: The Pact Rebound

In the heart of the dark forest lies the Grove of the Secret, where the newly proclaimed Huntress of the House of Beauty brings the chosen child of the Belle line. In this grove, the Alpha of the forest pack comes to accept his chosen mate. For over fifty years, Theresa Belle had served in this role, sacrificed to secure the peace between her family and the dark shifters of the forest. Unknown but long suspected by Camille, Theresa had died around the time of the accident that sidelined Camille as huntress. The magic didn't recognize a change of huntresses, because Camille still had magic, so it held until the day Kieran Belle Oisín-Cooper stripped away Camille's magic and claimed the full heritage of the House of Beauty. The magic shattered, alerting the Alpha of the pack that the old huntress was no longer in place. The time of the test was at hand.

The Beast felt the magic that had bound him to the forest since the day he'd challenged and killed the old Alpha shatter. However, much to his surprise, the binding spell reformed. He remained a prisoner in the forest.

"I do not understand this strange magic that binds me to this forest," he bellowed.

"Ancient One, it is the magic of the pact between the House of Beauty and the pack. It binds the Alpha and the pack to this forest. We are bound by a blood spell tied to the lineage of the Alpha," replied the shaman of the pack.

"I am not of the lineage of your last Alpha. How does this spell bind me?" the Beast demanded.

"You are not descended from the line of our Alphas; they are descended from your line. Blood calls to blood and binds all of the bloodline," the shaman said.

"Then there is some ritual involved to seal this pact with each Alpha?" the Beast asked.

"There has been in the past. If the binding has broken, then the huntress who made the sacrifice is no longer among the living or has used her Silver magic. A new candidate will come to the test, and if successful, will bring a new sacrifice to the Grove of the Secret to meet with the Alpha and renew the pact," the shaman answered.

"The binding broke, but then it was renewed in an instant," the Beast retorted.

"Then the House of Beauty had a hidden huntress and a new sacrifice already in place in the grove. It is not required that the Alpha receive the sacrifice, only that one is made."

"Where is this grove?" the beast demanded.

"It is known only to the Alpha and his designated successor," the shaman replied.

The Beast's rage was terrible to behold as he ripped the shaman to shreds. He'd killed both the old Alpha and the one who came forward to challenge as the Alpha's chosen successor. The location of the Grove of the Secret was lost. There was no way for him to go and break the binding spell. He would have to wait for the last child of the bitch to come to him. He took little solstice in knowing that his opponent's hidden secret was exposed. The boy was already the hunter, and with his death, all the enchantments both of Beauty's line and of the cursed ancient Silver mages would break.

Five Months Before
The Full Moon During Kieran's Spring Break

Five shifters lay dead at her feet. She'd felt a shift inside her, but none of the expected additional powers came to her, and more of the pack was closing in on her. She swept around her with the silver sword Kieran had given her, slicing through any shifter that got within reach. They were circling her now; it wouldn't be long before they attacked her from all sides. A huge dark gray wolf pounced on her from the left, knocking her to the ground and jarring the sword from her hand. She whipped out a dagger and tried to protect herself, but they were all over her, and claws were tearing through her leathers. God, was this the pain Kieran had felt when the shifters had mauled him during his tracker test? There had to be something she could do; she couldn't die here, not like this.

The magic tingled within her, and a spell of ancient might came into her head. She knew her time as a huntress was over whether she cast it or the pack tore her apart. Therefore, Rosie reached out and grasped the spell, letting the magic flow. She vanished from beneath the pile of the pack and spiraled across the forest to crash into a grove that contained a cottage, a dormant garden, and the remains of a corpse that might once have been a woman. Biting back a scream of terror at practically landing on the corpse, Rosie rose up and made her shivering way into the cabin.

Chapter Twenty-Seven

The ancient forest seemed gloomier than ever. Only two days after Camille's magic had been taken away, the full moon flickered through the waving branches of the trees. Dark shadows stretched from tree to tree, blocking all but the faintest hint of light. A young man stepped on the path leading to the heart of the woodland. The scene felt familiar to Kieran. Was it only four years ago that he'd stood here waiting for a shifter to come and begin the test for his status as a tracker? The dark forest didn't look any less daunting now than it had back then. This time he would follow the track to the clearing in the center of the forest to face the pack and its Alpha for the test of the huntress. There was a big difference for this test; he would not enter the forest alone.

At his left was the dark wolf that only a few hours ago had been Billy; at his right the bright and shining form of Cory in wolf shape. Kieran stood in his dark leathers, armed with not only his knives and new matching sabers, but also his father's silver long sword. He would have to start with the long sword since the sabers were heavily enchanted and the rules of the test only allowed minimal enchantments.

Behind him, he knew that his father, uncle, and grams were standing in silent support. They couldn't enter the forest, and unless he was victorious and broke the enchantment on the forest, Cory and Billy wouldn't be able to leave it because they shared part of the bloodline of the pack with their common descent from the Beast. Kieran drew a deep breath and then took the first steps along the path to his destiny.

The path ran straight through the forest to the clearing at its heart, and it took Kieran, Cory, and Billy only an hour to make the journey. Before they broke the cover of the forest, Kieran stopped Cory and Billy from going any further. He knelt between the two wolves and pulled them both close.

"I have to do this first part on my own. Once the first five shifters have gone down, then you can join in the fight. They're going to keep coming. Don't spare any of them, because they won't spare any of us," Kieran said to both wolves.

Both wolves whined but didn't move when Kieran rose, turned, and walked out into the clearing. When he stood near the throne of bone crafted by the Master, Kieran stopped. His anger rose when he saw the three human skulls, two of which were child sized. Here were the remains of Selene, Savannah, and Amanda. Callie's had been recovered from the edge of the forest nearest the house, but where were Rosie's remains? He would have all of his sisters back for proper burial.

"I am Kieran Samuel Belle, Hunter-candidate of the House of Beauty, and I've come for the test. Send forth your five chosen warriors, Alpha of the pack."

"Don't seek to fool me Child of Beauty, you passed the test of the huntress over a month ago when the minions I sent with the little owl attacked you. The magic of this forest tells the tale. The sacrifice made by the last huntress no longer holds us bound to this forest, but a new sacrifice by a new hunter does," came a growled response from the far edge of the woods.

"I have made no sacrifice; none of my generation meet the requirements for the ritual, and you've killed all of my sisters," Kieran replied through gritted teeth.

"Yet the sacrifice was made to and accepted by the forest. There shall be no test. Prepare to die Hunter of the House of Beauty," the voice called out.

The forest shifters poured out of the forest and raced to attack Kieran. He dropped into a defensive position and drew forth his sabers. The first shifter leapt to drive Kieran to the ground only to go flying in two directions as Kieran sliced it in half. His blades became a whirling wall of death, and shifter parts went flying in all directions. When it seemed as if the shifters would surround him—long after five shifters had died on his blades—Cory and Billy came racing out of the woods to tear into the shifters trying to get behind Kieran. Shifters howled and burst into flame from Cory's Silver bite or claws. Billy tore his victims apart with his greater strength. Soon, the pair of wolves was fighting off shifters right beside Kieran.

The number of shifters attacking doubled, and the weight of them drove the trio back for a moment. At one point, the shifters managed to separate Kieran from Cory and Billy, and he went down under their weight. Claws tore into his leathers, and despite the heavy enchantments, the claws reached the skin on his legs. Rolling to avoid a set of jaws trying for his hamstring, a bleeding Kieran reached a spot from which he chose not to be driven beyond. Silver magic swirled around him, driving back the shifters for a moment before it formed into his familiar silver armor, minus the wicked scythe blades. The shifters regrouped and came again. He began the dance of death. Ebony magic ripped across the clearing to blast Kieran from his feet, and the shifters leapt to try and pin him down, but Billy and Cory blocked their way. Kieran rose, and with a gesture, sent Silver magic racing across the clearing to burn anything with Ebony magic. Shifters burst apart as the magic cut through them, and at the edge of the forest, the magic hit a barrier of Ebony magic. It exploded, taking out a chunk of the forest.

Whirling back around, Kieran cut away several shifters trying to get close enough to take down Cory. Billy flashed past Kieran's shoulder and tore out the throat of a shifter going for Kieran's back. Kieran signaled to Cory and Billy, and the pair hit the ground at his feet as he set off a second Silver magic burst, illuminating the entire clearing and finishing off all of the shifters in the attacking force. A second bolt of Ebony magic came searing Kieran's way, but he was able to deflect it away.

"Come out and fight me, mage," Kieran called out. "I know you're the one behind most of the attacks against me on and off campus. I don't really know what you want from me, but I'm not going to let you keep attacking me or those I care for."

Silence greeted him.

Kethric Wilcox

Chapter Twenty-Eight

The Master and the Beast stood watching the battle in the clearing. When he thought he had an opening, the Master threw blasts of raw Ebony magic in Kieran's direction, hoping to put the boy out of commission. Nothing he'd observed of the boy in class, on campus, or his escapes from lesser foes had prepared the Master for Kieran's power. The blast of Silver magic the boy had flung in his direction took just about everything he had. The best he could manage was to deflect it and dodge the trees that came crashing down around him. Then came the boy's challenge.

"Come out and fight me, mage. I know you're the one behind most of the attacks against me on and off campus. I don't really know what you want from me, but I'm not going to let you keep attacking me or those I care for."

"This is what you wanted, mage, a chance to take on the boy. If you defeat him, then your plans move forward while mine will be impeded," the Beast said.

"Yes, and if I lose to him, then you have your shot at freedom," the Master replied.

The Master drew his darkest shadows around himself and stepped out into the clearing to face the boy. It was easy to find the boy; he was a gleaming beacon of silver in the center of the clearing, standing next to the throne of bones. The Master stopped when he was about twenty feet away from Kieran.

"Well, I'd say the evil mastermind finally steps out of the shadows, but since you're wrapped up in them, that would be a tall tale," Kieran said.

"I'll give you the chance to kneel before me now, boy. Surrender to me and you will know only pleasure as my slave," the Master said.

"I know pleasure, and it comes freely from my husband. No slave can know pleasure, only a lack of pain. The only option here is which one of us will walk away from this place alive."

"When I walk out of here, boy, it will be with you on a leash," the Master replied.

"You aren't walking out of here alive," Kieran retorted.

"Then, as challenged, I call weapons for our duel, and I choose magic only. You will have to get rid of your weapons."

"Fine." Kieran began removing his weapons.

"Lose the armor as well, Mr. Belle," the Master added.

Silver magic swirled around Kieran, and his armor reverted to his now battered leathers. A nagging voice in the back of Kieran's mind said he knew the voice of the mage and the way he'd called him Mr. Belle. Only his professors at school called him that. He knew it couldn't be Professor Simms; the man was a Ruby mage. Professor Mason was an Emerald mage, so who could it be? At last, Kieran stood in just his leathers; all his weapons leaned against the throne of bones near his sisters' skulls. *Keep an eye on those for me, my sisters. I'll need them later.* Kieran silently pleaded to his sisters' spirits. He stepped forward to face the Master once again, and spread his arms to show that he was unarmed.

"Well, at least you can still follow directions, Mr. Belle, even if you do still have a smart mouth."

"It's been mentioned that my mouth gets me in trouble. It's a family trait on both sides. You might as well drop the shadows. I know who you are under them, Professor Jaynes," Kieran said.

The shadows unwrapped from around the Master, and he pushed back his cloak to reveal that Kieran had guessed correctly. Before him stood his English professor, who gave him a mocking bow for having figured out the puzzle.

"What gave me away, Mr. Belle?" Professor Jaynes asked.

"Little things, Professor, like calling me Mr. Belle. What clenched it was referring to my smart mouth. Only two professors have ever commented on my snide comments. You and Professor Mason. No mage can fake the powers of another kind of mage, so I knew it couldn't be Professor Mason," Kieran replied.

"You are a star student, Mr. Belle; that along with your beauty sparked my desire to own you, and when Professor Simms offered to procure you, I couldn't resist. I grew leery of you when you gave your explanation of *Beauty and the Beast* and how reluctant you were to take it as your paper topic. I loved how you hid all kinds of tidbits in the paper you turned in, such a fascinating read. I had no idea how much truth was hidden in it until I discovered the Beast by accident."

"I don't really care, Professor. You've attacked me and mine. Your agents caused the death of my grandfather, and for that, I'm going to rip your heart out with my bare hands. Let's get on with the duel. I have a real monster to face," Kieran snarled.

Professor Jaynes made a gesture, and a wall of Ebony magic rose up behind him. Kieran mirrored him, and a wall of Silver magic rose up to match up and lock with the Ebony wall. The magic of the two walls swirled and formed into a dome of magic.

"Only the winner leaves this dome with his freedom," Professor Jaynes said.

"Only the winner leaves this dome alive," Kieran replied.

The two mages squared off, and the Master fired off a testing bolt of Ebony magic, trying to find out the power of Kieran's personal shields. He was caught by surprise when Kieran merely danced aside and let the bolt be absorbed by the shielding dome of magic. Kieran moved with fluid grace, and the spell he fired back wasn't a testing spell. Silver chains wrapped around his opponent and latched on with fiery hooks of Silver magic. Professor Jaynes screamed in pain and tried to muster a counter spell, but it was as if his own magic made the chains draw tighter. He watched in terror as Kieran approached.

"You should have heeded the warning I sent back to you with your dead apprentice, Professor. I am the Silver Witch, and your agents killed my predecessor and beloved grandfather. I'm going to do for you what I didn't do for Marissa when I trapped her in this same spell. I'm going to do as I promised and rip your heart out with my bare hand. I grant you a swift death," Kieran spit out.

Professor Jaynes screamed as Kieran's Silver-magic-wrapped hand slammed into his chest, piercing flesh and bone to grasp his heart. He felt Kieran grip his heart and squeeze before he tore it from the man's chest. Kieran looked up from the beating heart in his hand and watched as the spell, sensing the death of the victim, caught with tightened and incinerated the remains. Silver fire wrapped around Kieran's hand, burning away the heart and blood of his enemy. The magic in the dome swirled on last time before flashing pure silver and vanishing. Kieran staggered and fell to his knees as the vast use of magic caught up to him.

Across the clearing, Cory and Billy began to race toward him from one direction as more shifters poured out of the forest from the opposite direction. On hands and knees, Kieran didn't see either group heading his way. The howl of the approaching pack roused him to the danger headed his way. He pushed himself back up to his knees and raised his hands just as the first wave of shifters crashed into him, biting and clawing him. Cory and Billy crashed into the pile of shifters burying Kieran. Teeth and claws tore into the enemy shifters. From the bottom of the pile, a blaze of Silver magic came, driving off the pile and revealing Kieran in his full Silver magic armor, including the wicked scythe blades on each arm. Getting his legs under him, Kieran executed a powerful flip and landed on his feet, braced and ready to fight once again. A new dance with death began and continued until the corpses of shifters were piled high around Kieran, Cory, and Billy.

Out of the dark forest, a huge shape emerged. The Beast had finally come to fight. Kieran was reeling from blood loss, magic drain, and pure exhaustion. He braced himself to meet the Beast in combat.

Chapter Twenty-Nine

Kieran, Cory, and Billy stood facing the massive figure of the dark Alpha in his midway form. Fur as dark as midnight covered muscle double Cory's size in his own midway form. Kieran looked at the face out of his childhood nightmares and froze. This could only be the legendary Beast, whom both Beauty and the last male hunter had faced and banished across time. Now the darkness stood before him.

"So the latest of the bitch's descendants comes to face me. Are you braver than the rest of your family, little boy?" the Beast growled at Kieran.

"I've slaughtered my way through your pack and you doubt my bravery?" Kieran tried hard not to let his fear show through.

"I can smell your fear, little boy. All that strength, power, and training, you went through, and it's all for nothing. You're quaking in your boots, just like the last man to face me. Will you banish me to face another as the bitch and the coward did?"

"The time for running is over," Kieran growled back.

"You're drawing strength from this mongrel who smells of my lineage but is polluted with your Silver magic. Then, there is the more interesting pup at your side. My direct progeny, even if he smells like your mongrel lapdog here. You must be the child of that little bitch I caught trying to get it on with the human boy. They were both so much fun to play with. To bad the boy was so fragile, but that's the trouble with pure humans, they break easily."

"This is between us, monster," Kieran shouted to try and drag the Beast's attention back.

"No . . . these two are much more interesting than you are, Child of Beauty. They are the key to prophecy. They're a set of keys that will either lock or unlock the great spell. Silver to relock the spell, Ebony to unlock it forever. You, little hunter, are merely the lock. The choice of key is mine." The Beast's tongue lashed across his maw like he was licking his lips after savoring a tasty morsel.

Kieran screwed down his fear of the image from his nightmares of just that happening and lashed out, aiming to take the Beast's head from his shoulders with the swing of the scythe blade attached to his left arm. The monster dodged and slammed a huge fist into Kieran's back, sending the tired hunter sprawling face first into the pine needles covering the forest floor.

"Stay down, little hunter. I'll deal with you once I've locked away your little pets."

Kieran pushed himself to his knees. "If you're hoping that your Ebony mage is going to help you, monster, you're out of luck, because he's already dead."

"It doesn't matter. Once I make the little Ebony pup bred your ass, the binding spell will be broken," the Beast snarled. "Then, your Silver mongrel will rip you apart to finish off the House of Beauty once and for all."

"Well, that's not going to happen," Cory growled, shifting to his own midway form.

"You have no concept of the power of my bloodline, you pathetic pup. I'm an Alpha of an original shifter line; it gives me control over all descendants of the bloodline regardless of how diluted the bloodline has become. Bow to me, both of you," the Beast commanded.

Kieran had made it back to his feet only to watch in horror as Billy shifted to a midway form and bowed down before the Beast. He turned to see Cory struggling to fight the reflex to bow to a superior Alpha. Deep down in Kieran, he felt the tug as well through his bond with Cory. Kieran drew himself to his full height and banished his armor and clothes. He stood naked before the Beast, Cory, and Billy.

"You're mistaken about the requirements that break the binding spell. I am the last of the prime line that cast the spell. An Alpha of a founding line is the required key to unlock the spell. Billy just proved he isn't an Alpha by bowing to the Alpha of his line. Take me if you can, monster," Kieran said.

The Beast whirled with incredible speed to lunge at Kieran, thinking that he was vulnerable in his naked state. As he grabbed the naked hunter, Kieran drove his right hand into the Beast's gut just below the ribcage. Wrapped in Silver magic, his hand cut through the monster's flesh. The Beast reflexively drew Kieran closer, trying to rip out his throat, but only succeeded in making it easier for Kieran to change his angle and drive his hand up toward the heart of the Beast. He transformed the Silver magic from blade to fire and burned away the Beast's internal organs. Claws began to dig into exposed flesh, but Kieran ignored the pain as he wrapped his left arm around the Beast to hold them together as the monster struggled to break free.

"Kill him, my children." The Beast's words were a command neither Billy nor Cory could refuse.

"You've lost, monster. Killing me without having bred me leaves the spell in place." Kieran bared his teeth in a fierce grin as Silver magic burst forth from his body.

The pair leapt for Kieran with Billy howling as he tasted Silver magic; he tried to sink his jaws into Kieran's thigh. The Beast was surprised when Cory stepped through the Silver magic. Cory shifted to his own midway form and pressed up tight against Kieran, sinking his raging hard-on into Kieran's ass. There was an increase in Silver magic as the two lovers joined, becoming one, physically and magically. The Beast felt the mating bond between the two become a physical thing as Cory's strength flowed into Kieran.

"I am the Silver Shifter who is the key that closes the lock that is the Silver Witch. Together we make the binding. This night we choose to reseal the binding of old. To one animal form are those who were born to shift their shape bound. By the sacrifice of this Alpha of a first line, we bind and seal." Cory's voice was an odd cadence.

"I am the Silver Witch who is the lock that closes at the will of the Silver Shifter. Together we make the binding. This night we choose to reseal the binding of old. To one animal form are those who were born to shift their shape bound. By the sacrifice of this Alpha of a first line, we bind and seal," Kieran's voice answered.

The three became a blazing column of Silver magic that shot skyward and touched the moon before spreading to wrap around the world. Shifters everywhere felt the power of the binding spell clamp down on them and howled, hooted, growled, or made whatever cry of longing and pain as they felt the loss of potential freedom.

When the spell was completed, the Silver magic vanished, leaving Kieran standing only because Cory was holding him upright. Of the Beast, there was no trace.

****

Billy shivered and forced himself to finish shifting back to human form. He stood facing away from his uncles who were still locked in an adult position he shouldn't be watching. Eventually, he coughed to draw their attention.

"Umm, Uncle Kieran, Uncle Cory, are you guys done being a mystical lock and key?" Billy asked.

"Just a moment, Billy," Kieran said as Cory released him.

Billy felt the tingle of Silver magic he'd grown used to around Uncle Kieran, and then he felt a daypack being handed to him. His uncles had insisted he pack a change of clothes for moments like this. It suddenly dawned on Billy that he was as naked as his uncles. He practically ripped open the pack to drag out his clothes, and he dressed faster than he ever had in his life. He could feel the blush heating his face as he turned to face his uncles who were both at least dressed from the waist down.

"I think our nephew is shy, Wolf, although I bet if Ian were here, he wouldn't have been quite so quick to get dressed," Kieran teased.

"Nope, I'd have been even faster, Uncle Kieran," Billy replied. "Honestly, we're saving that stuff until we're of age. We change separately in the bathroom, and we each sleep in our own beds."

"Relax, Puppy. I'm teasing, and I'm glad you two are saving things until you're older. Now, on a serious note, what has to be done next is something you shouldn't see or be involved in. Your part is done. Go back to the clearing and carefully take the three human skulls out of that horrible throne and put them in our packs. Then, follow the trail we came in on back out of the forest. You will have to wait at the edge of the forest until I can bring down the magic binding the pack."

"Those skulls belong to your sisters, don't they, babe?" Cory said.

"Yes, Selene, Savannah, and Amanda. I don't know where Rosie's is, but it's not in that clearing," Kieran replied.

Billy gave both of his uncles a quick hug before heading back out into the clearing. Over his shoulder, he said. "Don't worry, Uncle Kieran. I'll be very careful with my aunts' remains." Then, Billy was gone. Kieran and Cory finished dressing, Kieran in a second set of his tracker leathers and Cory in heavy denim clothing and hiking boots.

"Kieran, do we really have to slaughter all of the rest of the pack? All the males and the Beast are dead; there's only females and pups left. Haven't we done a enough killing for a lifetime?" Cory asked.

"I wish I could spare them, Cory. They're as tied into the spell as the males and the Beast were. One side or the other has to be eliminated for the pact to be dissolved. I don't know about you, but after everything we've done, I'd like to live a lot longer," Kieran said.

"Yeah, I want you around for a long time," Cory said, hugging Kieran close. "Let's get this over with."

Kieran found the track to the lair of the pack, which was actually a small village deep in the woods. Tidy little cottages ranged around a clearing, where all of the remaining shifters were gathered. Young pups, gravid females, older females, and males too old to be of use in a fight. Kieran and Cory stepped into the village clearing and waited for the remains of the pack to focus on them.

"The Beast and your males are dead. Who ranks highest in the pack?" Kieran called out when he had their attention.

An aged female and limping male made their way to the front of the remaining pack and forced themselves to shift back to human. When their shift finished, they rose to face the Hunter of the House of Beauty and his shifter mate.

"I am the *Cainteoir don phacáiste*, speaker for the pack. This is *Eolas ar an phacáiste,* knowledge of the pack. We will lead now that the Ancient One is no more. What would you have of the pack, Child of Beauty?" the aged female said.

"How many of those now gravid with pups were bred by the Beast, *Cainteoir*?" Kieran asked.

"All of those you see, Child of Beauty. The Ancient One made sure that no other male came near a female in her season," the speaker admitted.

"And how many of these pups are the get of the Beast?" Kieran asked, feeling sick to his stomach.

"Again, Child of Beauty, since the coming of the Ancient One, no male save he has mounted a female when she entered her season. All of these pups are of the direct blood of the Ancient One."

"I'm truly sorry to hear that, *Cainteoir*. I had hoped there might be those I could spare. I promise to make this as swift and painless as possible for the pack."

"Child of Beauty, the pact between your house and the pack is still in force. A sacrifice was made and accepted on behalf of the current huntress. We cannot leave this forest," the lame man said.

"*Eolas ar an phacáiste,* I am the Hunter of the House of Beauty, and I did not make the sacrifice, although I know one was made. Unfortunately, my mate and nephew share the lineage of the pack and are trapped here as well unless the pact is dissolved."

"The House of Beauty would purge this pack in order to remove the pure taint of the Ancient One? There is another way."

"What is this other way, *Eolas ar an phacáiste?*" Kieran almost begged.

"You could sterilized the entire pack, from the pups in the womb to those males still fertile enough to bred. Then we will die out naturally," the lame male said.

"That leaves my mate and nephew trapped in here until they die as well. This is not an acceptable solution," Kieran replied.

"Then go to the Grove of the Secret and give magic to the one who has none," the speaker said.

Kieran started to say he didn't know where the grove was when the knowledge flooded his mind. Along with the location also came the awareness that giving the sacrifice magic wouldn't be enough to break the pact. The pack still had to die. Kieran closed his eyes for a moment, and when he opened them, they were pure silver. He raised his hands, and Silver magic glowed around them.

"I'm truly sorry, but the protection of the House of Beauty is withdrawn. I am Kieran Samuel Belle Oisín-Cooper, Silver Hunter of the House of Beauty and the Silver Witch. By my hand and magic, I pronounce your death sentence and carry it out."

Silver magic leapt from Kieran's hands and struck every shifter of the pack between the eyes, killing them instantly. Kieran wept tears of silver fire as he struck down the pack. When it was done, he turned on his heels and walked to the path that lead to the Grove of the Secret. Cory stayed behind, knowing that his husband and mate needed time and had to face the Grove of the Secret alone.

Chapter Thirty

Kieran entered the secret grove hidden away from the community of the shifters. He felt the tingle of magic as he crossed the boundary. In the center of the grove stood a cottage with a small garden plot in which a figure moved, tending the flowers and herbs growing there. The shape of the figure seemed familiar to Kieran as he moved closer. Hair as dark as his own hung in a braid over the figure's left shoulder, and the floppy hat this person wore obscured their face with shadow. Kieran called out so that he wouldn't scare the person by suddenly appearing by their side.

"Hello, I'm Kieran."

"I know who you are, silly," a familiar voice called out to him. "I've been waiting for you to come and find me, Brother."

Kieran stopped in his tracks. It wasn't possible. He'd seen her die, buried under a pile of shifters. Her throat had been torn out, and her sword had come to him when summoned, which it shouldn't have done if she was still alive. This couldn't be his beloved sister Rosie.

"Who are you?" Kieran called back.

"Did the shifters hit you so hard you don't know your own sister, Kieran?"

"You can't be who you sound like. Her sword came to me and showed me her death. It wouldn't have done that if she was still alive."

"It would if part of the spell that saved me also severed my connections to magic. It was the price I had to pay to survive."

The mystery woman turned to face Kieran as she removed her hat to reveal the familiar features of his beloved sister Rosie. Shock froze him for a moment before he was racing across the distance between them. He swept her up into a hug that lifted her off her feet. He spun her around until they were both dizzy.

"Kieran, stop spinning. You know I hate when you do that."

"Bright goddess, it really is you. How is it possible, Rosie? How are you here?"

"My one shot of Silver magic. I used the spell to shift me to the nearest safe place in the dark forest. I woke up to find myself in this grove and unable to leave," Rosie said.

"No, you wouldn't be able to leave once you no longer had magic. It's the nature of the Grove of the Secret. This place was used to maintain the pact between our family and the shifters. Every generation, the huntress would bring a relative with no magic here as a symbolic mate to the pack Alpha. The relative was always infertile, so there couldn't be any children."

"I'm not infertile, Kieran. I've had my—"

"I don't need to know, Rosie. It's because you lack of magic that you're trapped here in this grove. Are you alone, or is there another trapped here? I know Grandmother left her sister out here when she became huntress, but that was ages ago. I couldn't find any reference to Mother having done the same thing."

"I'm the only one here. I think our great-aunt was the last one to occupy the cottage; everything in there is about as old as the stuff Grandmother prizes."

"Well, it's time to get you out of here and back home. I have someone I want you to meet."

"I don't have magic anymore, Kieran. If what you've said is true, I'm here for the rest of my life."

"Oh, little sister, how I've missed your lack of faith in my men's magic. I'm the head of the family now. The pact shattered when I put down the last pup of the dark pack. The magic of this place is already fading and is easily swept away."

"You're the Huntress of the House of Beauty?"

"The Hunter of the House of Beauty, and more. I'm also the Silver Witch, and after all that's gone down over the past couple of weeks, I've become that old legend Gramps always talked about, the Silver Hunter."

"My, you've been busy since you escaped. You'll have to catch me up," Rosie said.

"I will, because there's a lot you've missed out on, being dead and all." Kieran laughed as he scooped his sister up and swung her around again.

With the wave of his hand, the warding spell shuddered and collapsed. Kieran led Rosie to the path leading back to the main house, and they stepped over the boundary together. Rosie laughed and slipped her hand from Kieran's and started racing down the path toward home.

"Last one home has to do all the explaining to Grandmother," she called out over her shoulder with a laugh.

"You'll have to do all your own explaining, Sister," Kieran called back as he passed her.

"No way, you've never been that fast," Rosie remarked as she pushed to catch up with her brother.

As they came around a bend in the path into a small opening in the trees, a handsome blond man stepped out of the woods and caught Kieran in an embrace that quickly became a very intimate kiss. Rosie stopped dead in her tracks as she realized the man kissing her brother was a shifter. She reached for the knife at Kieran's belt, but he moved with a grace much like their father. He turned in the blond man's embrace so that he was facing her and his weapons were out of reach.

"Oh no you don't, little sister. No sticking pointy silver weapons in my husband," Kieran admonished. "This is one of those things we have to catch up on."

"Did you say husband?" Rosie asked at the same time Cory was questioning him about calling this young woman sister.

Kieran grinned impishly at his sister and snuggled against his husband's chest.

"Corwin Oisín-Cooper, I'd like to introduce you to my not-deceased sister, Rosalind Oisín Belle. Rosie, this is my shifter husband, Cory." Kieran chuckled as Cory growled in his ear.

"It's a pleasure to meet you. Kieran has talked a lot about how special you were to him," Cory said while keeping Kieran close.

"I'd like to say the same thing, but Kieran and I have a lot of catching up to do. Like how you ended up married to a shifter?"

"We met at school and one thing led to another. We fell in love, discovered we were each other's mortal enemy, and said screw it because we loved each other more than opposing heritages between us," Kieran replied. "Oh yeah, there was Gramps' ancient prophecy that said we needed to be together in order to defeat the Beast."

"This is more than I can take. A shifter with free range of the family estate? What's next? Kieran moving the family some place else?" Rosie was close to screaming.

"Let's go back to the house, Rosie. Dad, Grams, Uncle Brom, and Grandmother will want to see you. We can talk when you've had a chance to catch up on everything that's happened since you took the test."

"I have as much right to lead this family as you do. More so since I'm a Huntress of the House of Beauty and took the test before you."

"Actually you don't, Rosie, but I'm not going to argue with you out here. I've been out in these woods all night. I've fought or just plain slaughtered the pack. Men, women, and children. I'm not the big brother you knew before, Rosie. That person died the day you went to take the test without my support. I'm the head of the House of Beauty, and I won't tolerate a challenge."

"I passed the test, and I'm the oldest living daughter of the last huntress; leadership of the family is mine by birthright."

"You're wrong on so many counts, Sister. Mother was never actually the huntress; the powers that make a true huntress never passed to her, because Grandmother never used her magic while mother was alive. I stripped Grandmother of her magic; you've used yours. Neither of you is qualified to lead this family by all the ancient traditions of this house," Kieran replied.

"As much as I love you, big brother, you can't lead this family. No man has ever truly led this family," Rosie retorted.

"It's time to go home so you can let the family know you're alive, and then we will find a role for you in my plans for the future of our family." Kieran's tone brooked no argument, and he and Cory turned, starting back toward the mansion.

****

Two nights after Kieran's victory over the Beast, the House of Beauty laid to rest the mortal remains of his sisters—Selene, Savannah, and Amanda—beside the remains of his sister Callie and their mother Miranda. A cousin, who was a minister, carried out the funeral service. Kieran did his best to hold back his emotions as he always had before the women of his family. It wasn't until the last ringing passages of scripture that Kieran felt the tears begin to escape his control. When the final prayer had been said, Kieran walked out of the family chapel and back to his suite, where he collapsed in tears and sobs against Cory. Now that his sisters were laid to rest, he could finally let go of his grief and mourn them.

Chapter Thirty-One

A week had passed since Kieran's defeat of the Beast, his discovery of Rosie in the Grove of the Secret, the burial of his sisters, and the departure of the Oisíns. The House of Beauty was in disarray as they attempted to adjust to the new reality. Kieran had been closeted in meetings with Grandmother Belle, Rosie, and several of the senior Matriarchs discussing the future. Factions were forming, and he knew the Council of Matriarchs had also been meeting without him present, debating his suggested course of action for the future of the House of Belle. His grandmother, Camille Belle, was still a formidable woman, with opinions of her own regarding the future of the family and their duties as the foremost hunting family. His plan set her on edge, and she was digging in to oppose it, because it meant leaving her home of nearly eighty years. He was sitting curled up in Cory's embrace on a sofa, in the suite reserved for the Huntress of the House, thinking. He was pulled from his thoughts by a knock on the door to the suite.

"Enter," Cory called out as he stroked Kieran's hair to keep his husband relaxed.

The door opened, and Rosie, Kieran's beloved younger sister, poked her head in.

"Kieran, can I speak with you in private?" Rosie asked.

"Come in, Rosie. This is as private as it gets. I don't have secrets from Cory," Kieran replied.

"Okay. I wanted to offer a suggestion for a compromise with Grandmother," Rosie said.

Kieran snuggled in tighter against Cory, hiding behind his own hair, as his sister pulled a chair closer to the sofa. He'd developed a weird tick over the last couple of days due to the stress of dealing with his grandmother and the Matriarchs. He tried to make himself relax, but Cory merely pulled him in tighter.

"Sorry, even though I'm head of this family now, she still has a way of making me feel like a little boy again."

"I never understood her hostility toward you, Brother. It was never rational, and it only got worse after Mom died," Rosie said.

"The list is so long, Sis. Trust me, Mom's death wasn't what she was angry with me about. She went over the edge when her brothers died with Mom. If she'd had her way, I'd have been on Mom's last hunt with her. Never mind I had barely started my training as a tracker. I'm the one who should have come home in the body bag, not her brothers and certainly not Mom." Kieran turned and tried to burrow beneath Cory.

"I'm sorry, Kieran. I know you were miserable here. We all missed you when you ran away, but most of us understood why you did it. I think Amanda was the only one who never really understood, but considering how young she was, it was forgivable that she was mad at you for leaving without saying good-bye."

"I wanted to say good-bye, but there wasn't time, and I didn't dare risk getting caught by the Matriarchs. I wanted to be here when Selene tested. I begged Dad to let me surrender to Grandmother when he told me you were going to the test before your time. He wouldn't let me. Told me you wouldn't want me to do that."

"He was right about that, Kieran. You escaped, found the man of your dreams, and had a chance at being happy. I still want you to be happy and free," Rosie said.

Kieran had surfaced, pushed back his hair, and turned to face her, but he was still snuggled in tight to his husband's chest, and Cory wasn't letting him go. She tried to hide a smile over how adorable her brother looked snuggled up with his husband. It didn't help when Kieran caught a glimpse of her hidden smile and stuck his tongue out at her. Laughter erupted from both of them, and Cory merely sighed. These two could reduce each other to giggles with a look.

"You said something about a compromise between Kieran and your grandmother?" Cory prodded when the giggles had gone on for several minutes.

Rosie drew in a deep breath to control her giggles. "Yes, let her keep this place; it's her home. Better yet, let me stay here to run the finishing school you want for your regional hunters and huntresses. It's my home as well, and as Huntress of the House of Beauty, I have the right to determine my own future."

At the fire in Rosie's voice, Kieran sat up straight, silver fire flashing in his eyes at her challenge. Cory was as alert as Kieran, and his amber eyes flashed a warning at Rosie. She drew herself up, refusing to back down from her position.

"You may be a huntress of the House of Beauty, Rosalind, but I am the Silver Hunter and head of this family. I know about the senior Matriarchs' plan to form a breakaway group centered here and on you. You all have no secrets in this house. Have you stopped and wondered why I haven't given you back your one shot of Silver magic? I could, you know, I'm the Silver Witch, heir of the woman who gave birth to both lines. I didn't do it, because I knew the traditionalists would rally around a daughter of the main line."

Rosie cringed back in fear as Kieran began to glow. His anger grew. The look of fear was what snapped Kieran out of his anger, because it was the one thing he'd never wanted to inspire in his sisters.

"Part of your advice is sound, Rosie. I don't need the money this estate would bring at sale. Grandmother will never support me if I don't let her keep something she values. I'm not sure about using this place as the finishing school for future hunters and huntresses, because our enemies already know where it is and I have to no desire to find another pack of shifters willing to make a deal for its protection."

"Actually, if you can ward this place, we can just let shifters roam into the forest and then use them for hunting practice without having to reestablish the pact."

"Wild shifters might be a better plan. We don't owe them anything, and we can test more than one hunter at a time. All right, Rosie, you have a deal with just two conditions in exchange for my giving you and Grandmother this place."

"Why do I hear wedding bells in my future?" Rosie looked at Cory for support.

"Don't look at me, Rosie. I support Kieran in this. I want lots of Belle nieces and nephews to spoil."

"Ugh, sappy love. I should have known you'd gang up on me," Rosie said.

"You and I are the last of the main line, Rosie. Your first-born child will become my official heir, superseding all my other arrangements with the cadet branches. I'm not going to arrange your marriage. I'm not even going to force you to get married. Just pick someone worthy to be the father of your children," Kieran said.

Rosie sighed and nodded her head. "Fine, I'll keep the line going, and I'll even bring my choice to Arkansas so you can approve or disapprove of him. What's the other condition?"

"All of the Matriarchs who support splintering the family by supporting you as a rival must step down. They will retire to the various estates in Europe, never to return to America."

"It's a deal," Rosie agreed without hesitation.

Kieran stood up and opened his arms to his sister. Rosie bounced out of her chair and wrapped herself around her brother. She felt herself wrapped in a double embrace as Cory hugged them both. Kieran looked down at her with a goofy grin on his face.

"You'll get used to it, Sis. Cory and I are a package deal, but I have a request to make of you as the new headmistress of the Belle Academy of Hunting," Kieran said. "I want you to seal off the library until Ian and Billy return here to take over the archives. They are Great-Uncle Jonas' true successors, and I've confirmed them as such."

"I'll do it on the condition that you agree to send me potential hunters and huntresses who aren't related to the House of Beauty. I don't think we should hoard our training anymore."

"I agree with you on that one, Rosie. Now I think it's time to go face Grandmother and see if she'll take the bait."

****

Kieran, Cory, and Rosie walked down the hallway to Camille's quarters. Kieran knocked on the door to his grandmother's suite. It creaked open, and the face of one of the younger cousins peered out. Seeing Kieran, she opened the door wider and bowed to him.

"I've come to speak with the Huntress-emeritus," Kieran said.

"I'll see if she will receive you, Hunter Kieran," the girl replied.

"Of course I'll see Hunter Kieran, girl. Send him in," Camille's voice called out.

Kieran and his party entered Camille Belle's elegant sitting room, tastefully decorated with heirlooms handed down over the generations from huntress to huntress. Camille herself was seated in a high-backed chair of Victorian provenance; legend said it had been a gift from the queen for services rendered.

Kieran glanced around the room quickly before focusing on his grandmother. This formidable woman had controlled his life since before he was born. Even though he was now the true head of the family, she still scared a part of him as if he was the little boy or even the teenager she'd dominated and hated. He drew strength from his bond with Cory and the presence of his sister.

"Honored Grandmother, thank you for taking the time to see us," Kieran said with a small bow to the seated woman.

"It gains me nothing to make you cool your heels, Kieran. I've acknowledged you as head of this family and tried to make up for some of my past actions by supporting your plans for the future. I'm willing to listen to what you have to say as you've been willing to listen to what I've had to say, even if all you really wanted to do was flee the room."

"You know me well, Grandmother. I listen because you have something I can only hope to have someday. You have the wisdom that comes from age and experience. Right now, I have knowledge that spans the ages on Father's side but not the wisdom needed to use it correctly. I've come to offer you a compromise that I hope will keep the peace in our family."

"You have wisdom, Grandson, to know that you lack experience. Your mother would be proud of the man you have become. Please sit. I will listen to your proposal."

"Is it safe to sit on the furniture, Grandmother? I'd hate to break something given to the family by King Solomon."

"Now you're being cheeky, boy. There's nothing older than Victoria's reign in this room. Sit. The couch is sturdy enough for you and your husband. Rosie, come sit beside me here."

Kieran and Cory settled on to the couch, an Edwardian settee from the look of it, and waited for Rosie to settle in beside their grandmother. Camille sent the cousin attending her to fetch tea and cookies.

"After a few discussions with Rosie and many with Cory, I've decided it isn't worth the fight to make you sell this place and move. Rosie also pointed out that this place with proper warding spells around the main buildings would actually make a good location for my proposed finishing school for hunters and huntresses. Rosie asks to be in charge of the school, but I'd like to add a twist to our agreement. I'd like Grandmother to administrate the school and train a select group in the administration of the vast wealth of the family."

"You want me involved in the future you envision for the family?" Camille said in surprise. "I thought you'd rather I retired to some small country home to be forgotten in all, save a name in the chronicles."

"You've been running the family business empire since you were a young woman, Grandmother. It would be foolish of me to retire you out of the financial end of things. Besides, someone needs to inspire a little fear in future generations of hunters and huntresses. Rosie and I are too soft to do that right now," Kieran replied.

"What about the stubborn faction that opposes all the changes you propose?" Camille asked.

"Exile back to Europe, where each branch of opposition will be given a different estate. We need to spread the family presence out as much as possible. I'm going to do a ritual to restore the Silver magic to each branch of the family. It should last several generations before it will need to be renewed," Kieran said.

"A masterful plan, Kieran. You are showing wisdom. I agree and accept your plans. In truth, Kieran, I would have given into your plans in the end. This place has many happy memories for me, and I hated the idea of parting with them. I hope you will come to forgive a stubborn old woman someday," Camille said.

"Perhaps in time I'll come to forgive you for the terror you inflicted on my childhood, but for now, you'll have to make do with my respect for your wisdom and experiences. Thank you for your support, Grandmother. I will see you tonight at the council's meeting."

****

Kieran had sent a couple of family members into the clearing at the center of the forest to clean up all the bones and corpses. They gathered them into a pile around the throne of bones. When all the remains had been gathered, they'd poured gasoline on the pile and set it on fire to cleanse the forest of its dark taint. Other family teams had gone to the shifter village and done the same thing. On the night of the dark of the moon, Kieran led a procession made up of a man and a woman from each branch of the family. He'd studied the family records, and with Great-Aunt Desdemona's assistance, had paired up couples that were far enough apart to marry without breaking laws. These couples would form the new Council of the House of Beauty. They would establish the regional houses and oversee all hunting activities in their regions. Once a year, they would come to Little Rock for a general council meeting with Kieran or his successor. Tonight, these couples would be touched with Silver magic, which would pass on down the generations. Tonight was just part of the new beginning for the House of Beauty.

Chapter Thirty-Two

Once everything had been settled and set in motion on the Belle estate, Kieran, Cory, Ian, and Billy had returned to the Oisín compound on the Maine coast to spend the rest of the summer. One night on the beach, Kieran stood in a circle of power and cast the spell that would set the potential for Silver magic in the exiled lines of the Belle family. The family spent time making arrangements to move to Arkansas and plan for the future of the lineage of the Silver Witch. During their final week in paradise, Kieran, Cory, Ian, and Billy were packing up their belongings for their return trip to Arkansas. To Cory, it seemed as if Kieran didn't want to leave Maine . . . or was it just the Oisín estate he didn't wish to leave?

"We could keep this place, Kier. You don't have to sell off all of your memories."

"I wish that was true, Wolf. Our enemies know about this place, so it's never going to be as safe as it was before Marissa destroyed the original wards. Better to turn it over to the National Park Service than try to maintain it."

"What about Grams? Where will she go?" Cory asked.

"She and Uncle Brom are coming with us to Arkansas. Uncle Brom found a place for sale up in Eureka Springs that he and Grams are going to turn into a bed and breakfast as well as setting up a store to sell his creations. They're both going to take Grams' maiden name as their last name," Kieran replied with a sigh.

"Well, they won't be that far away from us then. We can visit on weekends," Cory said, trying to cheer Kieran up.

"We won't be able to visit all that often, Cory. I'm sure we'll be busy taking the boys to various activities," Kieran said with a look at Ian and Billy. "There's also the fact that I'm now the Hunter of the House of Beauty; the last thing I want is to put Grams and Uncle Brom in danger.

"Babe, don't cut yourself off from Grams and Uncle Brom; they can protect themselves, especially since Brom's magic is coming back to him."

"I don't want to, Wolf, especially not after I do what I have to do to Dad to ensure the survival of the line of the Silver Witch. They need to forget me, at least for a while. When it's safe, I can send the counter to the memory spell."

"What about the relationship between your uncle and Professor Mason? If you alter memories, won't you mess with that?" Cory asked.

"Considering the explosive argument they had just before the professor got on the same plane as your parents to go back to Arkansas, it might be for the best if Uncle Brom forgets him too."

"You don't mean that, Kieran Oisín-Cooper." Cory stopped for a moment and made eye contact with the boys, who left the room to find someplace else to be. "You care too much for both of those men. They need a chance to work things out for themselves. I know that what you're going to have to do to Kellen is tearing you up, but don't make it harder by doing this to Grams and Uncle Brom. There are members of my family's pack that would jump at the choice you gave Billy. Offer some of them the collar in exchange for becoming guards on your uncle's new place."

"All right, Wolf, I'll leave it be on most of the recent memories for Grams and Uncle Brom. I'm still going to kick Uncle Brom's ass for messing up with Professor Mason. Those two are meant to be with each other."

"I know, and I'll help. There's a question the professor asked that nobody's ever answered," Cory said.

"What question is that, Cory?"

"He wanted to know why your father's eyes were the violet of an Amethyst mage when his magic was Silver."

"Silver eyes mark the heir to the power of the Silver Witch in our family. Dad wasn't supposed to be Gramps' heir. Uncle Brom was always meant for that role, at least until I was born. Dad was meant to marry an Amethyst witch or mage; that's why his eyes are violet."

"But he met and married your mother, who wasn't an Amethyst mage."

"Yes, but that was on the orders of Gramps. When Uncle Brom came out as gay and then ended up with his powers all messed up, Dad had to take Brom's place in everything. Gramps wasn't paying attention to the prophecy he set so much store in."

"When the lines of white do twist and twine, the firstborn of the second son shall of two Houses be."

"Yep, that would be the part Gramps missed. You want to know the real kicker, Wolf?"

"Somehow, I bet this is a major plot twist in our little personal fairy tale," Cory replied.

"Dad met the Amethyst witch at the same school where he and Mom were going to school. He told me she was the most beautiful woman he'd ever met. He knew they were supposed to be together, but he did his duty to the family instead of making himself happy. Don't get me wrong, he loved Mother, but they weren't soul mates. The real kicker is the witch went on to become a fashion model, a career Dad wanted to pursue."

"He'd have made a fortune with his looks and those eyes. So who is this witch?"

"Vivian Mason."

"The one they compare to Elizabeth Taylor because of the color of her eyes?"

"She's the one."

"Vivian Mason is beautiful."

"You're not catching the plot twist, Wolf."

"Okay color me dense, Kier."

"Vivian Mason is Professor Mason's older sister, and if things hadn't gone the way they did, I might be calling the professor Uncle John."

"Wow, that is a twist. You may end up calling him that anyways if he and Uncle Brom patch things up," Cory said with a grin.

"I'm going to end up calling him that for two reasons it seems."

"What's the second reason?"

"I'm going to give Dad the life the prophecy took from him. I'm going to give him his dream of being a fashion model and let destiny take its course on the runway."

"But won't that undo the magic you're going to work on your father tonight?"

"No, only Professor Mason will know the truth, and I'm pretty sure he'll never tell his sister that her boyfriend—or whatever status they're at when she brings him home to meet the family—has a son and a daughter from his previous marriage still living."

"That's putting a lot of trust in the man and giving him a terrible burden to carry."

"I know, and I hate to do it, but I want my dad to have the life he should have had twenty-two years ago."

"Well, I'm glad he's getting it now, but I'm glad he didn't get it back then, because I wouldn't have you." Cory sniffed back tears.

Kieran stepped around the bed and wrapped Cory in a tight hug. "I'm glad too, Wolf, because without you, my life wouldn't be worth living."

Kieran turned Cory around so they were face-to-face and drew him in for a kiss. Their embrace shifted as they each reached to undress the other. They didn't take long in getting each other naked and then fell on the bed together. Kissing and stroking each other, they rolled around the bed until Cory pinned Kieran to the bed, his cock hard and ready in the crack of Kieran's ass. His husband's equally hard cock was trapped between their bodies. It had been awhile since Cory had been in the dominant role, but they'd promised each other equality in their relationship. They were family, not pack; there was no hierarchy between them, just as there were no barriers between them. Cory leaned down and took his weight on his forearms as he pressed his body along and on top of Kieran's until they could kiss again. Cory's hips rocked, dragging the head of his cock over Kieran's hole and drawing a moan from the man pinned to the bed. Kieran adjusted his hips and wrapped his legs around Cory's waist, lining up his hole with the head of Cory's cock. The next thrust of his husband's hips pushed cock into ass, and Kieran bit down on Cory's shoulder as his muscles gave way to the hard cock. The burn helped to center him on his husband. Cory lifted up enough to lock his amber eyes on Kieran's silver ones, making sure he wasn't hurting his husband. A warm smile greeted him as hands moved down his back to cup his ass and encourage his rhythm. It was amazing to be inside the heat of Kieran's ass with no condom in between them. They lost themselves in each other's pleasure until finally Kieran's spine arched and a wet heat pulsed between them as he moaned loudly in pleasure; his orgasm soaked both of their bodies. Kieran's spasms tightened the muscles in his ass and pushed Cory over the edge, pumping his massive load deep into Kieran. The lovers collapsed together on the bed.

****

After dinner that evening at the main house, the family sat around the dinner table talking. Kieran excused himself and asked his father to meet him in the study.

"We need to have a very serious talk, Dad."

"Of course, Son. I know you're worried about protecting your grandmother, but Brom and I can protect her."

"Grams' safety is important, Dad, but so is the future of the lineage of the Silver Witch. I know you were forced to marry Mom when your heart had found a different match. I want you to have the life you should have had," Kieran said.

"That life is long gone. I'm sure Vivian found someone else and married. I'm beyond the fashion model age range. I can manage the family fortune for you and Cory and help Brom and Mother run their bed and breakfast."

"No, Dad. Vivian didn't find anyone and get married. She's a major fashion model, and her agency is looking for a semi-mature gentleman to work with her on several shoots and as her escort to events. I checked up on her, and when I found out she was Professor Mason's sister, I asked him about her."

"She never married?"

"There wasn't any reason for her to do so, Dad. She and the professor are the youngest of five children, and their siblings have already given their parents lots of grandchildren. You two were meant to be together. The only drawback is that I need you to continue the family line. You'll still have to father the next Silver Witch."

"All right, Son. What's the catch to this perfect life with the woman I should have married?"

"You can't be allowed to remember your old family until after I'm dead. You'll be heir to the power of the Silver Witch in a caretaker role for your children—and you'll have to have several. The line has become too narrow with just you for breeding stock. All of your children will inherit the full powers of the Silver Witch, with the eldest inheriting the title regardless of gender."

"Time to do what our ancestress did when she gave the power to a male line: mix it up and hide it. It's a very practical plan, Son." Kellen drew a deep breath to steady himself before asking, "What happens if I die before you do?"

"Then I'll find your eldest child and unlock the channel myself." Kieran's breathing became ragged for a moment, before he continued, "I'm sorry it has to be this way, Dad."

Kellen sat in one of the leather chairs his father had decorated the study with. He picked up his wine glass and took a large swallow. "Do Brom and Mother know what you have planned for me?"

Kieran moved one of the other chairs closer to his father. He settled into it and rested a hand on his father's knee. "No, and they'll believe you died in the same accident that claimed Mom and my sisters. If we ever meet again, you won't recognize any of us as family, nor will Grams or Uncle Brom remember your relationship to us. That will only change if Professor Mason and Brom reconcile and the professor chooses to unlock their memories and yours."

Kellen leaned forward to lay a hand on his son's knee. "When will you do this?"

Kieran pointed to the wine glass his father held. "It's already done. I enchanted the wine. Only you, Uncle Brom, and Grams had it with dinner tonight. When you leave this room, your new memories of the last twenty-two years will come into being. You'll find a suitcase and briefcase by the front door along with the keys to your SUV," Kieran said as the tears started to flow.

Kellen wrapped his son in his arms and hugged him as both of them wept over their mutual loss.

"I'm sorry it has to be this way, Dad. I have to protect the future of two houses, and I can't spare anyone's feeling, even my own. I love you, and I will always remember you."

"I love you too, Son. Tell your sister that I love her too. Good-bye, Kieran."

"Good-bye, Dad."

Kellen walked out of the study, and his memories shifted until he only knew himself as Kellen MacDonnell, up-and-coming male model. Unseeing, he picked up his suitcase and briefcase and walked out of his old life and into his new one. Behind him in the study, Kieran sank to his knees weeping for the loss of his father. In many ways, Kieran had just given Kellen the kind of life he wanted for himself. One free to be his own person.

About a half an hour after Kellen left for his new life, Cory entered the study to find his husband a soggy mess, eyes red-rimmed from his tears. He pulled Kieran into a tight embrace and let him compose himself. Kieran finally lifted himself off of Cory's shoulder and looked at his husband with red-rimmed silver eyes.

"It's done, babe. Grams and Uncle Brom only remember your dad, mom, and the rest of the family as dim memories."

"I only wanted to create, not to destroy. Where did I go wrong, Wolf? How did I end up destroying so much?"

"You haven't destroyed things, Kier. Altered them beyond recognition maybe, but not destroyed. We still have a future to build, and we're going to start by going back home to Arkansas and finishing our college degrees. You'll never get a good job and be able to support me in my old age if you don't have a college degree." Cory tried to lighten the mood.

"Wolf, between the fortunes I'm inheriting, neither of us will ever have to work a day in our lives if we don't want to. Do you think my dad will be happy in his new life?"

"I do. You've given him his dream, even if he never learns it was you who did it. Be happy for him. Come on, let's get you cleaned up before Grams and Uncle Brom wonder what you've be doing in here and why you were crying."

They stepped into the half bath off of the study, and Kieran took one look at his reflection in the mirror and knew there was no cleaning up the blotchy mess he'd made of his face with his crying. He ran the cold water and soaked a washcloth to try and cool down his eyes. It didn't really do much to help. There was no hiding his red-rimmed eyes without the use of magic. A minor disguise spell would allow him to safely make an exit from the family evening. Cory watched as Kieran swiped a glowing hand over his face and the damage from his tears vanished. Cory hugged him again before they returned to the dining room where Grams was just setting out dessert at the four places. Kieran looked at the dessert and almost lost his magical covering. Grams had set out a dessert that had been the favorite of both Gramps and his father, Apple Brown Betty with vanilla ice cream. Kieran choked back the new tears that threatened to flow, drawing his family's attention.

"What's the matter, *mo stór*? I thought we'd honor those who have passed. This was your grandfather's favorite, because it reminded him of your father. I wish you'd had more time with Kellen; he'd have been so proud of you."

"I'm sorry, Grams. I just miss Gramps so much. There's so much to do, and now I don't have him to turn to for advice. He was always such a good balance to Grandmother Belle. I just feel like the weight of the world has been dropped on my shoulders."

"Well, you don't have to worry about your uncle and I, *mo stór*. We'll be close to you in Arkansas."

"I know, Grams, and I promise Cory and I will come up to visit every chance we get. There will just be times when we won't be able to get away."

"Kieran, we know you still have your own life to live, and we want you two to find your happily ever after. We love you, and there will always be a place for you come and hide when the world gets to be too much for you," Brom said.

"Thank you, Uncle Brom. Grams, dinner was wonderful as always. I think Cory and I are going to head back over to our cabin for the night. We still need to make plans and figure out what things we want to ship back to Little Rock," Kieran said as he pushed back from the table.

Both of the young men stood and then hugged Grams and Uncle Brom before leaving. Cory took Kieran's hand in his own as they walked back to their cabin. He could feel the tension in his husband. He pulled Kieran to a stop when they'd gone far enough from the main house to be out of earshot.

"Babe, take us to the cave. I can tell you still need to scream and yell about how unfair life is, and you can't do that here where Brom or Grams can hear."

They walked forward into a swirl of Silver magic, and their next step carried them out into the entrance of the caves above the beach. When they'd made their way into the main cavern of the system, Cory stopped them and turned Kieran to face him. Cory looked into his husband's beautiful silver eyes, which were dimmed to a dull gray and red-rimmed from all his earlier crying. He cupped Kieran's face in his hands and brushed away a pair of tears that fell from his eyes with his thumbs before drawing him closer and kissing the love of his life. Kieran shivered in Cory's grip, not from cold but with the repressed sadness inside. Stroking back strands of Kieran's amazing midnight locks, Cory drew his husband down toward the hot pools. At the edge, he stopped and began to undress an unresisting Kieran. He then eased his lover into the hot pool before quickly stripping off and slipping in behind. He pulled Kieran in close and settled them both on the bench submerged beneath the water. Instinctively,

Kieran settled between Cory's legs and curled into his lover's chest, hiding his face behind a curtain of hair as sobs wracked his body. Cory held onto him, stroking his hair and back, just letting him cry himself out. When his sobs dissolved into hiccups, Cory rocked him gently, encouraging him to breathe with him until they settled into the same breathing pattern and the hiccups passed. When he'd settled, Kieran brushed his hair out of his face and looked up at Cory who read the loss in his lover's eyes. A quick kiss and then Cory resumed stroking Kieran's hair.

"I understand, babe. I know how much doing what you did tonight hurt you, and I share your pain. I'm so proud of you for doing this incredibly brave thing. Right now, you feel like you ripped out your own heart and stomped it into a paste, but we both know that your heart is protected and sheltered in me. In time, you'll see that this is a good thing. Your father is going to be happy in his new life. Grams and Uncle Brom are excited about their future, and I think with a gentle nudge, you can get Professor Mason back into Brom's life where we both know he belongs. We have time for just us. You can give the various branches all but the most important or highest paying hunts. Plus, you have your favorite sister back among the living."

Kieran stretched up and kissed Cory. "Thank you, Wolf, for being my anchor. You have no idea how much I wanted to drink that potion right along with Dad, Grams, and Uncle Brom tonight. To make myself forget all the pain we've been through. Your unconditional love is the only thing that kept me from reaching for that glass."

"Would it have worked on you? You made the potion and cast the spells. I thought you couldn't work magic on yourself."

"That potion and those spells would have worked on me just like they worked on the rest of my family. I might even have forgotten I was the Silver Hunter and all that entails."

"I can sense a 'but' in there, even if you haven't said it out loud, Kier."

"The 'but' is I'd have forgotten you as well. You'd have been a stranger to me. You're the best thing that's ever happened to me, Cory, but you're also wrapped up in the thing I'd most like to forget, and because of that, the potion and spells would have stolen the memories of you from me along with all the crap that went down because of the prophecy."

"Let me be your potion and spells then. I'll help you forget all the darkness and only remember the good times. We're going to build a bright new future for ourselves, Kieran Oisín-Cooper. You promised me a happily ever after."

"The happily ever after starts by us dropping the Oisín from our name, Wolf. The Oisín clan died tonight. Would you object to being Mr. and Mr. Belle-Cooper?"

"Shifters and hunters, please welcome to the world Corwin and Kieran Belle-Cooper." Kieran was laughing at Cory's silly introduction as Cory continued, "I like the sound of the new name, and I love hearing you laugh again, *mo chroí*."

"My heart, I see you had Grams teach you a bit of the old tongue. With you at my side, *mac tíre óg*, I plan to laugh a whole lot more," Kieran said as he snuggled in closer.

"I think we should dry off and go to bed, Kier. We have a lot to do tomorrow."

"Five more minutes like this, Cory," Kieran murmured against Cory's chest.

"Now, babe. In five minutes, you'll be asleep," Cory replied.

"Spoilsport," Kieran said as he disengaged from his perch and made a gesture.

Silver magic wrapped around both of them and whisked them and their clothes from the cavern back to their bedroom in the cabin. Both men were dry when they arrived back in the bedroom. Kieran pulled Cory over and into the huge bed, and they snuggled into the covers and were fast asleep before either of them could tell the other good night.

Epilogue

Kieran and Cory looked at the huge Christmas tree, which filled the corner of the front parlor of their stately Victorian home. It was their turn to host the friends and family party this year, and they'd been busy getting all the decorations out, food cooked, and the table set. It was hard to believe that four years had passed since they'd defeated the Beast and the evil mage known as the Master. They'd both finished college, earning their bachelor's degrees. Cory was weighing plans to go for his Master's degree in economics, so he could help Kieran better understand the vast family fortunes he controlled. Of all those coming to their home for the holidays, they were most excited for the arrival of Billy and Ian, who'd started their first year of college. Under Ian's influence and the stern eyes of his uncles, Billy had become an excellent student, and both boys had been accepted to Oxford. Kieran and Cory were looking forward to hearing all about their studies and lives in England.

The doorbell announcing the arrival of their first guests interrupted their study of the tree. Cory went and answered the door to find his parents loaded down with presents and food.

"Mom, Dad, we said no bringing food this year. Kieran and I have done all the cooking."

"That's why your mother insisted on bringing food; she didn't want your other guests to starve to death," Jonathan Cooper said with a laugh.

"I wanted you to have your favorite pecan pie, Corwin," Tamara said.

"Well, since it's pie, I'm sure Kieran will forgive you," Cory said as he took a stack of gifts from his father's arms. "You know where the kitchen is, Mom; just set it on the counter with the other desserts."

Once presents were settled under the tree and the pie found a home in the kitchen, Jonathan and Tamara wrapped both young men in a hugs before settling in with a glass of eggnog. They were just beginning to relate all the news from the farm when the doorbell rang again. Kieran went to answer the door and was engulfed in a double bear hug from Billy and Ian.

"Well, look who's here, our Oxford scholars," Kieran proclaimed loudly.

Billy and Ian were swept up in hugs and kisses from Jonathan, Tamara, and Cory.

"You boys know where your room is; go drop off your things and come back down. You can unpack later," Cory said.

Up the stairs, the boys vanished to put their suitcases and coats in their room. They noted that the twin beds had been replaced with a queen-sized bed, and they grinned at each other. They set down their suitcases and pulled out the presents they'd packed away before heading back downstairs to join the family. They arrived downstairs to find that Grams and Uncle Brom had arrived and were piling presents under the tree as well. More hugs and kisses were exchanged as the boys put their gifts under the tree as best they could.

"Boys, will you take Grams' and Uncle Brom's bags up to their rooms please?" Kieran asked as he came back into the parlor from the kitchen.

"We've got it, Uncle Kieran," Billy called out.

Ian and Billy grabbed Grams' and Brom's luggage and carried it upstairs to the rooms assigned to Kieran's family. Kieran had left the suites on the second floor like they'd been when he first met Cory. He'd given Grams the suite on the left-hand side at the front of the house overlooking the street. Uncle Brom had the suite on the same side at the rear of the house and across the hall from the boys' suite. Jonathan and Tamara usually occupied the front suite on the right-hand side. This year they'd opted to get a hotel room, leaving the suite available in case of unexpected guests. The boys came back downstairs just in time to catch the door as the bell rang.

"Professor Mason, wow, Uncle Kieran didn't tell us he'd invited you this year," Billy said as he stepped aside so that John and two others could enter the house.

"My goodness, Billy and Ian, I didn't know you were back from England already. Kieran mentioned you were coming home for the break," John replied.

"Can we take your coats?" Billy asked.

"Of course. Viv, Kel, these are Kieran's wards, Billy and Ian. Boys, this is my sister Vivian Mason and her friend Kellen MacDonald," John introduced his guests.

Both boys stopped in their tracks as the pair removed the coats and dark glasses. Both had to take a moment before blurting out a wrong word at the sight of Kellen. Because of their role as the

Archivist of the House of Beauty, Kieran couldn't wipe or even fade their memories when he'd done so to Kellen, Grams, and Brom. Ian regrouped first.

"Ms. Mason, Mr. MacDonald, a pleasure to meet you both. We've seen several of your promotions, and your last appearance during Milan Fashion Week was all over the television at school," Ian said as he took their coats.

"Oh, they're just as adorable as you said they'd be, John," Vivian said as she hugged a still stunned Billy.

"Uh, everyone's in the parlor, Professor," Billy said when Vivian released him.

"Professor, you should know that Brom is here," Ian said.

"I expected he would be. Kieran was kind enough to warn me in advance," John said before leading his guests into the parlor.

"Professor, you made it. I was hoping you'd come," Kieran cheered.

"I told you I'd come, Kieran. You know you're not my student anymore; you can call me John now."

"Nope, not the way I work, Professor. Besides. I'm thinking of coming back to school for my Master's in photography," Kieran replied.

"Well, if you do, I'm going to work you even harder as my lab assistant teaching freshmen," John replied.

"Ugh, freshmen. Now who are your guests?" Kieran asked as he turned to greet the professor's friends. He stopped when he saw his father behind the woman. "Oh bright goddess, Vivian Mason and Kellen MacDonald in my house. Be still my heart, and where the heck is my camera?"

Cory came out of the kitchen with a tray loaded with glasses of eggnog to catch the end of Kieran's conversation. Hearing the extra names was the only thing that saved him from dropping the tray at the sight of Kellen.

"Never mind the camera. Just get them to sign any available piece of paper, babe," Cory called.

"John, you didn't tell me this was a house of fans," Vivian said, blushing slightly at all the attention from such beautiful men.

"We should have been more better prepared, Viv. If we'd known we had so many fans stateside, we could have brought press kits for them," Kellen said. His familiar voice ripped away the scabs that had grown over the wound in Kieran's heart.

Swallowing hard, Kieran remembered his hosting duties and introduced the newcomers to the rest of those gathered. He marveled at how well the spell he'd crafted four years ago was holding up under the surprise arrival of his father under the same roof as his uncle and grandmother. It was as if all of them were meeting for the first time. The reunion between Uncle Brom and Professor Mason even seemed to be going smoothly. He was glad he had given both men a heads-up about the other being invited. Cory finished handing out the eggnog and stepped up beside Kieran, slipping one arm around his husband's waist as he raised his glass of eggnog.

"Everyone, Kieran and I want to say thank you all for coming to spend the holiday with us. It's a joy to have friends and family with us at this time of the year," Cory said.

"We have a very special announcement and someone we'd like you all to meet. Angelina, would you come join us?" Kieran called out.

A young woman waddled out into the parlor from the kitchen. Her advanced pregnancy was obvious to everyone gathered around the beaming couple as they parted to wrap her between them.

"This is Angelina Belle, one of my distant cousins on my late mother's side of the family. She very kindly volunteered to be the surrogate mother for the child Cory and I decided we wanted to have. Much to all our surprise, Angelina is pregnant with twins, boy and a girl, who will join our family in February."

Kieran, Cory, and Angelina were swamped with hugs and kisses from a very excited pair of grandparents, a great-grandmother, a great-uncle, and a pair of cousins to be. The questions and suggestions competed with each other until Kieran finally managed to get Angelina to a chair so she could get off her feet.

"Please, we'll answer questions in due time. Let Angelina get some air, please," Kieran said. "This is our big Christmas gift to everyone."

"How did you two manage to keep this a secret from everyone?" Grams asked.

"By going up to Maine for our last vacation. Grandmother Belle and Rosie were a big help in helping us find a cousin willing and able to become a surrogate mother. Angelina came down here just last weekend, which is why we couldn't come up to Eureka Springs or down to the farm," Kieran replied.

"We were busy getting the old servants quarters cleaned up and ready for Angelina's arrival. Not to mention all the work we've been doing converting my studio into a nursery," Cory said.

While all the women gathered around the happy couple and their unborn children, Professor Mason drew Brom aside. Jonathan had taken Kellen aside to pump him for details on his modeling career.

"I think you and I should talk, Brom. We had some pretty harsh words for each other when we last saw each other," John said.

"I know, and I've really taken a long hard look at myself over the last couple of years. Kieran kicked my ass around the new forge a few times too," Brom said.

"Yes, he's talked to me in the darkroom a couple of times as well," John replied.

"I'm sorry for treating you like you were less than a person, John. I was an idiot, and if you never want to have anything to do with me again, I'd completely understand," Brom said.

"Thank you for that, Brom. I was just as big of an idiot for not standing my ground on some things before they got out of hand. So if you'd rather not deal with me after this, I'll also understand," John replied.

"I think what I'd really like is for us to start over on equal footing. We kind of rushed into things. I enjoyed talking with you when we just talked, not that I didn't enjoy all the other things we did together, but I really miss having another guy to talk with," Brom said.

"I miss our conversations as well, Brom. How long are you staying in town?" John asked.

"Through the New Year. Mom and I closed the B&B for the holidays this year," Brom replied.

"Good. How about we start slow, and meet for coffee, say the day after tomorrow?" John suggested.

"That sounds like a plan to me, John," Brom said, extending his hand to the other man.

John and Brom shook hands, and only John noticed the smile on Kieran's face that had nothing to do with the fact that he was going to be a father soon. The family and guests all gathered around the dinning room table, which Kieran quietly expanded with a little magic so that Vivian Mason and his father could be seated with them. Kieran and Cory—with help from Billy and Ian—brought out all the food, and the gathering fell silent as they blessed the meal and then began to dig in. When everyone pronounced themselves stuffed, they adjourned back to the parlor to do a round of gift exchanges. Vivian and Kellen found a quiet corner out of the way of the chaos of family gifts—or so they thought. They were surprised when Kieran came over and presented them with a gift each.

"Kieran, you didn't have to give us gifts. You didn't even know we were coming with John today," Kellen said.

"We have a funny family tradition in this house. Well, it's something Cory and I came up with, and we've done it every year since we got married. We get a couple of gifts and set them aside in case we have unexpected guests or we hear of a family in need. This year we have unexpected guests. Please come and join in the family chaos," Kieran said.

"Thank you, but we don't have anything to give you in return," Vivian said.

"Actually, you've given me a gift just by being here, but if you feel you need to do something, would you consent to pose for me sometime while you're in town?" Kieran asked.

"We'd be honored. If you and Cory join us in a couple of the photos, I'm sure I can get John to shoot them for us," Vivian said.

"Would you include Angelina in the group shot?" Kieran asked. "She'll be the envy of all the family back in Maine."

"On one condition," Kellen said.

"Name it," Kieran replied.

"You let us come back to visit and take a picture with you, Cory, and your children," Kellen said.

Kieran choked, trying to hold back the tears he so wanted to shed. Cory came to his rescue. "Of course, we would. My goodness, the children will be famous before they're able to crawl," he joked, taking the attention off of Kieran.

"I have one other favor to ask of you as our hosts?" Kellen asked.

"Sure, you've made our day special already," Cory said.

"Everyone, I don't want to upstage the happy parents to be, but I'd like you all to witness something for me," Kellen said, drawing the focus of the room to their little group as he sank to one knee before Vivian.

"Kellen MacDonald, what are you doing?" Vivian asked.

Kellen pulled a small velvet box from his pocket and held it out to Vivian. He then opened the box to reveal a gleaming diamond and amethyst engagement ring.

"Vivian Mason, before all of these witnesses, I ask you the question I've wanted to ask you for twenty-six years. Will you marry me?" Kellen said as he took the ring from the box and held it toward Vivian.

Vivian was struck speechless until Kieran leaned in and whispered in her ear. "The correct answer is yes." She was galvanized, and her amethyst eyes locked onto a matching pair staring back at her. "Yes," she replied.

Kellen slipped the ring on her finger and then drew her into a kiss. Cheers broke out as the newly engaged couple broke their kiss and looked at the assembled room.

"So how big of a deal do you want to make of this marriage?" Kieran asked. "You are both famous after all."

"Oh my, I really hate the idea of being swarmed by the press on our wedding day," Vivian said.

"Well, this is your lucky Christmas. Grams is a licensed minister. We can slip down to the county courthouse on Monday when they reopen and get all the documents squared away. Then, we can do everything here at the house. Kellen can spend the night before the wedding here, so he doesn't see the bride before the big day," Kieran said.

"You are a keeper, Kieran," Vivian said. "Thank you so much."

"See? You got us a gift after all." Kieran gave her one of his famous smiles. "Now, speaking of presents, there are way too many under that tree. Billy, would you and Ian please play Santa's helpers and start passing out the loot?"

Finally, the holiday Kieran had dreamed of all his life, and he let all the joy fill his heart. When all those who weren't staying at the house had departed—and Kieran and Cory had seen Angelina to bed—they retired to their own suite on the third floor. In their private sanctuary, Kieran finally let all of his emotions slip free. Tears streamed down his face, and he cuddled into Cory. Some of the tears were from the sadness of not being able to fully share the truth with Kellen about how much the photos would mean to him. Yet, many of the tears were tears of joy at having been witness to his father's happiness and the prospect of having a family photo of three generations. His children would have at least one picture with their grandfather.

"It seems so odd, being around Dad and yet not being able to share all of our joys with him," Kieran said.

"I'm glad for the surprise guests. Too bad Grams won't know that she's performing the wedding ceremony for her youngest son," Cory said.

"I know, but this is still all for the best. You know I never realized just how famous Vivian and Kellen were in the modeling world. If any of those photos we're planning go beyond the family, we'll be swamped with press and modeling contracts," Kieran said.

"Send them to Grandmother Belle. She'll drive such a hard bargain they'll run for the hills and leave us alone," Cory replied.

"I like that idea," Kieran said. "This has been a perfect Christmas."

Cory reached over, grabbed their water bottles off the nightstand, and handed one to Kieran before tapping them together. "Here's to many more prefect Christmases."

They took a drink and put up their waters before snuggling in for a long winter's nap.

Dear Reader,

Thank you for reading my first series. I hope you enjoyed it. Please take a moment to leave a review. I hope you'll join keep following my stories. Coming up next, I'll be exploring the vampires of my world from their origins into the far future looking through the eyes of shifter and vampire hunter, Richard St. Martin, and Cain, father of all vampires.

Thanks,

Kethric Wilcox

Kethric Wilcox

About the author

Kethric Wilcox (1966-) was born in Melrose, MA to average middle-class parents. Growing up, he did normal kid things, cub scouts, and boy scouts earning the rank of Eagle Scout. He graduated high school, went to college as a computer graphic design major, in the days when the field was more programing than design, for a while before dropping out to go work in the travel and tourism industry for four years. Kethric relocated to Little Rock, Arkansas in the early 1990s and went back to college earning a B. A. in both graphic design and history. He currently lives with his partner, whom he officially started dating in 2008, in a 1923 house they renovated in 2012, and works as a graphic designer doing museum and trail exhibits. In his spare time, Kethric writes church dramas and paranormal gay romances. When he's not at a computer, writing, designing, or doing research, Kethric enjoys playing in the kitchen, creating healthy versions of some of his favorite desserts and dinners. He is an avid camper and loves to get away from technology from time to time to recharge his spiritual and creative energies.

For upcoming releases and more about the World of the Silver Hunter books, follow Kethric's blog, World of the Silver Hunter, at http://www.kethricwilcox.com.

On Twitter @KethricW

E-mail: kethricwilcoxauthor@gmail.com

Other Books by Kethric Wilcox

The Legend of the Silver Hunter Trilogy:

Tracker

Legend of the Silver Hunter
Book One

Once upon a time, there was Beauty and there was the Beast. The spinners of tales would have you believe these two fell in love and lived happily ever after.

The spinners lied!

The Beast was a shifter and Beauty became a huntress and founded a long line of huntresses aided by the power of silver magic.

Kieran Belle is a descendant of the House of Beauty and a tracker who longs to live a life free of killing shifters. Aided by his father he escapes to college in Little Rock, Arkansas where he meets the boy of his dreams, Corwin Cooper.

Corwin Cooper is a descendant of a clan of shifters, who has never shifted himself. Having finally decided to go to college, Corwin arrives and meets the mate his inner wolf cries out to claim for his own in Kieran Belle.

Ancient prophecy says Kieran is destined to become the legendary Silver Hunter. Dark forces seek to derail prophecy and end the House of Beauty. Can a child of the shifter-hunting House of Beauty and a descendant of shifters find love and happiness or will dark forces and opposing heritage tear them apart?

Witch

Legend of the Silver Hunter
Book two

Darkness, fear, and power stalk the wilds of coastal Maine.

Kieran Belle has brought his boyfriend, Cory Cooper, home to meet his father's side of the family, the secretive Oisín Clan. Descendants of the most powerful of the ancient Silver mages, the head of the Oisín is known as the Silver Witch.

Plots are not reserved for the bad guys alone. Unknown to Kieran and Cory, Grandpa Oisín the current Silver Witch, and even Kieran's own father are plotting to use them to fulfill an ancient prophecy, and bring forth the Silver Hunter.

Outside the seeming safety of the Oisín compound, the dark forces lead by the mysterious Ebony mage known only as the Master and a dark Alpha shifter plot to destroy the House of Beauty and break the ancient spell binding shifters to one animal form.

Kieran and Cory's love is threatened from within as they struggle for either balance or dominance in their relationship.

Will prophecy or fear rip these two star-crossed lovers apart, or will their enemies rip them to shreds first? What tales will the Spinners tell about the newest Beauty and his Beast?

Hunter
Legend of the Silver Hunter
Book Three

Nobody ever tells you how hard it is to become a legend.

When Cory Cooper came to Maine with his boyfriend, Kieran Belle, to meet the family, he never imagined the chaos that would engulf their summer break. The seeming safety of the Oisín compound has been shattered. Kieran's grandfather, the powerful Silver Witch is dead and Kieran has been severely injured fighting off the shifters who invaded his family home.

The dark forces arrayed against the young lovers aren't the only forces in opposition to their quest for Happily Ever After. Camille Belle, reigning matriarch of the shifter hunting House of Beauty, and Kieran's maternal grandmother, also stands in their way.

Can these descendants of rival houses over come the forces that oppose them or is this version of Beauty and the Beast doomed to repeat the sad ending of the past?

Coming Soon from Kethric Wilcox:

The Curse:
The Origin of the Vampires

The ancient holy books written to make my brother Seth and his descendants look better than they were are packed with lies about me. I have created this journal over my immortal life. Included is the truth of origin of the beings you hunt, the vampires.

How can I know the ancient origins of these monsters of the night, you ask. That is the easiest question to answer and the hardest answer to believe. I am Cain, son of Adam and Eve. In Seth's holy books, I am the brother of Abel and the first murderer, cursed by God to roam the earth.

They got parts of it right. In this journal is the truth. I hope that you were not a follower of any of the faiths of the people of the book, for you will scream at what is contained here. Your faith is about to be tested.

If you're reading this journal, you have my either my sympathy for you are now cursed in my place. I hail you Lord of all Vampires. I am Cain and I was the first of our kind.